Entwined Publishing books by K.E. Turner

The Wolves of Langeias
Wolf's Keep
Wolf's Prize
Wolf's Redemption
Wolf's Return

The Descendants
The Wolf and His Witch

The Wolves of Langeais

WOLF'S RETURN

K.E. TURNER

ENTWINED PUBLISHING

Wolf's Return
ISBN # 978-1-80250-260-2
©Copyright K.E. Turner 2025
Cover Art by Erin Dameron-Hill ©Copyright September 2025
Interior text design by Entwined Publishing
Published by Eternal, an Entwined Publishing imprint

Published in 2025 by Entwined Publishing, United Kingdom.

Entwined Publishing is a division of Totally Entwined Group Limited.

WOLF'S RETURN

Dedication

To my mum,
Patricia Constance,
who always puts everyone else first.

Acknowledgements

Some books are harder to write than others. Wolf's Return is one of those. It's an emotional story, for one, and it came about at a time where things in my personal life were a little on the stressful side. So I'm extra grateful for the support of my family, and my beta readers— D.D. Line, Victoria Brown and Georgine Luke. You cheered me on when I got things right, and you cheered me on louder when things needed work, never doubting this story *would* get there in the end. Thank you to my editor, Rebecca Scott for answering all my questions and for your guidance, helping me make this book everything I had envisioned it would be. To my cover designer Erin Dameron-Hill, for your amazing cover. D'Artagon has a special spot in my heart, and you've brought him to life. And to my readers—thank you for choosing to go on this journey with me. Getting emails from you, eager for the next book in this series, always warms my heart and makes my day.

Author's Note

Dear Reader,

When I encounter foreign words, I do not know the meaning of in a book, it causes me to pause each time I see them in the text, taking me out of the story. Here is a brief list of foreign words and meanings I have used in this book.

Bretaigne – Britain

Aumônier - Chaplain

Archeveque – Archbishop

Chevalier – Knight

Comte – Count

Comtesse – Countess

Dame – Lady, i.e.: La Dame Adeline - Lady Adeline

Eveque – Bishop

Ereyesterday – The day before yesterday

Franceis – French (in Old French)

Grand-mére - Grandmother

Grand-pére - Grandfather

L'enfer – Hell

Lous Garous – (Old French for Loup Garou) werewolf

Ludenwic – Port area of London (as known in the 10th century)

Ma Dame – My Lady

Madame – Mrs.

Mademoiselle - Miss

Merde – Shit/fuck

Mon Dieu – My God

Monsieur – Sir/Mr

Mon Seigneur – My Lord

Mon Seigneur Comte – My Lord Count

Puterelle – A medieval insult meaning a woman of loose morals
Rus – Russia (as known in the 10th century)
Yestreen – Last evening

As Old French is, well, an old language, there are many variations. I've chosen the terms I think best applies. In some instances, when I've not been able to confirm a word or phrase in Old French, I have taken the liberty of using modern French.

Langeais Keep and Langeais are real places. However, they have been used in a fictitious manner. There was a chapel at Langeais Keep, but it was not built until the 11th century. Its ruins can be seen in grounds of Chateau Langeais.

There were many Comtes de Anjou over the centuries (none named Lothair that I am aware of, although Lothair was a popular name at the time). One of them, Comte Foulques de Noir, built Langeais Keep to guard the crossing point of the Loire River.

Comte Foulques de Noir, The Black Falcon, was notorious for his wars with other comtes—as were many comtes of that era. His power base was in Tours, and Langeais Keep, one of the first stone keeps built, was just one stronghold for him. An important one.

He did, however, dress his wife up in her wedding gown and burn her at the stake. She was also his cousin. They did things a little differently back then. Burning people at the stake was a popular way of ridding yourself of your enemies while making a statement to the masses at the same time. He wasn't the only one to use such methods.

My Comte Lothair is a fictitious Comte de Anjou created from a compilation of many comtes of that era.

Theban is an alphabet attributed to the 16th century text Polygraphia by Johannes Trithenmius. I have used it here in a fictitious manner. There is no link, to my knowledge, of Theban to the 10th century.

There are many mentions of spells and herbs used to heal in this book. I am not a qualified herbalist, nor a practicing witch. All references to such things, while researched, are used in a fictitious manner. And, as much as there were myths and legends of the *Loup Garou* (werewolf) in medieval France, there are no documented instances of werewolves in 10th century Langeais. In case you were wondering.

There are nights when the wolves are silent,
And only the moon howls.
George Carlin

Prologue

Constance Voyante pushed inside her mud brick cottage and slammed the rickety door behind her, bringing dust and bits of straw fluttering down from the thatched roof. She leaned against the rough timber planks, grateful the room was empty, and let her tears flow.

How could I have been so blind? How did I not see this coming?

She had seen everything else. The baker's wife giving birth to twins. The failed uprising against the new tax five years previous. Comte Lothair's swift and terrible retribution. Little Emilie's fall from a tree and her broken arm. What use was her second sight if it never helped *her*?

Constance choked back a sob. The stares, the laughter, and the not-so-subtle mutterings of 'witch' reverberated in her mind. At the forefront of the crowd,

13

his lips twisted in silent mockery, had stood Tristan, her only friend and confidant. In a village full of suspicious fools, he had been her one stalwart supporter. Until he hadn't been. She clutched her hand to her chest, her dream of a happy life with him no more than ash from a cold fire.

Constance brushed away her tears with the heel of her hand and shoved away from the door. She should have known better than to dream of a life no different from everyone else. She sniffed. A foolish, *foolish* hope. Now she must pack up and leave. Again. She should have grown accustomed to it. *How many huts have we called home now?* But she and her mother had spent more time here than in any other place. It was not much — a single room, a dirt floor, two sleeping pallets, a table with a bench seat and a fire to cook over — but it was home. She had thought, for the first time... Her and Tristan could...

With a shaky breath, she snatched up her spare dress and stuffed it into a sack along with her apron, her coat, her darning needle and the pretty colored rocks she kept beside her sleeping mat. She hesitated over the hawk's feather. Tristan had given her that. He had found it in the field and had thought she would like its pretty stripes. She had. She did. But taking it with her would surely only be a reminder of the life she was leaving behind. A life not meant to be hers. Pity her visions had not warned her before she had so trustingly given him her heart and her...

Constance shook her head, banishing the memory of their tryst by the millpond, and turned her back on the hawk's feather. She thrust bowls, mugs and cooking pots into her sack. She wanted everything of importance, anything she and her mother might need, packed and ready to go when they came to force them out. Irate villagers cared naught for your worldly goods, nor your feelings, when they were desperate to see you gone.

The door creaked open as Constance grabbed another sack and began filling it with her mother's meager things and any stored food they had.

Her mother's pinched face was a picture of confusion. "What are you doing, Constance?" Barely four decades old, her worn skin stretched tight over her thin body and her eyes, once likened to the pretty blue of cornflowers, had dulled.

"We are leaving, Mother. The aumônier will be along at any moment. The villagers want us gone."

Her mother's lips thinned a little more, and she ran her fingers through hair long faded from a golden blonde to wisps of white. "Have you been telling stories about the Black Wolf again?"

Constance jerked around. "What? No."

She shoved the last of their salted meat, barely enough for one more meal, into the bag. People were superstitious by nature, and they could be cruel. It took little for their distrustful gaze to turn on a woman alone with her daughter. A daughter with two different colored eyes. They soon forgot the woman had tended their illnesses and healed their wounds. Herbal tinctures and poultices so easily became the work of the devil in the minds of the suspicious. No, she had not understood then, that tales of the man who could turn into a wolf, that sharing her visions of future events, would be cause for alarm.

Constance was no longer that child, and she had learned that lesson well. Years had passed, and she had not spoken of the Black Wolf to anyone since. Nor shared her visions. Not with Tristan. Not even her mother. She had not had a vision of the Black Wolf for a long time.

"The Marchand boy took a turn for the worse yestreen. He died not long before sunrise." Constance's fist clenched at the injustice of it all. "And the tanner swears his cow's milk dried up this morning."

She stuffed a coarse, blackened loaf of bread the baker—in an act of charity—had given her only yesterday into the bag. This morn he had stood behind Tristan, his round face no longer jovial, and hatred burning in his usually merry brown eyes. Her mother healed people. Why would she want to curse the tanner's cow with a dry udder when the people of Langeais were their only source of coin and food? It made no sense.

"As villagers are wont to do, Mother, they are looking for an explanation." Constance did not mention Tristan. Her bond with him was over, and her naïve, romantic imaginings of a life with him served no purpose but to goad her anger.

"Come, Mother. Help me pack all that we can carry. I doubt anyone will be kind enough to lend us a horse and cart for our travels."

Her mother sagged, shrinking inside herself. "Where are we going to go?"

As clear as the interior of their hut, Constance's vision struck—a small meadow with a cottage and a freshly piled mound of dirt decorated in flowers. Constance stood beside it, her head bowed. Alone. She sucked in a breath, tears smarting her eyes again.

"Due east about five leagues, there is a cottage." The words flowed, and she knew the truth of them before she had finished speaking. It was often the way of her visions, of her second sight. Knowledge was simply there. "It is where we are meant to be, Mother. Where I am meant to be." She stopped her packing and stared at her mother, knowing her next words would only anger her, but no more capable of stopping them than she was of ignoring her visions. "The Black Wolf will find us there, and we will once again have his protection."

Anger flared in her mother's faded blue eyes. "The Black Wolf is *dead*." She snatched the sack from Constance's hands and shoved the remains of their scant supplies in it. "Jacques d'Louncrais died in battle a year ago. And with him, his protection."

"I know, Mother, but his son —"

"Has abandoned us to our fate." Her mother's shoulders sagged, and she let the sack slide to the floor. "We are no longer in reach of their gaze, Constance. These little girl fantasies will only bring you heartache."

"But, I have —"

Her mother huffed out a breath. "You are young and untrained and are yet to learn how to separate true visions from that which your heart longs for." Her mother picked up the sack and squared her shoulders. "Come, Constance. It is best we are gone before the aumônier arrives. I have no wish to face another crowd armed with pitchforks and flaming torches."

Constance pressed her lips together and kept her silence. There was no point wasting precious time arguing with her mother. She hoisted her sack over her shoulder and grabbed their most prized possession from the table. A book, old, the edges of the pages stained with ingredients from the herbal preparations it detailed. Centuries of knowledge passed down through this one book. And in its pages, hidden within the swirls of their secret language, the legend of the Black Wolf and the spells the coven used to aid them.

She clutched it to her chest. Jacques d'Louncrais might be dead, but his son was not. A new Black Wolf walked the earth. According to village gossip, he was more powerful than his father. Despite what her mother said, there *would* be a time he would seek her out. He *would* need her. Her visions did not lie. The Black Wolf would come to her in the dead of night. Her heart stalled as another image flashed across her mind. A clearing, a cottage, a black wolf, her and...someone else. She gasped. A child. With flowers in her hair and grass stains on her feet, she danced around them. Their child.

Constance's heart soared, banishing the tightness in her chest. He *would* come for her. One day. She *would* have the life she wished for. She would not be alone forever.

Chapter One

Nine years later
Frankia 999

Constance closed the big book shut on the page dedicated to the Black Wolf and swallowed the lump in her throat. Her mother had warned her about the heartache she could bring upon herself, but she had not listened. Her mother had not the gift of sight. How could Helene have possibly understood the deep, unshakable belief that accompanied her visions? Constance had cast aside her mother's words of wisdom, trusted in her own truth, and paid the price for her foolishness.

She rubbed her hand across the book's worn binding. The Black Wolf *had* come. He *had* needed her. She had opened the door to him and the love and longing in his dark eyes had been everything she had hoped for. Everything she had envisioned. Only… She heaved out a sigh. It had been for the woman in his arms. For Erin. Not for her. A woman far from her own time, wounded and in the throes of a turning. His mate.

The Black Wolf had needed Constance's skills as a healer and her knowledge of his kind. Nothing more. The flame of hope that had sustained her through long years of solitude had been snuffed out in an instant. The one vision she had hoped above all was true, and it was but a delusion of her childish dreams.

Constance set the book aside. There was naught she could do to change it. Naught she *would* do. Only a fool would attempt to separate a wolf and his mate. What she *should* spend her time on was helping the Dufont boy, and perhaps save his life.

She assembled the ingredients she would need on the table — garlic, rosemary, horse chestnut, horsetail and honey — and set about grinding them into a sticky paste. She would make the journey into the village at first light, give them the remedy and impress on the boy, and his mother, the importance of following her instructions closely. With any luck, they would journey to meet her, and she would encounter them part way on the path. Then she would have no need to spend a night in an empty stable stall with naught but a rough horse blanket for warmth.

A sennight ago, Madame Dufont had sought her services for her son's cough. Constance's most recent vision told her the foolish boy had gone swimming in the millpond against her advice, though he had not confessed such to his mother. Now he was wheezing, and Constance suspected his lungs were filling with fluid. If the boy were to die… Well, Constance had experienced such circumstances before, and it would not be the boy's disregard for his own health the villagers would lay the blame on.

It had been many years since villagers had last forced her from her home, but the memories remained. Of their angry faces and the taunts of 'witch'. The village aumônier knocking on their door. Their frantic packing to save what they could before someone set fire to their humble home. At least now, she would have somewhere to go. Someone to turn to. The Black Wolf. Constance would call on him if she had a need, but bearing witness to the bond between him and his new mate would be almost too much to bear.

She paused in her grinding. *Enough wallowing, Constance. You should be grateful.*

Her reconnection with the wolves of Langeais was not without benefit. Having a wolf in her home for a time had ensured a ready supply of meat. That the wolf was Seigneur Gaharet d'Louncrais, the alpha of the pack, had afforded her much more. Luxuries she had never known until now. Though he had forsaken his title, his estate, and had fled the Comte de Anjou, he had support still. He had seen to it Constance had everything she could need.

She ran her hand down the bodice of her new dress. A lovely deep blue and of fine, soft wool, unmarred by constant darning and patching. Another two of similar quality lay folded neatly near her sleeping cot. Her baskets of vegetables and fruits and her salt pot were all full. The barrel of mead nudging the wall beneath her shelves was rich and strong, unlike the watered-down wine she had exchanged for healing the merchant's sleeplessness. On the table, several new knives gleamed, their edges sharp and their elaborate handles beautiful beside her plain and well-worn ones.

She had stores of dried and salted meat, a pot full of venison and a deer hide and horns to trade with. She could not remember living so well. Yet one thing had not changed. Constance was still alone and still an outcast.

Tears pricked her eyes, and she blinked them back, taking in her little hut. The slab table with its nicks and stains, the dirt floor she swept daily, her pots of herbs, her collection of pretty rocks and feathers she had started as a child — they held so many memories. Good and bad. For nearly a half score years she had called this place home. Eight of those years she had lived here alone, her mother gone. Yet it had never felt more empty than since her reconnection with the Langeais wolves.

A tingling up her spine and a pounding of hooves from approaching horses snapped her from her melancholy. Someone had crossed her warning ward beyond her clearing. Villagers rarely approached on horseback. The Dufonts did not own one. Nor their neighbors, and she had received no other vision of a sick child, or a villager in need of care.

Unease prickled up her skin. Seigneur Gaharet had warned her to be wary. Could this be the unknown presence from the night of the storm? The night Seigneur Ulrik and his mate had sought her out? The one who had crossed her ward, yet not revealed themselves?

Her gaze skipped to the length of timber resting beside the door. *L'enfer.* With wolves beneath her roof, she had gotten into the habit of not barricading her door. Nor had she resumed her practice of replenishing the protection spell over it every morning. She swiftly hoisted the block of wood across it, headless of splinters, and slammed it into its slot. It would hold, but not forever. There was no time to compose a spell. She skirted the table, putting it between herself and the door, and grabbed one of her new knives. With it hidden in the volumes of her skirt, she faced the entrance and waited.

The rider dismounted, and footsteps approached. Her heart thudded in her chest and her hand, gripped around the knife, grew slick with sweat. Was it the keep guard? Or others of Seigneur Gaharet's pack?

A heavy fist pounded on the door. "Constance."

Her body trembled, but she stood resolute. For all that it was not much of a life, and lonely living out here in the forest, she had no wish to die today.

"Constance." The man banged on the door again. "I know you are in there."

Her grip on the knife tightened. He could smell her. It could only mean one thing. A wolf was at her door. One she could trust? Or one she could not?

Her bottom lip quivered. "Who are you? What do you want?"

"It is I, Aimon. The white wolf."

Was it truly the young white wolf, so loyal and dedicated?

Oh, where is my second sight now? What use is it if it does not warn me *of danger? If it helps everyone* but *me?*

"I am sorry I have frightened you, Constance, but Gaharet has sent me to fetch you."

Constance wavered. His voice *did* sound familiar. "How do I know you are who you say you are?"

Seigneur Gaharet was in hiding from his own pack. Two wolves had tracked Seigneur Ulrik through the storm.

"Do you remember when we first met? When you found me slouched in the grass watching your cottage? I had hidden myself at the edge of the forest, but you found me all the same. As though you sensed I was there."

She remembered. A white wolf with bright blue eyes. He had followed Seigneur Gaharet. A protector, bound to his maker by a bond of blood and teeth only death could break.

"Do you remember what you said to me that night? You said, '*Heed my words, wolf. That which was thought lost you will find. Hidden in plain sight, it is time for its presence to be felt. Guard it well and the reward shall be yours.*'" He chuckled. "I dismissed your words as some nonsensical riddle. But you were right, Constance. I found that which was lost. It was Kathryn. A she-wolf unknown to us. My mate."

Another wolf had found his mate? Yes, she could sense it around him now, and it only added to the deep knot of misery sitting heavy in her chest. Yet, he had spoken true. She *had* predicted it. The man who stood on the other side of her door was Monsieur Aimon, the white wolf.

Constance set the knife down, removed the wooden barricade and opened the door. Blue eyes framed by white-blond hair stared down at her.

"Gaharet has requested your presence at the d'Louncrais Keep," said Aimon. "We have need of your skills."

"Seigneur Gaharet has returned to his keep?"

"Yes. Much has changed since we last met." Concern flickered in his eyes. "Will you come, Constance?"

"Of course I will come, but is there not a healer in the d'Louncrais village? It is quite a journey from here."

"No other healer will suffice. We need *your* particular skills, and your knowledge of us."

Oh. Constance stepped away from the door. "Come in. Let me set you some food and drink while I collect my things."

With Monsieur Aimon seated at her table, a bowl of venison stew and a mug of mead in front of him, Constance grabbed a small sack from a hook on the wall. "Tell me of the injury or illness so that I may bring the correct herbs?"

"It is not an injury of body, but…"

She raised her eyebrows. "Another turning?"

She had received no vision of it. She had already prepared an herbal potion for Seigneur Ulrik's mate, Rebekah's turning, when a d'Louncrais' servant had arrived requesting one, but they had not asked her to deliver it in person.

Constance collected the herb pots she would need, wrapped them in cloth and placed them carefully in her sack along with the preparation for the Dufont boy. They would pass through Langeais Village, and she could deliver it then. She put out the fire and grabbed her cloak. From memory, the d'Louncrais keep was a half day's ride.

Monsieur Aimon shook his head. "It is not a turning. It is…" His forehead settled into a frown. "Best you see for yourself."

"Oh." Her gaze darted to her grimoire. "I shall bring this then."

Constance scooped up the book and cradled it against her chest. She had a feeling she was going to need it.

Chapter Two

The black wolf yawned and stretched out his body, the heat from the flames in the central fire pit easing some of the stiffness in his old injuries. It had been many winters since he had enjoyed the warmth of a blaze, a rug beneath his bones and the security of four walls surrounding him. He could take a moment to enjoy it.

The familiarity of this hall soothed him, with its large oak table where he had enjoyed many a meal, the fresh meadowsweet rushes that covered the floor and the flicker of the oil lamps that gave the air a smoky haze. But his keen eyes noted the changes. There were wolves here he had not met, living in this keep, if his nose did not betray him. It never did.

The uproar his arrival had produced had died down. His brother had stopped asking him to shift, and they had all settled at the table to discuss him, resigned to await the return of a white-haired chevalier he did not recognize. Gaharet had sent him for a healer the moment his brother had set eyes on him.

D'Artagnon huffed. His scars were old and he had long grown accustomed to them. There was nothing even the most skilled of healers could do for them now. Nor would he want them to. They were a reminder of his purpose, of his failure. Every twinge, each time the skin pulled tight, every time he blinked his one good eye, it fueled the coals of his rage and stoked his determination. He had no need of a healer.

The thin, balding human who had shown him to the hall — he remembered him, though the servant's hair was grayer and thinner now. The sandy-haired wolf had once been a childhood friend. Ulrik? They had sent him away after some trouble.

There was a human male, vaguely familiar, who he could not quite place, and with him a redheaded she-wolf. An image of another redheaded woman, one with eyes blue like his own and a fiery temper, hovered in his mind. His mother. This she-wolf reminded him of her. *Is this female my sister*? He did not remember having a sister. From the matching color of their eyes, she was kin to the human male. The human male was most definitely *not* his father. That was a face he remembered well.

Another unfamiliar she-wolf had fled the hall the moment the kitchen maids arrived with the midday meal, one hand on her stomach and the other covering her mouth. His brother's scent on her had been strong, though not strong enough to mask the pup growing in her womb.

In his absence, his brother had found his mate. A good thing, a wonderful thing, but it gave him pause. He had come here with the purpose of reuniting with his brother, of fighting side by side with him once again, but his brother's circumstances had changed.

His brother had a mate now, and the future of the d'Louncrais line to protect.

He eyed the hall entrance. It had been a mistake coming here. His father had entrusted this task to him and, as before, there were valid grounds for *not* including his brother. The burden must be his alone. He rose and padded silently across the hall, only to have his path blocked.

Gaharet. His brother. A bigger black wolf than him. Alpha of the Langeais wolves. Though his brother's love for his new mate coated every word he uttered, there were deeper lines of worry around his eyes and a hardness about him he had never seen before. Not even after the death of their mother, or their father.

Gaharet crossed his arms, one eyebrow raised. "Thinking of leaving so soon, D'Artagnon?"

D'Artagnon. His brother meant him. It had been many seasons since he had thought of himself as a man. As D'Artagnon. Years since someone had called him by his name.

"It is good you have returned. For now, more than ever, we need you here. Much has happened since you last set foot in this keep. Stay a moment, and I will tell you of our troubles."

Troubles? Could things be worse than when I left? He stared at his brother's boots, debating his course of action.

"No longer are we the strong pack you once knew," his brother continued. "Our numbers are few, and the only females we have are those in this keep. Our pack is on the verge of extinction."

D'Artagnon jerked his head up. On the verge of *extinction?* He sat his haunches down. What had happened in his absence? Had he stayed away too long and his pack suffered for his silence? Why was his brother only telling him this now? It seemed he was not the only d'Louncrais wanting to spare his sibling a heavy responsibility.

"I see I have your attention. An archeveque named Renaud set about capturing one of us for his own purposes, and has killed most of our pack in doing so," explained Gaharet.

Archeveque Renaud? Not my enemy?

"The only wolves left of the pack you knew are Ulrik, the twins Edmond and Aubert, Godfrey and Lance."

His nemesis was one of the few this Renaud had spared? Coincidence? D'Artagnon thought not.

"Aimon became one of us three years ago." Gaharet motioned to a wall hanging where embroidered figures danced across the fabric in the flickering firelight.

Where once one embroidered panel had hung on the wall, now there were two. The second, a battle scene where his fellow pack fought on horseback. There, embroidered into the fabric, was his enemy. He pared his lip back and a low growl rumbled in his throat. That man, that *traitor*, had struck him down, and yet still he remained a trusted member of the pack. Trusted enough to grace the walls of what was once his home.

He studied the figures on horseback—his brother, the twins, Ulrik, Lance and Godfrey. At the bottom of the piece, the young, white-haired chevalier. He lay in a pool of blood. Dying. This must be Aimon. The redheaded she-wolf reeked of him and the scent of mating. Had his brother turned this Aimon? The pack had not sanctioned a turning since… D'Artagnon could not remember a turning.

He eyed the entrance again.

Gaharet squatted before him, blocking his view. "How did Renaud slay so many werewolves, you might ask?"

D'Artagnon peeled his gaze from the doorway.

"One of our own betrayed us. I am betting" — his brother's dark stare bored into him — "that does not come as a surprise to you, brother."

D'Artagnon met his stare, unflinching. His brother knew of the traitor, suspected he had aided this Renaud, but did he know of the true depths he had sunk to?

"The traitor's deception did not end there, did it, D'Artagnon?" His brother's voice was soft, but dark shadows flitted in his eyes and a muscle ticked in his jaw. "He killed our father. He killed our mother, and in doing so, he turned Kathryn." Gaharet pointed to the redheaded she-wolf sitting at the table. "I suspect you knew of his treachery, and that is why he tried to kill you."

D'Artagnon swiveled his gaze to the female. Kathryn. The she-wolf who reminded him of his mother was Kathryn. He had heard that name before, yet... A memory floated up from the dark recesses of his mind. Of a little girl with flaming red hair, hazel eyes and a nose covered in freckles chasing him through the keep corridors with unrestrained glee. Kathryn. Not his sister. His cousin.

He turned his eye back to his brother. Kathryn had been there when his mother had died? She had seen her attacker? And he had let her live?

Gaharet rose and paced the floor. "Kathryn was but a child during her turning. She remembers only that her attacker is dark-haired, my height, and carries a sword with a stone on the pommel. That is all we know."

"I keep trying to remember, but..." Kathryn hung her head, and her father laid a comforting hand on her arm.

"What Kathryn has been able to remember has narrowed it down to two," said Gaharet. "Godfrey and Lance. And Godfrey is missing."

D'Artagnon swiveled his ears forward. *Godfrey is missing?* Since when? He had followed Godfrey and Lance through the forest, only to lose them both in the storm. Had only one of them returned?

He tracked his brother's agitated steps. Gaharet wanted him to shift, to return to human form and give him a name. That *had* been his intent, but now...

D'Artagnon stared unblinking at Gaharet.

"Can you tell us, D'Artagnon? Give us a clue?" His brother walked over to the wall hanging, tracing the figure of Godfrey with his finger. "I never would have thought Godfrey would betray us. He has stood by my father's side, and now mine. He has always given me sound advice, but his absence at this time is damning, and his behavior of late has been unpredictable."

His hand shifted to Lance. "But Lance, after all these years of his support, of putting my trust in him as an adviser, has *lied*. At a time when honesty and the truth are so imperative. I have always believed both of them to be good men. Loyal pack members. I do not want to think either of them could be guilty of such a thing."

His brother turned his back on the wall hanging. "Or is it, as someone suggested, a wolf from Ludenwic or further afield? From Rus? Wanting revenge for all that happened centuries ago?"

"I do not believe this is the work of the Ludenwic wolves. Victor would not risk their alliance with us," said an unfamiliar voice, husky to the point of a harsh whisper.

Intrigued, D'Artagnon turned to the group at the table. Who did that voice belong to?

"The Rus pack? Maybe," said the voice.

Ulrik? Scars crisscrossed the man's throat. Scars made not by a sword, but by teeth. From his time in Bretaigne?

Uncertainty flickered across his brother's face, his shoulders tense. "Maybe. Whoever it is, they possess knowledge of the amulets. The pack split into three so long ago, and the alpha stripped the amulets from all who left. Would either the Ludenwic or the Rus pack remember any of the lore surrounding them?"

D'Artagnon glared at the embroidered figure on the wall. Their traitor was far closer than Ludenwic or Rus. All D'Artagnon had to do was shift and speak his name. Or cross the hall and touch his nose to the wall hanging. Point out the man who had killed his parents and betrayed them all. His brother would then have the answer he craved, though the truth would be a pain all of its own.

Indecision swirled in his gut. Things had seemed so much clearer in the forest, his mind consumed by his wolf and his decisions made on instinct alone. Should he tell Gaharet and risk his brother's unborn pup growing up without a father?

Gaharet threw up his arms. "I know you are in there, D'Artagnon. What needs must I do to reach you? To convince you to shift?" Gaharet crossed his arms, leaned against the table and scowled.

Movement in the doorway and the scent of freshly baked bread, raw meat and herbs drew D'Artagnon's eye. A large woman in a flour-dusted apron, her bulk weighing heavy on her knees and a genuine affection brimming in her eyes, shuffled toward him. Her name floated into his mind. *Anne.* The cook.

She held out a raw deer haunch. "Here you go, D'Artagnon. Sorry it took me so long, lad. I had to send the stable boy out for a fresh kill. I was not expecting to be feeding a wolf. And you look like you could use a good feed. Never fear. Old Anne will look after you now you are back." Her eyes brimmed with tears. "It is good to have you home again, lad." She placed her hand on her chest. "When I thought you were dead, it near broke this poor old woman's heart."

"D'Artagnon, please. Stay." His brother sighed and gestured at the haunch. "At least until you have eaten."

His shoulder twinged. A good meal by the warmth of a fire would do no harm. He carefully took the haunch in his teeth. The old woman beamed, then patted him on his head.

D'Artagnon jerked his head back, dropped the meat and snarled. Gifts of food or no, he was no pet. Nor a harmless pup. He bared his teeth and snarled at her again. The fire crackled and spit, loud in the sudden silence in the hall.

Gaharet's eyebrows shot up. "You are taking your life in your hands there, brother mine."

Anne stood before him, hands on her ample hips, with a glare so ferocious a seasoned chevalier might balk. D'Artagnon peeled his lips back further.

"Now you hear this, young man." Anne wagged a plump finger at him. "I will tolerate none of your nonsense now any more than I did when you were a boy. I will grant you some leeway, given all you have been through, but this will be your only warning."

Haunch forgotten, he crouched, ready to pounce, his hackles raised, his ears flattened against his skull and his growl a promise of violence and retribution. Any hint of the man he was, of the brother he had once been, he had pushed so deep there was little left but wolf.

Do not threaten me, *old woman.*

With more speed and strength than was right for a woman of her age and bulk, she struck, slapping him across his snout.

D'Artagnon lunged.

He caught a blur of movement from the side, then his brother's strong hand gripped the scruff of his neck, threw him to the ground and held him there. He thrashed, snarling and snapping at the hand that pinned him to the floor.

"Stop, D'Artagnon!"

The order rolled over him and he fought it, fought against the strength of his brother's hold. A thick, musky scent filled the air. His brother's wolf was close, readying for a shift.

Gaharet's grip tightened. "D'Artagnon, *enough*! Do not force me to confine you to the training room until you can get yourself under control. I will not have you attacking Anne, nor anyone else here, no matter your suffering."

His brother was strong. Even in his human form. A true alpha. Still, with all his years spent as a wolf, D'Artagnon could best him. But... The memories of his youth broke through. Of them shifting into their wolves and racing through the forest together. Of plotting against Anne to steal treats from the larder. Training together. Competing for available females. This was Gaharet. His *brother*. With a snarl, he conceded to Gaharet's authority and relaxed his body beneath his brother's hold. The grip on his neck eased, though his brother did not let him go.

Gaharet's weary sigh washed over him. "This will not do, D'Artagnon. You *must* shift back so we might talk with you. We need to hear what happened, where you have been and why it has taken so long for you to come home." The hand against his ruff gentled, stroking his fur. "Tell us who attacked you." His brother released him and stepped back, giving him room. "Shift back. Talk to us. Tell us what you know, and we will hunt this wolf down together."

D'Artagnon rolled to his feet and locked gazes with Gaharet. He made no effort to bring forth the change.

Gaharet placed his hands on his hips and frowned. "One last time, I am asking you to shift, D'Artagnon. Do not make me order you."

D'Artagnon ignored the request. He had not shifted since that fateful day he had crawled from the bloody battlefield. His brother's determination to seek the man who had cut him down only stoked his resolution to remain a wolf. If he could do one thing, he would protect his brother.

Gaharet's shoulders sagged. "Very well. I did not wish to do this, but you leave me no choice. D'Artagnon, *shift.*"

The order rolled over him—the compulsion, the command. He braced against it, flattening his ears. Gaharet scowled and loomed above him, dark shadows in his eyes as his wolf hovered barely below the surface. A strong wolf, powerful, more so than their father.

"Shift, *now.*"

The words, little more than a guttural growl, rumbled deep in his brother's throat. The group gathered around the table shrunk into themselves. Kathryn shivered. Ulrik's nostrils flared, and he gritted his teeth. The thin, balding servant's eyes bulged and Anne, the woman who had dared slap him across his snout, gulped and retreated. Not D'Artagnon. Though his knees shook and the urge to obey his alpha sizzled up his spine, he remained resolutely, doggedly wolf.

His brother's jaw rippled, dark hair sprouted across the bridge of his nose, and the sharp point of a canine peeked out beneath his top lip. His brother's control was slipping, his wolf pushing forward, angry at D'Artagnon's defiance.

"*Shift.*"

The command, ground out through gritted teeth and a mouth part transformed into a muzzle, hit him with the force of a granite boulder thrown from a catapult. He whimpered, but did not obey.

A startled gasp from the doorway had them both turning.

Two wide eyes—one blue, one green—stared at them. With tendrils of blonde hair escaping from beneath her hooded cloak, the woman stood in the glow of an oil lamp like an angel sent from the heavens above, clutching a book to her chest. *Her.* The woman from the cottage in the woods. The one he could not banish from his thoughts. That tingle of familiarity that had scratched at his mind since he had spied on her at her cottage in the forest burned through his brain like wildfire.

"D'Artagnon. *D'Artagnon!*"

He ignored his brother and took several steps toward the woman in the doorway. All the other occupants in the room ceased to matter as he took her in. Her worn coat, her sun-warmed skin, the way she clutched the book to her body as though it were her most prized possession.

What is it about her that commands my attention so?

He raised his snout and sniffed the air. Horse, herbs, flowers and a soft earthiness—she smelled of the forest. Of...home. He shook his head. What a ridiculous thought.

The white-haired wolf, Aimon, stepped into the room and nudged the woman forward with a gentle hand to her shoulder.

No. He will not touch her.

D'Artagnon lunged, his teeth snapping and his hackles raised.

Once again, his brother threw him to the floor and held him down. The woman retreated, her eyes wide, her knuckles white as she gripped her book. Aimon, his hands held up, backed away from her. D'Artagnon stopped fighting his brother's hold.

Why do I care if Aimon touches her?

Gaharet's grip on his scruff eased. "D'Artagnon, this is Constance, our healer. Constance, this is my brother, D'Artagnon." Gaharet's attention flicked between him and Constance. "Have it your way, brother. For now." Amusement coated Gaharet's words as his gaze settled on Constance. "At some point, something, or some*one*, will make you shift."

Chapter Three

Constance's breath whooshed from her lungs, and her heart stalled. *Another* black wolf. Staring at her. Seigneur Gaharet's *brother*? Constance almost dropped her grimoire. A fluttering in her chest eased some of the tightness that had been her constant companion the last few months. Could this be…?

She gaped at the black wolf. "I… I do not understand. I thought—"

"That we had lost him?" Seigneur Gaharet's hand remained on his brother's neck. "So did I. By the scars he bears, we nearly did."

The wolf, Monsieur D'Artagnon, blinked.

Oh. He has only one eye.

A large, puckered scar, a savage white line against black fur, slashed across his head where his other eye should have been. Another one curved behind his shoulder, down across his ribs and disappeared beneath his body. Either of his injuries would have killed a human. Two of them would have posed a significant challenge to a werewolf. This wolf was lucky to be alive.

The black wolf fixed his singular blue gaze on her.

"Where…? What…?" She shook her head, trying to wrap her mind around this new development. D'Artagnon was supposed to have died almost a decade ago. He had *survived*? Where had he been all those years?

Seigneur Gaharet shrugged. "We do not know. I would ask him if he were to shift, but he has not."

Is he stuck? Constance frowned. *Is that even possible?*

"I am uncertain if that is by choice." Seigneur Gaharet turned his attention to his brother. "I tried ordering him to shift. Few can resist an alpha's command. Whatever force is holding him is stronger than I am." He unfolded himself from his squat. "I need to talk to my brother, Constance. I need to know who did this to him. My instinct tells me it is the same wolf that has betrayed us all. Can you help us? Help him?"

"I…" She met the unblinking gaze of the one-eyed wolf. The wolf was angry. At her, at the world? Did he even wish for help? She clutched her book tighter to her chest. "I will do my best, Seigneur Gaharet."

L'enfer. A wolf who could not, would not shift. She had never heard of such a thing. But a black wolf, another black wolf… She banished the memory of her vision before it took root. She had mourned that loss once. Was she foolish enough to believe in it again?

Seigneur Gaharet nodded. "That is all I ask, Constance. Thank you." He gestured toward the table. "Come. Sit. We will talk."

A servant took her cloak and her bag and Constance followed Seigneur Gaharet to the beautiful oak table large enough to fit half a small village. She slid into a seat, conscious the wolf was not the only one staring at her.

She eyed the fancy goblets and the platters of meat, fruits and cheese laid out on the table. The room was grand. Far grander than anything she had seen in her lifetime. A fire roared in the large central fire pit. On the wall, two magnificent scenes with brightly colored figures engaged in battle. She imagined its only rival would be Langeais Keep.

She set her grimoire down and curled her fingers in the soft wool of her dress. For all she had benefited from her recent connection with the wolves of Langeais, she was still a peasant, and an outcast one at that. Being here amongst all this wealth set her on edge.

"You have already met Ulrik," said Seigneur Gaharet, inclining his head in his direction.

Seigneur Ulrik. The sandy wolf. A storm had raged the night he had sought her out, his mate, a woman from the future in his arms. Constance breathed through the tightness in her chest. There was no sign of his mate, Rebekah, but if she had used the potion Constance had prepared, most likely she was still recovering from her turning.

"And Aimon."

Monsieur Aimon took a seat beside a woman with glorious red hair.

"This is his mate, Kathryn, and" — Seigneur Gaharet indicated an older man — "her father, Farren."

Dame Kathryn smiled at her, and Seigneur Farren nodded a greeting. Monsieur Aimon slipped Kathryn's hand into his and kissed her knuckles. Kathryn glowed. Constance balled her hands into fists beneath the table and smiled. Mated pairs everywhere. Watching them together stung more than if she had poured mead into an open and putrefying wound. Her gaze slid to the black wolf, still fixated on her.

"This is Gascon, my steward," continued Seigneur Gaharet, indicating the thin, balding man who had shown them to the hall. "And Anne, the cook." He pointed to a large woman in a flour-dusted apron.

Anne's eyes narrowed. "I remember you. A little girl with blonde curls." She wagged her finger at Constance. "I will never forget those eyes."

Constance stiffened. Always it was her odd colored eyes that people noticed.

The cook's kind and wrinkled face considered her. "An age of wisdom in them, uncanny for one so young."

Constance's breath hitched. No one had ever said that about her before. Freak. Blind. Dumb. Wretched. Cursed. Witch. All words she had borne with stoic acceptance, though they had cut deep and compounded her sense of otherness. But wisdom... Constance gave Anne a tentative smile.

"You came here with your mother many years back," said the cook. "In the dead of night. Jacques brought you in through the kitchen."

Seigneur Gaharet's eyebrows rose. "She *did*? He *did*?"

"Yes," confirmed Anne. "When you and D'Artagnon were both boys."

The black wolf was still staring at her, shadows flitting across his eye. How far gone was he? Did any of the man remain? How much did he understand?

"Anne is correct, Seigneur Gaharet." Constance did her best to ignore the black wolf's regard. "Seigneur Jacques summoned my mother. A woman from the future had appeared. The first one I encountered."

"The first..." Seigneur Gaharet's eyes narrowed. "*Marie*? Gray eyes and freckles?"

Constance nodded.

Seigneur Ulrik gaped at her. "*Victor's* mate? The alpha of the Ludenwic wolves has a mate from the future?"

"I believe so, yes." How did they not know this? Wait. Someone did. She caught the gaze of the black wolf and a certainty settled in her bones. *He* had been there that night. He had seen her, though she had not seen him. And he remembered.

Seigneur Gaharet turned to Seigneur Ulrik. "Did you...?"

Seigneur Ulrik shook his head. "No. This is the first I am hearing of such. Victor, nor Marie, gave any hint. Not to me. And none of the Ludenwic wolves made mention of it. All I knew was Marie was a former maid here, and she had mated Victor when he visited from Bretaigne."

"Anne, were *you* aware of this?" asked Seigneur Gaharet.

"No. All I was told was that Marie was in desperate need of work and a roof over her head. I assumed she had arrived from another estate, a product of some scandal."

"I think Victor and I are going to have a little talk about him keeping secrets." Gaharet turned back to her. "So, my father knew of you and your mother."

Constance nodded. "Oh, yes. As did your mother. She was there that night."

Should she reveal the black wolf's secret? His blue gaze bored into her. She kept silent.

Seigneur Gaharet rubbed a hand across his chin. "And your mother was also a witch, like you, with knowledge of our kind?"

"Yes."

"Did you know this, Anne?"

Anne pursed her lips. "As if I would keep such knowledge from you if I did. All those months poring over those scrolls in the library... And Aimon. As if I would let him suffer like that had I known there was a way to ease him through the turning." Anne huffed. "You wound me, Gaharet. Jacques kept this a secret. Even from me."

"A feat in itself," muttered Seigneur Gaharet. "But...did you not help my mother through her turning?"

"Why, yes. I did. But Jacques banished me from his chamber for the first few days. He said he wished to care for his mate. Alone. Growled at me when I tried to insist on helping the lass."

Seigneur Gaharet sighed. "For whatever reason, Constance, my father took his knowledge of you and your mother to his grave. And we, as a pack, have been the poorer for it." Seigneur Gaharet placed his elbows on the table and leaned forward. "Soon, Constance, you and I are going to have a long overdue discussion about all that you know of us, of our kind. Right now, however, I need your help. D'Artagnon needs your help."

The dark eyes of the man she had once thought would take her as his mate regarded her. They did not plead. They were not solemn. Rather, they held a certainty more familiar with *her* visions. He believed in her, and in her ability to help his brother.

The skin on the back of Constance's neck prickled. The black wolf had moved closer and was barely steps away. She stilled. He focused on her, as though she were the only person in the room. What was going through his mind? Did he resent her presence? Or was he merely curious?

The black wolf sniffed and turned away. He picked up a raw haunch of venison and padded over to lie by the fire. This wolf was damaged — physically and, if he truly was stuck, possibly mentally. Would he *want* her help? But, if they could not help him, he may never return to human form again.

Chapter Four

D'Artagnon lay by the fire chewing on the haunch, swiveling his ears from one voice to the next, listening to the conversation at the table. The tall thin man had silently slipped away, as a good servant does. Gascon. Brother to Anne, steward to D'Artagnon's father and now to his brother. All the servants were from one extended family, if his memory served him. They overran the whole keep.

Anne, a not-so-good servant, had retreated to the kitchen. A wise thing, because he had yet to forgive her for the slap across his snout. Mayhap he had let her treat him such as a young man. As a wolf, he would no longer tolerate such an affront.

The others sat around the table discussing him as though he were not only a wolf, but also hard of hearing.

"Maybe he has been a wolf for so long, he does not want to return to human form," suggested Aimon. "It is exhilarating being a wolf, running through the forest and chasing prey."

D'Artagnon grunted. The white wolf was young, in body and in wolf, still but a pup filled with the exuberance of his new existence.

"Tell me you felt nothing, Aimon, when Gaharet commanded D'Artagnon to shift?" demanded Ulrik. "My wolf *cowered*, and *I* was once foolhardy enough to challenge Gaharet for leadership of the pack."

D'Artagnon dropped the haunch. Ulrik had *challenged* Gaharet? That would explain the scars at his throat and the raspiness of his voice. His brother had faced so much while he had been gone. Alone. His lip curled in a silent snarl. One more thing his enemy would pay for.

"No," said Ulrik, the certainty in his voice ringing clear. "The D'Artagnon I remember as a boy was a follower, not a leader. He is stuck."

D'Artagnon sniffed and resumed chewing on the bone, tearing at the sinew.

"Perhaps…" A rap of fingers on the table.

D'Artagnon swiveled his ears toward the older man. The one Gaharet had called Farren. Kathryn's father. His mother's brother.

"I confess," said Farren, "I know little of being a werewolf, but would I be correct in assuming those scars on his body would ordinarily have been enough to kill a werewolf?"

His brother tilted his head and regarded Farren. "Possibly."

"And being in your wolf form, you are stronger, are you not?"

His brother nodded. "All our wolf senses and abilities are stronger in that form, yes. What are you suggesting, Farren?"

"Could it be he is choosing to stay in wolf form because he is afraid?"

Ulrik snorted. "He is here." He gestured at their surroundings. "In his home. Surrounded by his pack. What is there to fear?"

Gaharet held up his hand. "Let us hear Farren out, Ulrik. He may be onto something."

His brother had not changed. Still the same responsible man he remembered. Cautious, thoughtful, smart enough to know he did not have all the answers and willing to listen to all ideas and opinions before making a decision. Unlike Ulrik, who seemed as impetuous as ever.

"I do not suggest he is afraid of us, or anyone." Farren inclined his head at Ulrik. "As you pointed out, he stood his ground when Gaharet commanded he shift. Many a warrior, werewolf or no, would be hard-pressed not to obey. It made the hair on the back of my neck stand on end. But what if what he fears is being human? It was as a man he fought on that battlefield, and it was as a man he nearly died. If we are right in thinking the person who attacked him was also a werewolf, this traitor to the pack, perhaps he feels stronger facing him as a wolf."

D'Artagnon leveled his eye at Farren. He was not afraid. And he was *not* stuck. At least, he did not think he was stuck. He could shift any time he chose. To prove his point, he called forth the change, letting it hover close below the surface.

Gaharet's nostrils flared, and he turned, watching him.

D'Artagnon ignored him, his heart thudding loud and fast in his chest, and his stomach curdling. A tremble started along his spine, and the darkness of his nightmares threatened. He pulled back from the shift, letting his human half slip back into the depths of his subconscious. The sensation subsided.

He could not meet his brother's gaze. Could Farren have the right of it? He shook his head. No. He was out of practice, nothing more.

His brother was not the only one who had sensed his attempt to shift. The healer jerked her gaze away, a flush rising up her neck. The woman from the cottage in the forest. With her wheat-colored braids and her unusual eyes. Nary a day had gone past since he had watched her through the storm had she not slipped into his thoughts, distracting him from his purpose. And he had the right of it. He *had* encountered her before. He had not needed Anne's confirmation to know he had seen her in this keep. Once, long ago. Though she had been but a child and he on the verge of adulthood, he remembered.

A mere half-score and four years, he had snuck out from under the sharp eyes of his brother, avoided the kitchen should Anne catch him and box his ears, and gone to the village. A pretty, dark-haired human girl, whose name he could no longer recall, had agreed to meet him at the edge of Old Tumas' cabbage patch. It was the night of his first fumbling kiss, all teeth and tongues and inexperience.

Sneaking back in, he had spied his father and mother in the library and the three strangers gathered there with them. One, a woman in a snug black dress that left her legs bare, and strange red shoes that had her standing on her toes. He would come to know her as

Marie. The other two, a mother and her child — a little girl with blonde curls and eyes of different colors — one blue, one green. The little girl, now a woman, sitting at the table.

But recognition alone was not enough to warrant his reaction to her.

The woman, Constance, snuck a peek in his direction and caught him staring. She flushed again and looked away, rubbing her hands across her book, her heartbeat elevated. Did he frighten her? With his scarred body and missing eye, he was no longer the handsome youth many had once proclaimed him to be. As a wolf, he had borne the evidence of his failings, but...

D'Artagnon gave a shake of his head. *Why do I care what she thinks of me? And why am I still here?*

He should leave now while they were all otherwise occupied. He had agreed to a meal, and there was little meat left on the bone. D'Artagnon could be out of the door before any of them, alpha or no, could stop him. He had a promise to keep. Deaths to avenge. A wolf to hunt and kill. He would spare his newly mated brother the responsibility of this. See vengeance done himself.

Yet, he could not force himself to move toward the door, nor shift his gaze away from the woman. From the loose strands of hair that escaped from beneath her head veil and her upturned nose. From her sun-kissed skin and calloused hands. The woman eked a living out in the forest. It was written all over her, though the quality of her dress belied it.

Her scent tickled his nose, drawing him in. He focused, narrowing in on her alone, and did what he had longed to do back at the little cottage in the forest, taking her in with all his enhanced senses. A chasm of pain and loneliness so deep it almost matched his own flowed from her. Whereas anger and his need for vengeance colored his, hers was dull and smothered, as though she had resigned herself to the vagaries of her existence. Life had not been kind to her. That made him want to rend, tear and destroy.

A deep growl rumbled in his chest, and all eyes turned to him. He ignored all but hers.

D'Artagnon abandoned his place by the fire and padded across the floor to the table. To her. No one moved, nor made a sound, but he sensed their scrutiny in the prickle across his ruff. Her fingers fluttered against the bodice of her dress, but she did not shrink away. He opened his senses again and this time the aching loneliness was subdued by curiosity and thin tendrils of...hope?

Interesting.

He edged closer, sniffing at her feet and working his way up her dress to her knee, taking her scent deep into his nostrils. There was something about this woman. He sniffed her hand, and her fingers curled into her palm.

"He will not hurt you." His brother's voice, deep and confident, cut through the baited silence.

He narrowed his eye at Gaharet. What made his brother so certain? He was not the same man — wolf — he had been when last they had fought side by side. After the incident with Anne, Gaharet should be more cautious.

Constance eyed him, wary and yet still curious. "I believe you."

Her soft, melodious voice washed over him, soothing some of the sharp edges in his mind. D'Artagnon flicked his ears forward, longing to hear her speak again. He inched closer and settled his chin on her knee, fixing his gaze on her face.

"Would you look at that?" Ulrik rasped. "*L'enfer.* Could this mean…"

"I believe it could." Awe tinged his brother's voice.

His brother's words should concern him, but when Constance raised her hand and set it on his head, gently stroking his fur, D'Artagnon no longer cared.

Chapter Five

Beneath Constance's hand, the wolf's fur was thick and coarse, not soft and luxurious as it looked. He was real, present, not a notation in her grimoire or a character in the tales of her ancestors. His blue eye, with dark shadows flitting across it, held a pain so deep she may never comprehend the depths of it.

She brushed her hand across his fur again, avoiding the scar. The wolf may not be sensitive about such things, but the man might be. Monsieur D'Artagnon. She should think of him as Monsieur D'Artagnon. For as much as he appeared a wolf from the wild, in truth that was who, what, he was. A man. One who had once lived in this keep. Who had survived much to return all these years later. For whatever reason he persisted in his wolf form, the man inside remained. Somewhere.

She set her free hand on her grimoire and turned her attention to Seigneur Gaharet. "There are only two things I know of that can affect a wolf's ability to shift." She absently picked at the edge of the worn leather-bound book. Were they desperate enough to go to such extremes? "Wolfsbane and silver."

Monsieur D'Artagnon snatched his head from beneath her hand and retreated, his lips peeled back to reveal large canines. Seigneur Ulrik snarled. Monsieur Aimon reared back. Seigneur Gaharet's gaze never wavered.

They had asked for her aid, and she must give them all the information, no matter how unpleasant. Constance pushed on. "I would counsel against wolfsbane, for it elicits an inability to maintain form—human or wolf. As you well know, shifting requires energy. Too long an exposure to wolfsbane, too high a concentration, and a wolf will soon collapse from exhaustion. Neither wolf nor human have a never-ending supply of energy. Silver, however, *will* subdue a wolf."

Seigneur Gaharet tugged at his beard. "Not entirely."

"I assure you, Mon Seigneur, it will." She tapped the grimoire. "According to my ancestors' experience."

"Not according to mine. During a turning, a wolf is so strong it is possible for them to break free of any bonds of silver."

What? Constance opened her book and flicked through the pages until she came to the one she was searching for. She ran her finger beneath the curling script, reading it line by line. There was no mention of any wolf breaking free of silver.

"Are you sure, Mon Seigneur?" Constance dropped her gaze, her cheeks heating. "I am sorry, I do not mean to question—"

"No apology is necessary, Constance. You are right to doubt it. I would not have believed it myself had I not seen it with my own eyes."

Constance slid her gaze to Monsieur D'Artagnon. The wolf seemed to grow larger, broader as he stared her down. If Monsieur D'Artagnon had resisted his alpha's command to shift, could he resist the power of silver? He raised his head, a determined set to his shoulders and jaw, and a certainty settled in her chest, common with her visions and her second sight. Whether his fear of being human was preventing him from shifting or something else, it mattered not, for her mention of silver had set her against him. It could well see him refusing to shift on principle.

"Be that as it may," continued Seigneur Gaharet, "I would not use silver on any werewolf. Especially not my brother, who has been through so much. What sort of welcome home would that be? We need to find another way."

That made her task more difficult. "Of course. I will study my grimoire and see if I can find something else that may assist."

Monsieur D'Artagnon huffed and retreated, though he did not take his eye off her, and a new wariness flickered in its depth.

"Anne." Seigneur Gaharet beckoned the old woman. "Show Constance to a room." To Constance, he said, "You have had a long journey. Rest and refresh yourself. We will discuss this again anon."

Constance closed her book and got to her feet.

The old cook's eyes narrowed at the black wolf. "May I suggest the room at the top of the stairs, Gaharet?"

A slow smile spread across Seigneur Gaharet's lips. "A splendid idea, Anne. Make it so."

D'Artagnon jerked his head to stare at his brother. *The room at the top of the stairs? My room?* He glared at the little healer. She had drawn him in with her soft voice and her sense of otherness that mirrored his own until her mention of binding him with silver had snapped him from his stupor.

Anne gathered up the Constance's bag and cloak, her eyes twinkling. "Come, come now, dear. Let us get you settled in."

There was a knowing look in Anne's eyes that had D'Artagnon's hackles rising. The old cook was planning something. He gritted his teeth. Had the woman not learned anything after what had happened earlier? He snorted. What did it matter? Why should he care what Anne was plotting, or where Constance would sleep? Now was his chance to leave.

Constance followed Anne. "Time alone would be good. I must study the writings of my ancestors. I have not seen, nor read, of such a case as Monsieur D'Artagnon before, but..." She paused, and glanced back at him, consternation flickering in the depths of her eyes. "I will endeavor to resolve it."

D'Artagnon snarled. *I am not a problem for you to solve, little healer.*

His brother's shrewd gaze settled on him, as though sensing his resistance. It was difficult to hide anything from a wolf, especially one as perceptive as his brother.

Let him see. Let him make of it what he will. I am not staying.

In the guise of following Anne and Constance, he slipped into the corridor.

"D'Artagnon." His brother's voice followed him.

D'Artagnon paused and looked over his shoulder.

Gaharet leaned against the door frame. "Nine long years you have been gone, and you think to leave already?"

L'enfer. His brother always had been too observant, too canny.

"I *could* confine you in the training room. Force you to remain here," said Gaharet. "But I will not. I am asking you, not as your alpha, but as your brother, to stay. Please. Whatever ails you, we can help you. Whatever burdens you bear, you no longer have to shoulder them alone. You are safe here. And we could use your help to find this traitor."

The large door of the entrance loomed close, mere steps away. All he need do was pad down the corridor, push the door open and return to the forest. Would Gaharet follow him? Perhaps, but he had learned a few tricks over the years. It would be a simple matter to evade his brother.

"Will you not stay the night? A few days?" A shadow crossed his brother's face. "I have missed you, D'Artagnon. We all have."

His brother's words tugged at him. He had missed him, too. The steady calm his brother exuded. The feeling of having him at his back. His solid and unwavering support. And he had missed his pack. With Ulrik returned, it would almost be like it was before. He had been gone nine long years. What were a few days? It was a small thing. He could do this for his brother.

D'Artagnon turned, intending to reclaim his place by the fire. In the periphery of his vision, he glimpsed Constance before she rounded the corner of the stairwell—her slight frame and the gentle sway of her hips. He narrowed his eye on his brother. Gaharet wanted him to shift. Staying for a few days would give the little witch time to find some way to force him. Already she could be hatching a plan. Anyone wishing him to shift, or thinking they could use silver on him, was not to be trusted.

Best to keep my enemy close. His father had taught him that. Though it had not worked so well for him.

With a snarl at his brother, D'Artagnon loped up the stairs after the women, the scent of his brother's relief following him.

He caught up to Constance and Anne at a doorway at the top of the stairs and pushed past them into a large room. His room. The aroma of old meadowsweet rushes hung in the chill air, giving it a stale, abandoned feel. Cold coals lay in the brazier in the corner. A half-burned candle sat beside an open book on the table by the bed, and his clothes remained haphazardly thrown about. Everything was the same as the day he had awoken, donned his armor and prepared for battle, answering the summons from Comte Lothair. As though not a single person had crossed this threshold since that fateful day.

So long ago. So many years living in the forest, sleeping on the ground and hunting for his food, yet he still remembered the feel of sinking into the soft downy mattress. It seemed only yesterday he had sat in bed reading into the late hours, having no inkling of the betrayal the following morn would bring.

Anne motioned Constance into the room. "Come, child. You will sleep in here."

D'Artagnon leaped onto the unmade bed, the covers still thrust back as he had left them. He flopped on the cool linen sheets, rested his chin on his paws and watched her. The healer. Constance. The woman who had threatened to bind him in silver. He shuddered and his heart hardened. Even had his brother not rejected her suggestion, he would never allow it.

She had his brother and the other wolves charmed and had almost ensnared him, but he was awake to the danger now. He would keep watch. Ensure she did not attempt something despite his brother's decree.

"This was D'Artagnon's room," said Anne. "Gaharet forbade me from touching it after... Well, that is all in the past now." The old cook beamed at him. "He has returned."

Constance moved about the room, her shoulders stiff. "Are you certain Seigneur Gaharet would want me to sleep here?" She turned in a slow circle, her gaze flitting from one open chest, the books haphazardly stacked, to another with tunics and breeches spilling out onto the floor. "I expected a sleeping mat in the hall, or in the larder or the grain store. Maybe an empty stall in the stables? Not a room as grand as this. Not...*his* room. Where is Monsieur D'Artagnon going to sleep?"

"Oh, heavens no, child." Anne crossed to his chest of books and dropped the lid with a *thunk*. "You are our guest. Here to help the young lad. If he insists on staying in wolf form, then he can sleep on the floor by the brazier." She gave him a sly smile. "Or curl up on the end of the bed, if he must." She picked up a tunic, shook it out, folded it then placed it neatly away. "Always such a messy boy, this one. Even as he grew, he never had a care for neatness and order." She scooped up a pair of breeches. "Not like his older brother at all."

"But—"

"Now, shall I have the servants bring you a bath, child? There is a marvelous barrel I can have the boys roll in and fill with hot water. You can soak away the rigors of your journey."

Constance caught his stare, and color infused her face. "A jug of water should be ample, thank you."

The flush of her cheeks stirred something within him. He gritted his teeth and ignored it. The woman was too beguiling for her own good.

"Mm, perhaps you are right. No need to give this young man more than he deserves. At least, not until he has *earned* it." Anne shuffled about the room, scooping up the clothes from the floor, folding them and stacking them neatly in the chest. She made a shooing motion at him. "Come now, lad, the girl needs a rest before supper. Remove your furry self off the bed so I can straighten it."

More color rose across Constance's face and down her slender neck. "There is no need, Anne. I could not possibly sleep in this bed. A sleeping pallet with the other servants is all I require."

"Nonsense, child. You *shall* sleep in this bed. What say you, D'Artagnon?"

Constance, snug in between bedsheets thick with his scent? It appealed to him far more than it should.

He glared at Anne. He was not keen to cower to her demands. She was but the cook. In this, though, they were in agreeance. The little healer would sleep in his bed. Where better than in his territory so he could keep a close watch over her, a witness to whatever plan she made? And that was the only reason. He rose and slipped off the bed.

"Now, there will be no more talk of sleeping pallets, or whatnot." Anne straightened the covers. "Gaharet has ordered it so, and you have D'Artagnon's permission. That is enough for me." Anne shifted his unfinished tome aside. "You can put your precious book on the table there. None will touch it, I assure you."

After a moment's hesitation, Constance set her grimoire down on the table beside the half-burned candle.

Anne picked up the empty water pitcher and a crumpled, used linen. "I shall send a maid up with some warm water and a clean cloth for you to freshen up. And since our furry lad here refuses to shift and prove useful, I will send one of the boys with fresh coals for the brazier."

D'Artagnon ignored Anne's dig at him. It would take a lot more than a snide remark from an old woman to prompt him to shift. She waddled out of the door, pitcher in hand, then he was alone with *her*. The woman from the cottage. In his room. Soon to be sleeping in his bed.

He fought the confounding sense of satisfaction that lodged in his chest and made himself comfortable beside the cold brazier. The last nine years had taught him much, but the most useful was patience. He would give his brother his few days, then he would return to hunting for his nemesis. Nothing, not his brother's entreaties to remain in the keep, to shift, nor this woman who intrigued him so, would stop him from fulfilling his promise to his father. He would avenge his parents' death, and *his* near death. If it was the last thing he did, D'Artagnon would see it done.

Chapter Six

Constance stood awkwardly in the room. She had never slept in a bed so grand. She had never slept in *any* man's bed, and certainly not one belonging to a member of the nobility. Monsieur D'Artagnon, no less. A black wolf. *Another* black wolf. The thought had her heart fluttering.

The bed looked soft and the covers warm, but she would not be sleeping here alone. Her childhood vision poked at her mind, and a swirl of heat rushed across her skin. She placed her palm on her forehead. Was she coming down with some sort of fever? She dropped her hand. No. As a healer, she knew better. The reminder of her vision, and the intensity of his regard, had more to do with the tingling in her body than any possible malaise.

Awareness flickered in the black wolf's eye. Not only the knowing of a wolf, but the intelligence of a man. A battle-hardened chevalier, and a man who, she presumed, had spent years as a wolf surviving alone in the woods. Constance had firsthand experience of how hard it was to eke out a living from the forest. It was only through the charity of the Langeais villagers she could manage it.

As a wolf, he would have advantages she did not. His ability to hunt, for one. But Monsieur D'Artagnon had lived his whole life on a wealthy estate with far more comforts than all but a few would ever experience, surrounded by people—his brother, the servants, the villagers. There were hardships beyond the physical with a life lived in the forest, as Constance knew well.

A manservant arrived with a scoop of glowing coals and placed them into the brazier, before departing without a word.

A young maid followed, with a pitcher of water and a fresh linen. "Shall I assist you with your clothes, Mademoiselle?"

Constance shook her head. "Thank you, no. I can manage." She had managed for almost her entire life.

The servant girl curtsied before Constance could stop her.

"Please. There is no need for that." *L'enfer*, she was but a peasant.

The girl curtsied again. "Of course, Mademoiselle."

Constance sighed. What would the servants think of her when they discovered she was no more entitled to such treatment than they were?

"If that is all, Mademoiselle…"

"Thank you."

The girl beat a hasty retreat, leaving her alone with Monsieur D'Artagnon once more.

The black wolf had not taken his eyes off her for one moment. He did not trust her. That much was clear.

Not since she had outlined the choices for a cure to Seigneur Gaharet. His resistance would make her task harder, and she did not want to fail. Could not *afford* to fail. Her life was precarious enough. She *needed* the protection the Langeais wolves could give her.

"Your brother is very concerned about you, Monsieur D'Artagnon. About your inability to shift."

The black wolf cocked his head, ears pricked.

"About what has happened to you, and where you have been all these years." Constance unpinned her head veil, set it aside, and unfurled her braids from around her head. She untied the bands around the ends and raked her fingers through the braids, teasing them apart. "Do you not feel safe surrounded by your pack? Seigneur Gaharet is a strong wolf. Together, and with Seigneur Ulrik and Monsieur Aimon, surely one traitorous wolf could not prevail."

Constance turned her back on him, though the skin on her neck prickled, and poured water from the pitcher into the bowl. There was something teetering on the edge of her vision, a sense that there was more, but it would not reveal itself for her to see. Sometimes that was the way of her visions. Nothing more than a vague sense — something beyond the reach of her understanding. A foreboding.

"Whatever you may believe, Monsieur D'Artagnon, I am trying to help you."

The wolf gave an indignant huff.

Constance pulled at the stays of her dress. "My ancestors knew much about your kind. My grimoire is full of records of our dealings with the Langeais wolves. Something in there is bound to assist us. Something far kinder than silver."

Constance was not so sure of that. As a young girl, enamored with the Black Wolf, she had devoured those pages. Nothing she had read — in the records, the spells, the potions, or in the legend of the first Black Wolf — would aid her now. She would search through them all the same. Maybe she had missed something.

She slipped her soft wool overdress off and laid it across a chest. "Do you not want to tell your brother of the man who gave you those scars?" If only she could command a vision forth of the traitor's face, or the knowledge of a name. "It would be of great help to your pack. They have suffered much at his hand."

Was he watching her still? Her fingers trembled. Did she want him to be watching as she prepared for bed? It was not like she would be naked. She was wearing her chemise. It should be no different than if she bedded down with the servants, sharing a room and a sleeping pallet. But her body was convinced this was different.

With her mouth suddenly drier than the bark of an old river birch, she removed her underdress and set it aside, too. Goosebumps prickled across skin laid bare.

Pull yourself together, Constance.

She dipped her hands into the water and splashed it onto her heated face, neck, arms and legs. She dried her damp skin with the fresh linen, having regained some measure of calm, and turned to face him. He had not moved.

"Why have you returned, if not to speak of these things?"

His gaze held firm, but within his eye, shadows shifted. Again, that sense of foreboding.

What am I not seeing?

Curse her second sight. She let the feeling go. Forcing a vision never worked. All she could hope was it would become clearer in time. She gathered up her book and slipped beneath the covers of the bed.

Constance sank into its softness with a sigh. A mattress stuffed with feathers, not straw. She pressed her hand into it, awed by the downy lightness. "It is so soft." She plumped a pillow, marveling at the smooth suppleness of it before propping it against the headboard. It was as heavenly as the mattress. She closed her eyes and leaned into it.

Do not get used to this, Constance. It is but temporary.

Soon enough she would be back in her humble cottage, sleeping on her hard cot with her straw mattress and her patched blanket, and this would all seem like nothing more than a beautiful dream.

Constance opened her eyes and reached for her grimoire. She flicked through it, past recipes for potions and pages of herbal lore, until she was near the back of the book. At the section devoted entirely to the wolves of Langeais, where the curling secret script of her ancestors replaced Latin.

She ran her hands over the page, written long before she was born. Curls and shapes danced across it. It was childlike in quality—letters with tails, repeated patterns. Indecipherable to anyone who did not know it. The perfect way to hide secrets. Twins, her mother had told her, had created this language. A secret language between the two of them. For years, it had remained little more than that. As time went on, and the knowledge entrusted to the coven became too important to be forgotten, and too dangerous to be scribed in the language of the church, it became the secret script of the wolves. Of the Black Wolf.

Each generation had one. Indeed, it had all begun with a single black wolf.

Constance turned the pages, skimming over the legend until she came to the description. Dark hair, dark eyes and a strong nose. Like Seigneur Gaharet. It seemed they bred true in the d'Louncrais family. She glanced over her book at Monsieur D'Artagnon. At least, one of them had. Monsieur D'Artagnon had his mother's eyes. Dame Elise d'Louncrais was not one easily forgotten. With her bright copper hair, unblemished skin, blue eyes and regal demeanor, to a young Constance, she had seemed like a queen.

She ran her calloused fingers through her own hair, the color of straw. That she was entertaining a d'Louncrais finding her appealing seemed ridiculous. With her different colored eyes, her peasant's hands and sun-browned skin, she was the furthermost thing from an ideal mate for a d'Louncrais. She had only to look at the others — copper-haired Kathryn, cultured Erin with her astounding knowledge of the past and the future, or Rebekah, with her green-streaked hair and colorful skin markings, so exotic and bold — to know she was but pale in comparison.

She rubbed a hand over the woolen bed covers. But here she was. In Monsieur D'Artagnon's room. In his *bed*. And there *he* was, sitting by the brazier, watching her.

The wolf snarled. A divide as wide as the county gaped between them, placing them at odds. She had a task to complete. One, from the stiffness of his shoulders and the determined set of his brow, he would do everything he could to thwart. Constance dropped her gaze to her grimoire. Something in here had to give her the answer.

D'Artagnon watched and waited. Constance's eyelids drooped. Her book dipped once, then again, before slipping from her fingers as she drifted off to sleep. When her breathing deepened, he slunk over and leaped up beside her. Perhaps now he could uncover what it was about this woman that fascinated him so. Or forestall any plans she might have for him.

He sniffed at the book and contemplated destroying it. No, the book held purpose for the healer, was precious to her. Leather-bound, with pages of vellum. How had peasants afforded such a luxury? A gift, perhaps? From one of his ancestors? It was clear her family had a connection with his own. That his father had died before passing on this knowledge was but another strike against his nemesis.

The book had fallen open, and he eyed the familiar script scrawled across the pages. The same script as on the pack's sacred amulets. This, however, was far more complex than the simple lines his father had forced D'Artagnon to memorize when he had presented him with his amulet. A simple spell to recite when in mortal danger, to bring them back to their alpha. He had not needed to read it, nor have knowledge of the language, merely recite its verse as he smeared his blood into the amulet's grooves.

D'Artagnon still missed the weight of his amulet around his neck, though he had lost his long ago. In battle. Cut from around his neck before he could utter a word. His nemesis had seen to that. Before he could recite the spell, fall at his brother's feet and reveal who had killed their father and mother. The man who had cut him down.

Whether fate or luck had intervened that day, D'Artagnon neither knew nor cared. But it had. In the form of a chevalier from the opposing army. Attacked from behind, his father's murderer had turned to block a killing blow and D'Artagnon had crawled into the forest, shedding his armor and shifting form, determined to survive. Vowing he would one day have his vengeance. It had burned within him, warming him through the icy clutches of winter during the long years of his self-imposed exile. It had kept him alive.

Constance shifted in her sleep, curling on her side, her face softening in repose. The cares and worries, the wariness, the aching loneliness that tainted her scent slipped away. She sighed and smiled. Whatever she dreamed, it was pleasing to her.

She sighed again. This time, a slight frown creased her forehead. "That which you think you want was never meant to be yours."

He stilled. Was she talking to him? Her eyes remained closed. Part of her dream, perhaps?

"What *is* meant for you is far greater reward" — her voice firmed, and she grimaced, as though the words pained her — "if you have but the courage and the room in your heart—"

His hackles rose. It was eerie listening to her talk as though she were conscious.

" —to make the right choice." Her face smoothed out, her last words fading to a whisper, and she rolled away from him.

He shook his fur. The woman spoke in riddles. Mayhap her words were nothing more than a product of a strange dream. Not meant for him, despite the chill that had gripped his bones. He turned his attention back to the book and, with his nose, he flipped through page after page of the curling script. He had no hope of reading whatever secrets it held. Not without the key to a language his pack had long forgotten.

He nudged the book shut and pushed it away, stepping toward the edge of the bed. Constance shivered beneath the covers. Was she cold? The coals in the brazier glowed, giving off ample heat. Was it something in her dream? The beginnings of a nightmare? D'Artagnon had had more than enough experience with those. He eyed the floor beside the brazier. The spot where he had intended to sleep.

Constance moaned. Indecision burned through him. She called to him, to his wolf. Never had he felt a pull so strong.

D'Artagnon turned away from the brazier and curled up on the bed beside her, laying his head across the leather-bound book and his body snug against hers, giving what little comfort he could offer. Perhaps he would gain comfort from her presence, too. Some relief from his own nightmares. As he closed his eye and drifted into a light sleep, it was not the usual visions of his enemy's vicious and twisted face, his sword arm raised, that flitted into his mind. Rather, the outline of Constance's body visible beneath a thin chemise as she washed. The curve of her hip, her tapered waist and her glorious golden tresses falling over her shoulder. The little healer, Constance, calling to him even in his sleep.

Chapter Seven

A gentle tapping on her shoulder startled Constance awake.

Anne, the old cook, stood over her, a candle in hand. "Time to eat, child. The evening meal will be soon served. No doubt you are hungry."

Constance pushed herself up and rubbed her eyes. Her journey must have exhausted her more than she had realized. She had fallen asleep. Worse, she had neglected to place a ward around the bed. Constance had not slept without the security of a ward since...well, never. Anyone could have come in here and stolen... Her heart in her throat, she hunted around for her grimoire amongst the thick covers.

Anne handed it to her. "It is here, child. No one has taken your book. No one would dare. Not with D'Artagnon on guard."

She grasped the book tight and searched the room for the black wolf. He lay by the brazier as he had before she'd fallen asleep.

"Come, child. Let's get you ready for supper. You could do with a bit more meat on your bones." Across Anne's arm was a bundle of blue cloth. She held it up. "I have brought you a dress. One of Kathryn's. You are similar in size."

"Oh, I have a dress. I could not accept anoth—"

"Of course you can. I will not have it gossiped about in the village that we did not take care of our guests. Come, now. I will help you into it. The color will suit you fine."

Constance suffered the unfamiliar sensation of having someone assist her to dress, smoothing her hands over the soft wool and running her fingers over the pretty embroidery along the edges of the sleeves. Unease settled in her stomach. They had given her several new dresses before, but this one had belonged to Dame Kathryn and was far fancier than anything she had ever worn. With its embroidered hem and cuffs, it was more suitable for a woman of the noble class. She did not belong in such finery. She tugged at the laces at her waist.

"Stop fussing, love. The dress looks beautiful on you. As though it were made with you in mind. Come, sit, and I will braid your hair."

Anne grasped her arm and propelled her into the chair, giving Constance little chance to protest. The old cook combed her hair, and with deft fingers, braided it, curled the braids around Constance's head and secured them in place. A lump formed in her throat. The last person to help her with her hair had been her mother.

Anne fixed her head veil in place. "There. All set. D'Artagnon will escort you down to the hall, and I will join you anon. Once I have checked on the kitchen." Disapproval creased her forehead. "One cannot leave

71

those young ones there alone for but a moment before they are getting up to mischief. Lord knows what state the food would be in were I not there to keep that kitchen running smoothly. Run along now, child."

With little choice but to do as Anne instructed, Constance scooped up her book. This keep was full of treasures which, if sold, would keep her fed and clothed for a lifetime, but nothing was more precious than the knowledge in her grimoire. Neither Anne nor Monsieur D'Artagnon said a word about her mistrust, and she followed the black wolf from the room.

The murmur of many voices spilled into the corridor from within the great hall — male voices, female voices and bursts of laughter. Constance paused in the doorway. *So many people.* Maids, farmers, chevaliers, all gathered at the large table. In their midst, Seigneur Gaharet and his mate, Dame Erin. Seigneur Ulrik, deep in conversation with a big burly man with a ruddy complexion, sat at one end of the table. At the other end, Monsieur Aimon and Dame Kathryn laughed with Seigneur Farren.

What she would have given to be wearing her old clothes. To wrap herself in their rough familiarity. She was but an impostor in this fancy dress.

Dame Erin beckoned her over. "Come and sit down, Constance. There's a spare seat here."

A furry muzzle nudged at her hand. D'Artagnon inclined his head toward the table and all the unfamiliar faces. Taking a steadying breath, she crossed the floor, the press of a large, warm body against her thigh a surprising comfort.

She slid into the seat Dame Erin had suggested and placed her book on the table. "Thank you, Ma Dame."

No one gave Monsieur D'Artagnon so much as a glance. As if having a big black wolf join them for supper was a common occurrence.

Beside her, a grizzled farmer with a wrinkled face and a scowl looked her up and down, his rheumy gaze flicking between her and her grimoire. "Interesting looking book. You a witch?"

Constance stiffened. All talk around the table ceased, and an uncomfortable silence settled over the hall. *To be ousted so soon.*

"Tumas." There was a warning note in Seigneur Gaharet's voice.

"I mean nothing by it, Mon Seigneur." The old farmer, Tumas, rubbed the back of his neck. "I have this boil here that will not heal. Anne has tried her best, but... This young lass looks the real thing, what with those eyes and all."

Constance stared at her hands. *Oh, why was I not born with normal eyes?*

"Tumas," Seigneur Gaharet growled.

"I mean no offense, lass. But I remember a time when we had witches in the village." He jerked his knife at Seigneur Gaharet. "Was one in yer grandfather's time. Not easily forgotten, that one. Handed out salves or potions if she had a mind to. Had eyes just like yers."

Constance jerked her head up.

"Had visions, too. Yer get those?"

Eyes like mine? Constance nodded, too dumbfounded to speak.

"Such a shame. Could have done a lot of good, but she chose different. I was a boy when the villagers cast 'er out for 'er evil ways."

Hope died a vicious death, stomped on by the superstition of others. What had she expected? That the d'Louncrais villagers were any different from those of Langeais? Or any other village in the county? Of course they were not. But she would like to know more about this woman with eyes like hers. Could it be all who were born with the second sight were marked so? Her mother had been less than forthcoming on the matter than Constance would have liked. As if she, too, was unsure how to manage Constance and her affliction.

"I shall prepare a salve for you, Master Tumas, and deliver it on the morrow." She glanced at Seigneur Gaharet. "If that is acceptable to you, Mon Seigneur?" She would like to talk to Master Tumas some more about this witch, but not here in front of all these people.

A big, black furry body pushed in between her and Tumas, forcing the farmer to shift along to make space. Monsieur D'Artagnon sat on the bench seat on his haunches, looking for all the world as though he planned to partake of the meal along with everyone else.

A hint of a smile crept across Seigneur Gaharet's lips. "I will have someone to escort you on the morrow, Constance. But let it be known" — he raised his voice so all at the table could hear — "Constance is here at my request. There will be no casting her out for whatever nonsensical reason. And, if you have ailments, you will consult with Anne first. Anne will decide if your complaint requires Constance's expertise."

Nods and mumbled agreements rumbled around the table. With the arrival of platters piled high with food, the conversation and attention turned away, much to Constance's relief.

Anne sat her sizable bulk on the other side of Constance, placed a bejeweled pewter goblet in front of her, and filled it with wine.

The cook handed her a knife with an elaborate carved handle. "Do not be shy, child. There is more than enough food to go around. And it all tastes wonderful, if I do say so myself." Anne placed a plate in front of Constance and filled it with meat, bread and spoonfuls of thick stew. "Eat up now."

Constance slid her grimoire beneath her bottom, safe from food spillage and prying eyes, and picked up the bread and dipped it into the stew. She did not have to look to know everyone was watching her. Maybe they were not staring outright, but from the corner of their eyes, or with furtive glances between bites of food, or over their fancy goblets. It was not the first time she had come under such scrutiny, so she did what she always did. She ignored it.

The big black wolf next to her was harder to ignore. His fur brushed her sleeve, and the warmth of his body seeped through to her skin. With his perpetual snarl, he stared down all who would look her way. If they were not already curious enough, having a scarred wolf, one of the d'Louncrais, sitting next to her and challenging everyone at the table, would assure her place in the village gossip tomorrow.

Constance shuffled the food about on her plate with the tip of her knife. More than she ever did when she visited the village of Langeais, she was conscious of her difference. It did not matter she was not the only peasant at the table. That beside her sat Anne, the cook, and across from her, the maid who had curtsied to her earlier. Half the village had to be here, comfortable in their place at Seigneur Gaharet's table. Eating his food.

Drinking his wine. Though she was here at his request, she was more an outsider than they were. What she would not give to be one of them. Someone who belonged.

"Tell me, child, what other herbs would you use to cure cranky old Tumas' boils?" Anne leaned closer and gave a conspiratorial wink. "Though I have a right mind to let him suffer this one on his own."

Constance set aside her knife, grateful for the distraction. "What herbs have you already tried?"

"Well now, I started with a warm compress, and while that helped some, it is a persistent lesion. I suspect Tumas, like most men, only adheres to my instructions when it suits him."

On the other side of Monsieur D'Artagnon, Tumas grunted.

"Then I used chamomile flowers to soothe the redness, willow bark for the pain and honey to prevent infection."

Constance nodded. "You have a good knowledge of herbs. I would only add scrapings from the bark of a slippery elm tree and wash it with some vinegar. Perhaps you are right, Anne. Many a patient ignores advice about their health."

This time, both Tumas and Monsieur D'Artagnon huffed. Across the table, Seigneur Gaharet bit back a smile. Beside her, Anne beamed.

Constance picked up her knife and poked a piece of meat and chewed on it without tasting it. No matter how congenial, how much they tried to include her, she longed for the comfortable solitude of her rickety little cottage in the forest. She glanced at the black wolf beside her. There she would be comfortable, but she would also be alone.

Chapter Eight

The little healer — Constance — was uncomfortable with the curiosity of the servants and the farmers, and with their attention. He had scented her unease the moment Anne had insisted she wear the blue dress, and her discomfort had only increased when they had entered the hall. Then Old Tumas had called her a witch. A growl rumbled in his chest, and he glared at the grizzled and grumpy farmer. Tumas had upset Constance.

D'Artagnon gritted his teeth. *Why am I defending her? Protecting her? Caring how* she *feels?* Why had he leaped onto the seat, squeezing himself between Constance and that which disconcerted her? This *witch* with her angelic braids peeking out from under her veil, and her pretty upturned nose, discussing herbs and poultices with Anne. He snorted. And his brother, openly grinning at him from across the table. Gaharet was as taken with her as Anne was. He had thought them both more shrewd than that.

Well, she would not fool *him* with her honeyed voice and her hesitant smiles. She would not work her magic on *him*.

Old Tumas shrugged at him and turned his attention to his supper. D'Artagnon eyed the rest of those assembled at the table, snarling at any hint of a furtive glance. It rankled that he did so, that he could not stop himself. His brother's continued amusement only infuriated him further. He growled at his brother. Gaharet chuckled.

His brother's mate frowned at him. "What's so funny?"

Gaharet leaned closer to her. "D'Artagnon."

She raked her gaze over him. "Oh?" Her focus slid to Constance and her green eyes widened. "Oh." A slow grin spread across her lips. "That's a good thing."

"It is," his brother agreed. "A very good thing."

What is? What were they talking about? Beside him, Constance toyed with her food. Other than her lack of appetite and her discomfort, nothing seemed amiss, nor struck him as something to be smiling about.

"D'Artagnon." Gaharet gathered the green-eyed woman's hand in his. "This is Erin. My mate."

D'Artagnon quirked the eyebrow over his remaining eye. Did his brother think him witless because he would not shift? His senses were stronger than they had ever been. Years of using them to survive had honed them. He focused them on the woman now, searching beneath his brother's musk, the heady aroma of sex and the scent of the pup in her womb. Confidence and curiosity surrounded her. Gaharet kissed his mate's hand, and she softened against him. His brother had found a good mate. A strong one.

An emptiness welled up inside him, a long-forgotten yearning threatening to consume him. As a young man, the desire, the *need* to mate had burned ever brighter as the years had passed, embedded in his psyche as much as his wolf, intertwined and inseparable from the instincts that drove him. As had his brother, nay all werewolves, he had strived to meet the one woman who would be his match in all ways. Like his father had found his mother.

Behind him, the wall hanging played out his parents' courtship. Something to aspire to. Something worth fighting for, to cherish. A constant reminder of what could be. Until the day they had lost their mother, and his father his mate.

His shoulder twinged. That had all changed on that sodden and muddy battlefield. Fate had another purpose for him, and a mate would be but a distraction. He had spent too many years strengthening his body and his mind, pitting himself against nature to give up on his quest. Let his brother have the joy of being mated, of being a father and carrying on the d'Louncrais line.

Beside him, Constance laughed at something Anne had said, and the sound sank deep, almost to the marrow of his bones. He shut his eye, leaned closer, and breathed her in. The ruff on his neck bristled, and he opened his eye to his brother's smirk. He jerked away from Constance.

D'Artagnon spent the rest of the meal on edge, annoyed at his brother's amusement, as much as at himself for his undeniable need to protect the little healer, and shield her from the attention she so obviously abhorred. It was a relief when the meal finally ended, when the staff departed and servants cleared the empty platters from the table.

Constance begged fatigue, gathered her book and slipped from the hall. He watched her go, an unexplainable urge to follow surging in his chest. The wolves and Farren remained, none making a move to leave. They would have discussions this night. About him and the pack's situation. About the traitor. Talk he should be a witness to. A lot had happened in the years he had been gone.

His gaze slid to the door. Constance's scent lingered, taunting him. The witch could be doing all manner of things now she was out of his sight. Such as creating a spell or thinking to use silver now she was beyond his brother's presence.

His brother watched him, waiting.

D'Artagnon huffed and leaped from the seat, padding after the little human, ignoring his brother's laughter that followed him from the hall. He had been cautious coming to the keep, sniffing around the village and the walls. Nothing had been amiss. No scent out of place. He had promised his brother a few days. There was time enough to hear what he had to say. Constance he could not trust to leave alone for a single moment.

He found her perched up in bed, flicking through the pages of her grimoire. This time, he did not wait until she was asleep to jump up beside her.

She jerked her head up with a gasp.

He stretched himself out and locked gazes with her, daring her to complain. She gripped her book a little tighter around the edges, but she did not attempt to shoo him from the bed. Satisfied, he rested his head on his paws and settled in for the night but remained alert. Only when her lids fluttered closed and the book slipped from her fingers did he allow himself to relax, to sleep.

* * * *

D'Artagnon moved closer to the warm bundle of soft curves beneath the covers. He nuzzled her neck and breathed in her soft, earthy scent. Constance sighed, snuggling into him. He stretched and slid his arm over her, tucking her along the length of his body, reveling in the brush of golden hair against his bare shoulder.

My bare shoulder?

D'Artagnon's breath seized in his lungs, and he popped his eye open. *I have shifted?*

Even without the aid of his enhanced senses, he knew the truth of it. Cool night air breathed across his skin for the first time in years.

Merde. I have shifted in my sleep.

Constance murmured, lost in her dreams, and he tightened his hold.

L'enfer. What am I doing?

She let out a soft, breathy moan, and for the first time in a long time, something swirled within his chest other than anger and the deep cut of betrayal. Emotions he barely remembered himself capable of. Tenderness and…desire. His cock stirred.

Merde.

With slow, deliberate movements, careful not to disturb her, he relaxed his hold and removed his arm, rolling away from her. He slipped off the bed onto unsteady legs, strange to him after all this time, his breathing harsh to his own ears. He glared down at his half erect cock. *What is this woman* doing *to me?* What had she *done* to him?

He had barely let her out of his sight from the moment she had walked into the hall. Not once had he caught her whispering a spell. Yet, here he was, shifted into human form, as naked as the day he was born. No. She had done nothing, and yet... He clenched his hands into fists. *I have shifted.*

She rolled in his direction, snagging the covers tighter under her chin. Her eyes opened, and she stared straight at him. His heart skipped a beat, and he sucked in a sharp breath. Then her eyes fluttered closed. D'Artagnon released his breath, allowing the tension to ease from his body. He slid his gaze over her sleeping form. The tight lines around her eyes, the press of her lips together and the tension in her shoulders were gone. A longing to gather her in his arms, stroke her hair and brush his lips across hers squeezed at his heart. To promise her she need not fear again.

D'Artagnon threw back his head and stared at the ceiling. This woman was dangerous, and not only because she was a witch. The pleasant memory of her sweet body pressed against him tingled along his skin and he swallowed a groan. If the state of his cock was anything to go by, pleasant did not go far enough to describe it.

It had been a long time since he had enjoyed the feel of a woman in his arms. Mayhap that was what had caused his uncontrolled shift. It was possible. It might well be what Gaharet had planned. To tempt him with the carnal pleasures of a woman. But no matter how enticing, how much his human body called for him to slip beneath the covers and pull her into his embrace, the darkness swelled within him and his body trembled. His wolf pushed forward, wanting—no demanding—the change, and he could no more control it, nor push it back than when he had shifted in his sleep. Perhaps Farren *was* right. He was afraid.

His bones cracked, his muscles popped, and coarse black hair sprouted across his skin as his face elongated and his spine and hips contorted. He dropped onto all fours, back into the form he had become more comfortable in than his own skin. The darkness eased, retreating into the deep recesses of his mind, as he sank into the familiarity of his wolf.

D'Artagnon leaped back onto the bed and settled himself at the foot. He would watch her from here. Getting too close had consequences. Ones he was not yet ready to face.

Chapter Nine

Constance awoke to darkness broken only by the soft, orange glow of waning coals in the brazier. Cocooned in delicious softness, a heavy weight rested on her chest. She blinked as her eyes adjusted to the gloom. *Monsieur D'Artagnon?* She could barely make out a lump of midnight fur, two twitching ears and the glint of his eye. His large head so close his breath fanned across her chin. He had slept beside her? *All night?* When had he moved from the foot of the bed? She had always slept lightly. How had she not stirred?

Suddenly the weight was gone, and the dark outline of a wolf slipped off the bed and materialized by the brazier in the corner. Constance felt the absence.

She might not have awoken, but she had dreamed. Of a man, a glorious, naked man, standing beside the bed. With one pale blue eye, and a lock of dark hair hiding the scar where his other eye should be, he had stared down at her. Her body tingled. Was that what he would look like were he to shift into a man? Muscled, strong, a little wild and untamed? It was a fanciful notion, but an appealing one.

Constance peeled back the covers and slipped from the bed. With the glint of the wolf's gaze following her, she crossed to the window and threw open the shutters. Light streamed in, the sun hovering well above the horizon. *L'enfer*. Below, the bailey bustled with activity — servants, farmers, workers on the estate — all going about their daily business.

"I have slept late." Constance splashed water on her face, washed the sleep from her eyes and toweled herself dry. "What will Seigneur Gaharet think of me?"

The wolf tilted his head at her, his ears flicking forward.

"He did not call me here to laze about in bed all day. I have a task to complete."

The black wolf growled. He might have slept curled against her side, his head on her chest, but that had not changed how he felt about her reason for being here. Constance sighed and dropped the damp linen beside the washbowl. Dreaming about Monsieur D'Artagnon might be the closest she would ever get to him.

Constance hastened to dress, snatched up her grimoire then headed down the stairs. Monsieur D'Artagnon, like an ominous shadow, trailed along behind as she followed the sound of voices to the hall.

She paused in the doorway. They were all here. Seigneur Gaharet and his mate, Erin. Monsieur Aimon and his mate, Kathryn. Seigneur Ulrik and his mate, Rebekah. Pale with dark shadows beneath her eyes, Rebekah leaned against Ulrik, a contented smile on her lips. The green streaks in her hair remained, but the silver jewelry in her ears and nose were gone. She had undergone her turning.

The only other human in the room, Seigneur Farren, sat by his daughter. She could only presume his mate… wife…had passed. She looked closer. Yes. The aura of grief long borne hovered over him, etched in the lines on his face and the acceptance of loss in his eyes. Her heart reached out to him. Sitting amongst all the happily mated couples would be hard for him, too.

A tight band squeezed at Constance's chest, all the more constricting as a certainty settled over her. Another presence was making itself known. She shifted her gaze to Dame Erin. Yes. There. Dame Erin was with child. A little girl. Her nostrils flared. Could she have… Had her vision been of *Erin* and Seigneur Gaharet and *their* daughter? Had she mistaken Erin for herself all those years ago? She glanced at the black wolf beside her. Was it wrong to hope she had not?

The conversation halted, and Seigneur Gaharet turned. "Good morrow, Constance. I trust you slept well."

Constance dipped her head. "Thank you, yes." Too well. She forced herself to walk over to the table. "I am sorry I slept so late and kept you waiting. The bed was…"

Seigneur Gaharet waved her excuses aside with a smile. Relieved, Constance slid into a seat beside Seigneur Farren, finding comfort in solidarity. Monsieur D'Artagnon made himself comfortable by the fire pit. She set her book on the table.

Seigneur Gaharet steepled his fingers and leaned toward her. "Have you found anything more in your tome, Constance? Anything that may assist D'Artagnon to shift?"

Constance opened her grimoire, flicked through it until she came to the pages of the secret script, devoted to the Langeais wolves.

Erin rubbed her hands together, her eyes bright. "Ever since I spotted this in your cottage, I've wanted to have a look inside. An honest to goodness witch's grimoire. Oh, my!"

Before Constance could stop her, Erin leaned across, grabbed the book and slid it across the table. Constance stifled her dismay.

"Look, Gaharet. It's in the Theban alphabet. The script on your amulets. How is this possible?" Erin turned a few pages forward, then a few pages back. "All of it. No, wait. Some of it's in Latin." She paused on a page. "This is an herbal tincture for boils." She flicked to the next page. "Here's one for the Sweating Sickness." She turned another page. "And this one is for Bloody Flux. This is quite a comprehensive text, Constance. Far better, and far more advanced than Bard's Leechbook. Not a single recommendation to stick barley into one's ear, or to smear beetroot on one's face. Wait a minute. It's written in Latin." She looked up at Constance. "You read Latin?"

Constance nodded. "My mother tau—"

Dame Erin blushed. "I'm sorry. Of course you do. It's your book. It's just that…my knowledge of this time period was that most peasants were illiterate. But Theban…" Dame Erin turned more pages. "This script… There's no recorded examples of it until the *sixteenth* century." She fingered the pages reverently. "And this book is old. *Now.* In the *tenth* century." Two little frown lines appeared between her eyebrows, and she tugged at her bottom lip with her teeth. "I wonder where the alphabet truly originated fro—"

Seigneur Gaharet took the book from her hands and placed it back in front of Constance. "Now is not the time for that, Erin."

Dame Erin reached for it. "But—"

Seigneur Gaharet took her hand and kissed her knuckles. "Another time, love. We have more important things to discuss right now."

Constance swallowed down the lump in her throat and fixed her gaze on her book, the characters dancing before her eyes. She had once thought this man, Seigneur Gaharet, would take her as his mate. Seeing the two of them together, the bond between them—never were two people meant to be together more.

Constance had to force herself to not look at Monsieur D'Artagnon, to keep her focus on Dame Erin. She cleared her throat. "Twins."

Dame Erin raised her eyebrows. "I beg your pardon?"

Constance pointed to the characters on the page. "The sacred script of the Langeais wolves was a language created centuries ago by twins in my coven. They used it to communicate with each other."

"Twins. How intriguing. I wonder how it came to be—"

"Enough, Erin." Seigneur Gaharet squeezed Dame Erin's hand, taking the bite out of his command. He returned his attention to Constance. "This is all very interesting, and one day, when matters are not so pressing, Constance, we are going to have a long overdue conversation about everything you know about our kind, about our pack and about our lore. Now, however, we need to know what your grimoire says that can help my brother."

Conscious of everyone's attention, Constance flicked through the pages until she found the one she sought. "I have found no mention of any other wolf that could not shift. Not in all my coven's dealings with the Langeais wolf pack." She fidgeted in her seat. "And, as I mentioned yesterday, there are few things known to have the ability to affect a werewolf." Constance spun her grimoire around and slid it across the table to Seigneur Gaharet. She tapped a finger at the relevant passage.

He glanced at the page. "What am I looking at here, Constance?"

She muffled a gasp. Had the Langeais wolves fallen so far from their heritage they could no longer read the words of the secret language? She glanced at Dame Erin.

Dame Erin shrugged. "Sorry, Constance. Without Google, I have no means of translating Theban."

Google? Constance pulled the book back across the table. "It says here, *'a werewolf has but two weaknesses. Wolfsbane, which doth render the wolf unable to maintain his form. He will shift from one form to the other and, if not removed from the herb's presence, he will do so until all energy has been exhausted. Then he will die.'*" She ran her finger beneath another line further down the page. "*And Silver, which doth suppress the wolf as though the wolf ne'er had existed. Where so the silver should touch the skin of a werewolf, it will burn. Only the removal of the silver can return the wolf to the surface.*"

"I can attest to both," said Ulrik. "I was under the influence of the wolfsbane for mere moments, and it struck me down, leaving me unable to stand or catch my breath. And silver…" Ulrik shuddered.

Constance held up her hand. "But this passage" — she pointed at the script on the bottom half of the page—"details the potion I prepare to ease a werewolf's turning. Some herbs *do* work for werewolves. Many herbs have more than one use, and I am hopeful somewhere within these pages is one I can use. I may have to experiment with the dosages, but..."

Seigneur Gaharet nodded. "Whatever you need, Constance. Anne will help you source anything you require."

"Thank you, Mon Seigneur Gaharet. I should warn you, it might take some time, but I will endeavor to find a solution."

Seigneur Gaharet smiled. "I have every faith in you, Constance. My brother is in good hands."

Chapter Ten

D'Artagnon let the conversation flow over him, a forgotten participant slumbering by the fire. It would take time for the little healer to read through every potion and every page of her grimoire. More to test the dosages of any herb she thought might be useful. He yawned and stretched his legs, then rested his muzzle on his paws, his gaze fixed on the happenings at the table. He would be long gone before she found a solution.

Erin rose. "Well, if Constance is going to be busy reading her grimoire, I am going to get your father's journal, Gaharet, and see if I can find out about the witch Old Tumas spoke about."

Constance paused, a page part turned. She was as curious about the witch as his brother's mate.

"Perhaps she was part of your coven, Constance. Or one of your ancestors," said Erin, heading for the door. "Heterochromia—when a person has two different colored eyes—is a genetic mutation that often runs in families."

Constance stiffened. Talking about her eyes made her uncomfortable. Again, the compulsion to comfort her seized him, but he resisted it and kept his place by the fire. A few more days and such emotion would no longer trouble him.

Ulrik leaned forward, his elbows on the table. "Constance, when we met, you said Rebekah was not the first woman to come through time, and she would not be the last."

Erin returned with the journal and began paging through it.

"I assume Marie was the first. Then Erin, then Rebekah. There are more coming?" Ulrik asked. "Do you know when?"

"I believe there will be others, but"—Constance shook her head—"I do not know when. My visions are not always clear. Sometimes it is more of a knowing than a vision. I know there will be more women from the future, but I cannot tell you who they are, or where they will appear. That I was given to know this suggests I will meet them." She shrugged. "But that could be tomorrow, or when I am an old woman. Unless I get another vision, I have no way of telling. I am sorry."

Erin frowned. "I never believed in seers and the like. In my time, there are many charlatans telling gullible people what they want to hear while trying to fleece them of their money. But I will admit, from what I've heard from Gaharet and Aimon, you sound like the real deal. Though it seems to me it's not as helpful as it sounds. More like random snippets of information and half-assed answers. That must be *so* frustrating."

"Oh, yes," agreed Constance. "More than one time in my life I would have wished for clear knowledge, to be certain of exactly what the vision is telling me, but it is not my experience of how second sight works."

D'Artagnon's instincts perked up. She was holding back. Not lying, but hiding something all the same. Something about her visions. She caught his gaze and ducked her head down, her fingers fiddling with the cuff of her dress. Yes, she was definitely hiding something. But what?

Constance continued to study her grimoire, page after page. Occasionally, she would lean forward, her attention caught by a passage, or a word. Then she would press on. The tension in his shoulders eased. That she remained silent suggested she had yet to find anything of use.

Erin flicked through the journal, equally engrossed.

"Listen to this." Erin smoothed her hand across a page. "It's not about the witch Old Tumas spoke of, but it caught my eye and it's interesting. It says here a woman, dressed most unusually, turned up in your great grandfather's time, Gaharet. He was out for a run. He made special note of it here because, and I quote, '*I had not caught scent of her until the moment she suddenly appeared in front of me. Though I stood as a wolf, she showed no hint of fear, but held her ground and spoke to me as though I were a man.*'"

Gaharet tugged at his beard. "Spoke to him as though he were a man, not a wolf? That suggests she knew what he was. And he did not catch her scent until she appeared in front of him." He turned to Erin. "That is similar to how we met, though I shifted before you saw me as a wolf. I wonder, did this woman also travel through time?" He leaned closer to his mate, peering at the journal. "Does it say anything further?"

"Yes." Erin read on. "*Though she spoke Franceis, her inflections were strange to me, her accent broad and rounded, like no other I have ever encountered. As though she was from some faraway land. She asked me if I knew her, and I confessed I did not. Then she told me her name and waited, as though the mere mention of it should have meaning. It did not. She retreated, and I moved to follow her, but one of my pack called me back. A rivalry between two males over a female had turned deadly. On the morrow, I searched for her, but as with her arrival, her departure left no trace. I sent queries to the closest villages. None had heard of her either. Her name was Cordelia.*"

"It does sound as though she was from the future," agreed Gaharet. "I suspect the encounter was much like ours. I could fathom less than half of the things you said upon our meeting."

Erin worried her bottom lip. "I wonder what happened to her? Did she find her way home, or was she stuck here somewhere? And accent broad and round. Maybe an American?"

American? What was that?

His brother's mate was a knowledgeable one. Curious, and forthright in her opinions, too. A good match for his brother. Beside her, Constance seemed almost timid. Yet there was a quiet strength in her, a persistent resilience. She was a survivor, navigating life's vagaries with a fortitude more common of a seasoned warrior.

"Here's something about the witch Old Tumas said the villagers cast out." Erin looked up from the journal. "She was young. As in, young enough to have an infant."

Constance gasped and her hand flew to her mouth. His brother recoiled, his distaste thick in the air.

Ulrik shifted in his seat. "If your *grand-père* was anything like your father, I do not see him taking such a course of action without reason, Gaharet."

Neither did D'Artagnon. He had only heard of one person cast out from the village. By his father. A slovenly stable hand named Didier. He had attacked Marie, dragged her to the stables and tried to force his attentions on her. Didier was lucky her mate Victor had not killed him. And fortunate his father had decreed his punishment banishment and not death.

"And it says here her name was also Cordelia." Erin cocked her head. "That's an uncanny coincidence." She shared a look with Gaharet. "We should talk to Old Tumas. See what he remembers."

Unease prickled up D'Artagnon's spine. It *was* an uncanny coincidence. Two women of different generations, both mentioned in his father's journal. Both named Cordelia. It was not a common name. It might mean nothing, but the clench of his gut and the discordant clang in his mind had his instincts screaming. Did his brother feel it, too?

"We have enough trouble without borrowing more." Gaharet nodded at the little healer. "But I see no harm in Constance talking to Tumas if she wishes. There might be, as you have suggested, a family connection."

Anne lumbered into the room, a covered bowl scenting of herbs and honey in her hands. "If you need to speak to Old Tumas, I have the perfect excuse for you to go see him." Anne set the bowl in front of Constance. "This is the paste for the old grouch's boils."

D'Artagnon wrinkled his nose. He did not envy Old Tumas.

Gaharet's steward stepped into the room and handed a parchment to his brother. "From the Langeais Keep Guard, Mon Seigneur."

Gaharet snapped the seal and opened the missive.

His brother grunted. "It seems our time is up. Comte Lothair has summoned us all to Langeais Keep to renew our vows of fealty in three days hence." Gaharet stood. "Farren and Aimon, I leave it to you to ensure this keep is well fortified and the men are prepared. If we are to leave my pregnant mate, along with the other mates, I would know they are safe. Ulrik, get word to the others that we are to meet outside the keep. We will enter together. United. Send messages to the others, including Godfrey, if he has returned. If not, have our man ask around the Lagarde estate. See if anyone knows anything. And have him talk to Godfrey's steward and find out if Lance has been there."

Ulrik got to his feet with a scrape of his chair. "Perhaps I should go to the Lagarde estate in person."

D'Artagnon half rose.

"No," said Gaharet. "I am not willing to risk another member of our pack, nor leave Rebekah without a mate."

D'Artagnon eased himself back to the floor.

"But you sent Lance to check on Godfrey," said Ulrik. "After we rescued Rebekah from Langeais. It surprised me you did, since we cannot be sure we can trust him."

"I had little choice. I had to send someone. Lance and Godfrey were childhood friends. If I sent anyone else, he would have suspected something was amiss. If

Godfrey is the one who has betrayed us, then Lance is match enough for him."

Ulrik raised an eyebrow. "And if Lance is the traitor and Godfrey has fallen afoul of him?"

Gaharet scrubbed a hand across his face. "Then sending Lance to the Lagarde estate will change nothing."

"But what about Godfrey?"

"There is little we can do for him now."

The downturn of Gaharet's mouth, the tightness around his eyes a measure of the cost such decisions were taking on his brother.

"D'Artagnon, take Constance to see Old Tumas. He needs his boil poultice. I do not need him any grumpier than usual." Gaharet tapped the missive from Comte Lothair on the table. "Two women named Cordelia…"

His brother *did* feel it. D'Artagnon would go with Constance. He would hear what Old Tumas had to say. Perhaps he might learn something more and put to rest this uncertain feeling surrounding these two women. This was one burden he could relieve his brother of. Soon, he would relieve him of another.

Gaharet crumpled the parchment from Lothair as Constance, the bowl of pungent herbs in her hand, followed his brother from the hall. He wanted this traitor caught and held to account for his crimes. Needed the threat to the pack gone. But he wanted his brother back more. Constance was the best hope his brother would shift forms, and not because of her skills with herbs, her knowledge of their kind, or her second sight.

As the men departed and the women retired to the library, Anne came to stand beside him. "It is not my place, Gaharet, but…"

Amusement rippled through him, and he raised an eyebrow at his old cook. "Since when has that ever deterred you, Anne? From saying what is on your mind *or* taking action?"

"I…" She brushed at the flour on her apron. "Well…I confess I may have meddled a little with you and Erin."

Gaharet chuckled. "I know." He gave the old woman an indulgent smile. "And you have my eternal gratitude. Without your actions, Erin and I may not have sorted out our differences."

Anne beamed. Gaharet could afford the little untruth. Nothing would have prevented him from claiming his Erin.

"And I…uhm…"

Gaharet had never seen the old woman flustered like this.

"I may have meddled some more with Kathryn and Aimon."

He bit back a grin. "Mmm."

"But I have noticed D'Artagnon is rather fond of Constance. He has barely left her side since she got here."

"I have noticed that myself."

"He slept on the bed with her last night. Covered the blankets in dark fur that the maids had a devil of a time getting off."

"He did, did he?"

"For whatever reason D'Artagnon remains in wolf form, perhaps he just needs the right…encouragement?"

"I was thinking much the same." Gaharet crossed his arms and looked down at the woman who had been a constant presence in his life since he was a boy. "What do you have in mind, Anne?"

"Well, I had not thought of anything in particular…"

Gaharet doubted that was true. The old woman was a bigger schemer than Archeveque Renaud had been, but with Anne, none of her actions were self-serving. "Anne."

She harrumphed. "Well, I… I must confess, I *have* been giving *some* thought to D'Artagnon's problem. I think the only thing that will make that boy shift is that girl."

"You think so?"

"Are you telling me you do not think Constance is D'Artagnon's mate? What, with the way he follows her, unable to leave her side. How he looks at her when she is not paying attention." She pointed a flour-dusted finger at him. "The same way you look at Erin. The way your father looked at your mother."

"I will tell you no such thing, Anne, for I believe you are right. Constance *is* D'Artagnon's mate."

She fisted her hands on her hips. "Of course I am right."

"Then what is your plan, Anne?"

"Leave it with me, Gaharet. I will come up with something."

"Good." Gaharet turned to leave. "Oh, and Anne, from now on, you have my permission to meddle to your heart's content."

Chapter Eleven

Constance exited through the large entrance doors of the d'Louncrais Keep, her grimoire tucked beneath her arm, the bowl of boil poultice in her hand and Monsieur D'Artagnon at her heels. She was grateful for the reprieve on her task, if a little surprised. For all that Seigneur Gaharet wanted her to find an answer to Monsieur D'Artagnon's inability to shift, he seemed to lack any sense of urgency.

She brushed away her puzzlement. Who was she to question the ways of the nobility, of the alpha? And he had granted Constance her wish. She was getting to talk to Tumas. She shivered and tightened her white-knuckled grip on the bowl of poultice. As much as she wanted, *needed,* to know about the witch the villagers had cast out, this Cordelia, her stomach twisted in knots at the thought of what she might learn. Would she like what he would tell her? About this woman with the different colored eyes? The witch who had the second sight like her? Could there be, as Dame Erin had suggested, a family connection?

The gate guard smiled at them as they passed through, and they followed the road down the hill to the village. Tendrils of smoke curled from chimney holes in neat and sturdy cottages and farmers were returning from the fields for the midday meal, some with their baskets full of their harvest. The scent of cooking food and the murmur of voices filled the air. It was like any other village. And yet, it was not.

In every village Constance had lived — and there had been a few — there had always been a clear division amongst the peasants. Between those less fortunate than others. No less noticeable than the differences between comtes and kings, or merchants and nobles. A poorly thatched roof, clothes more worn with signs of constant mending and a pinched expression, the worry of where their next meal would come from difficult to conceal. Constance looked for the signs, the people and the cottages that mimicked her childhood. She could not find them.

A child waved as they passed, no fear of the big black wolf by her side. Constance waved back, and a smile lit up his little face. No hesitancy, no strange look. Only a smile. The little boy went back to playing his game of pickup sticks. Another young child joined him, and they giggled over their game. Not the whispered conversations and finger pointing she was used to.

A woman with a basket of wet clothing on her hip greeted them. A man outside his cottage whittling a stick nodded and smiled, muttering Monsieur and Ma Dame as they passed.

Now it was Constance who stared. At every villager, waiting, nay expecting someone to say something.

About her, this stranger to their village with the odd colored eyes. Or, at the very least, to mention the large scarred black wolf trotting along beside her. Apart from a friendly greeting, the villagers paid them no mind at all.

"What a most extraordinary village."

Monsieur D'Artagnon swiveled an ear in her direction.

"Do you not find it so? It is as if seeing a wolf walk through their village is neither here nor there. Nor am I stared at. Rumors must abound after supper last eve, yet nothing. Though I visit Langeais regularly, I am not afforded such grace as I am here. It is…" Her heart had never felt so…light. "Nice."

Would that she had lived here. Had grown up here, in the shadow of the d'Louncrais keep. If she had, that child, or that woman, could easily have been her. Yet she had not. Certainly not after Jacques d'Louncrais had died, but not before either, when they had served him and been under his protection. "I wonder why my mother did not choose your village to live in?"

How different would her life be if she had? The connection with the Langeais wolves might well have remained intact. Her mother was long gone, and she had taken her reasoning with her to the grave. "Perhaps the old farmer with the boils would know?"

The black wolf padded beside her. Perhaps this woman with the second sight, cast out all those years ago, had sealed *their* fate, and forced her mother to seek other villages to live in and call their home. Had things changed since then? Could they change now?

She glanced at Monsieur D'Artagnon out of the corner of her eye. If she found a way around whatever kept him as a wolf, broke through what was holding him back and convinced him to return to human form, she would have proved herself to the Langeais wolves. To Seigneur Gaharet. Could she then ask a boon of him? Ask for a place in the d'Louncrais village?

Her heart swelled at the idea—of a little cottage amongst these people. Villagers who seemed no more bothered by her eyes, or her status as a witch, than they were of the rising and setting of the sun. No more living alone, eking a life from the forest.

Seigneur Gaharet's word was law here. No one would cast her out, come for her with burning torches in the middle of the night. She would have more work, more means of putting food on the table. The village did not have a healer, and the d'Louncrais would benefit from having her close. No need to send a man on a half day journey should another turning require her skills. With more women coming from the future, Seigneur Gaharet would need her. What better place for her than in the d'Louncrais village?

First, she must do as Seigneur Gaharet asked. She eyed the black wolf again. And if doing so extinguished any chance of her vision coming true? She swallowed the lump in her throat. Or had her mother had been right, and her own hopes and dreams had swayed her second sight? Should she miss this opportunity to improve her life over something that would never come to pass? But...she was here. In the presence of *another* black wolf. That had to mean *something*.

Monsieur D'Artagnon nudged her with his shoulder, snapping her from her musings, and trotted toward a cottage second from the end of the row. Constance gathered her thoughts and followed. She had come here for a reason. Her reception here, what Master Tumas had to tell her, might change everything.

She rapped on the door, and it swung open to reveal a woman older than her, but younger than Tumas. "Good morrow. I am Constance." She held up the bowl. "Seigneur Gaharet has sent me with a poultice for Master Tumas."

The woman smiled and curtsied. "Monsieur. Ma Dame. Come in, come in. I am Georgette. Tumas is my father."

Constance held up her hand. "Oh, I am not—" It was the dress. No peasant or servant would own such a fine garment. While she wore it, she would get the same reaction.

Monsieur D'Artagnon brushed past her and into the cottage, leaving Constance to follow. She stepped across the threshold into a cozy hut of mud-brick and thatch, much like her own. But there, the similarities ended. While her cottage's thatched roof had gaps where the mice had defeated all her efforts to keep them out, this one had a tight weave. Where their table was of solid construction, hers was no more than discarded timbers cobbled together to provide something useful. Their bowls, pottery jars and mugs all matched. Their baskets and cooking pots were in good condition and by far more plentiful than her meager collection. And it was much, much bigger, with two sleeping nooks hidden behind fabric far thicker and of better quality than she had ever owned.

Tumas and his daughter lived as farmers, but it was clear the d'Louncrais looked after their people. She would not need a cottage as big as this one. Something small would more than suffice. She could have neighbors. And friends. She might never again feel the pinch of hunger in winter, when fewer people trudged out to the forest, braving the cold to see her. More reasons for her to want to live here in this village, cared for and watched over by the d'Louncrais.

Tumas roused from his seat. "There yer are, girlie." He pointed at the bowl. "Is that fer me?"

Constance offered him the bowl and Tumas sniffed it, wrinkling his nose. He jabbed his finger in the sticky paste and grunted. "Can yer not"—he wiggled his fingers at her—"say a spell, or some such?" He scooped up some of the paste. It slid from his fingers and dropped into the bowl with a wet plop.

"You...want me to cast a spell? To heal your boil?" The man had been witness to a woman cast out of the village for witchcraft and he wanted her to perform a spell? Was this some sort of trap?

The old farmer's scowl lifted. "Could yer? Save me walkin' around with this sticky stuff on my neck, smellin' like"—he sniffed at the bowl again—"whatever foul herbs Anne has mixed in this."

"I..."

"Father." Georgette heaved out a long-suffering sigh. "There are no simple solutions when it comes to healing. Your boils would be gone by now if you had only followed Anne's instructions in the first place." Tumas grunted and Georgette snatched the bowl from his hand. "Turn around and I will apply the poultice for you."

She smiled an apology at Constance, as Tumas did as his daughter requested. "Do not mind my father. He is an old grouch, but it is all noise. Please, make yourself comfortable. I was about to serve up the midday meal. Would you care to join us?"

Constance was at a loss for words. When had a villager ever asked her to sit at their table? She made tinctures and poultices. She tended their illnesses and their injuries. They only called on her when they needed her skills. No one had invited her to join them for a meal. Not ever. Not when she had helped birth the tanner's son or splinted the Fournier boy's leg when he broke it falling from a horse. Nor when she had saved the life of the Bassett girl who had eaten the berries of the deadly nightshade.

Perhaps it was the dress, or the presence of Monsieur D'Artagnon, but Constance longed to believe it was because this village was different, that being in the care of the d'Louncrais, of werewolves, made the villagers more tolerant of each other.

Monsieur D'Artagnon leaped onto a seat, and Constance smiled at Georgette.

"That is very kind of you. Thank you." Constance slid onto the bench seat next to him as Georgette applied the sticky paste to her father's neck. Would what she learned here change how she viewed this village, these villagers? She shored up her courage. "Your father mentioned a witch at supper yestreen. I was wondering if I could ask you some questions about her?" Her gaze flicked between Tumas and Georgette. "If you do not mind."

"Of course. And you have come to the right place. Father is the oldest in the village. I doubt anyone else would remember her." Georgette gestured to the bowl. "How often should I apply this?"

"Three to four times a day is best. And leave it on for as long as possible."

Constance pursed her lips to hide her smile as Tumas groaned and Georgette rolled her eyes.

"I will make sure he follows instructions this time," said Georgette. "Thank you. Although why my father was willing to risk Anne's wrath is beyond me. No one else in the village would."

"That old harridan," grunted Tumas. "I am not afraid of her."

Georgette poked her finger at her father. "Well, you should be."

Tumas crossed his arms. "No old woman is going to bully me." His expression softened, and a smile tugged at his lips.

For all his rough words and denials, it seemed Tumas had a genuine affection for Anne. Beside her, Monsieur D'Artagnon cocked his head and studied Tumas. He lifted his muzzle and sniffed the air. He yipped once, twice, then his jaw dropped open and his tongue lolled out. Was he...*laughing?* His grin widened. Yes. Yes, he was.

Tumas scowled at the black wolf. "Now, yer see here, boy. Do not go saying a word of what yer think yer know."

D'Artagnon yipped again.

Tumas threw his hands up in the air. "Argh! Cannot hide a damn thing from a wolf." He wagged a gnarled finger at Monsieur D'Artagnon. "Yer keep your mouth shut, yer hear? Anne is a good woman. She does not deserve to be the subject of gossip in the village or up there in yonder keep." He turned his astute gaze on Constance. "And I will have yer keep any vision you might have to yourself, girlie."

"Oh, Father. Everybody in the village already knows about you and Anne." Georgette plopped the bowl of poultice on the table, and turned to the pot over the fire. "You are a fine pair, the both of you. Do you think the villagers care if two old fools find some happiness together?"

Tumas huffed. "Well...well..."

Georgette ladled stew into four bowls and set them on the table. "I, for one, am happy you two finally decided to do something about the feelings you have for each other, instead of dancing around it like you have for the last score years."

Tumas' face flushed a deep shade of red and he fixed his gaze on his stew.

Georgette set a loaf of crusty bread on the table and carved it into chunks, then placed two pieces in front of D'Artagnon and the rest on a platter in the center of the table. "Now, you said you have some questions?"

Beside Constance, the black wolf licked at the bowl of stew with studied care.

A wolf with manners? Constance shook herself. "Ah, yes." She swallowed, trying to ease the tightness in her throat. "The woman...the witch...with eyes... eyes like mine..." She took a deep breath, rubbed her sweaty palms on the soft wool of her dress, and faced Tumas. "You said she had the second sight, and that she used her ability for evil. That the villagers cast her out. We...that is...*I* would like to know more about her abilities. If you could tell us all you remember about her. Please."

Eyes full of a sharp intelligence glittered at her across the table. "Yer cannot fool me, girlie. I may be an old man, but I can see the truth of things. Yer wants to know why we cast her out." He jerked his head at Monsieur D'Artagnon. "The young wolf here wants to know, too. As keen as any lad for the harvest festival, he is."

Monsieur D'Artagnon abandoned his stew and fixed his gaze on Old Tumas.

"I may not have your senses, young wolf, but I have lived a long life. I have your measure."

Monsieur D'Artagnon sniffed and resumed eating.

Constance nodded, her hands shifting from her dress to the smooth timber of the table, so unlike her own rough, splinter-ridden one so far away in her humble little cottage.

She dipped her head. "I...I confess you are right." Monsieur D'Artagnon wanted to know? Because Seigneur Jacques would not have cast a woman and a babe from the village without just cause? What *had* this witch done? Constance had more personal reasons for learning all she could about this witch, and after what Dame Erin had said, she could not help but wonder if the woman *did* bear some relation to her. "I have never met another woman...witch...with the gift of second sight. Nor someone with different colored eyes like mine. I did not realize there was a connection between the two."

Tumas nodded and dropped his spoon into his bowl. "I was only a boy at the time, but I remember the talk in the village." Tumas sighed. "It did not sit well with my parents, and many other villagers, that they had cast her out with a babe in her arms. But in the end, after what she did, the fear she brought to the village, she left 'em no choice."

Chapter Twelve

D'Artagnon licked the stew with a delicacy more suited to the man he had once been. It had been years since he had sat at a table to eat—as a man—but he had not forgotten the etiquette his parents had instilled in him. For all his apparent focus on his food, it was the conversation that held his attention. And Constance. And the wily old farmer.

Old Tumas and Anne. Who would have thought? He chuffed between mouthfuls of meat and vegetables. *Does my brother know?* Probably. As Tumas had pointed out—there was little you could hide from a wolf.

"Ah, she was a strange one, all right." Tumas pointed at Constance. "And not just because her eyes were two different colors, either." A faraway look settled in Tumas' eyes. "It was a long time ago, but I can still remember the strange way she spoke, as though she had come from a distant land." He waved a weathered hand at them. "She spoke our language fair enough, but yer could always tell when she was talkin'.

Stuck out like a bristle on a badly tanned hide, it did. And for a healer, the woman was cold. She could chill the air with a look, a word, sometimes just by breathin' the same air as yer."

Tumas shivered, and D'Artagnon abandoned his stew. Unease threaded through his gut. Even as a memory, this woman affected Tumas. The old farmer would have experienced much in his long life. Had lived amongst werewolves, served them since he was a boy. Lived in the village of an alpha werewolf. That Tumas feared a human woman, witch or no, was a little concerning.

"Cordelia, her name was, and she scared all us young 'uns," continued Tumas. "And not a few of our parents, too. Whenever us children saw her coming, we done drop everything and run. All of us. Not a damn one of us brave enough to face her. Yer dared not get sick, because then she had reason to visit yer cottage. To visit yer."

Constance sat in stunned silence, concern tainting her scent. He shuffled a little closer and pressed against her arm. Like he had pressed into her soft curves last eve. The memory sliced through his brain, bringing a heat to his body difficult to ignore. He should retreat, but he could not force himself to move.

"Yer *grand-pére* must 'ave sensed somethin' about her, for he took his time decidin' if he should let her in the village. But the woman was with child, and like yer father, yer *grand-pére* was never one to turn away a woman in need." Tumas lapsed into silence and focused on his stew.

Constance took in a deep breath and let it out slowly. "Can you tell me what she did that finally had the villagers casting her out?"

D'Artagnon was glad she had asked the question. Memories had a way of distorting things over the years, becoming bigger, more potent in the mind than in truth. Tumas *had* been but a child.

"There is not much I can tell yer. Yer must understand, I was a boy, not privy to the talk of adults. But, like most young boys, if my parents forbade me anythin', it only made me more determined. One night, when my parents rushed off to old man Brun's hut, threatening me with a whippin' if I left the cottage, it set a fire under me like no other. I followed 'em and peered through the window."

His chest heaved. "To this day, I wish I had listened to me parents and stayed on me sleeping pallet, warm by the fire. What I saw..." He raised his gaze to D'Artagnon's. "In all my years, I have never seen the likes of it. Not even when yer father tore apart that good for nothin' servant Anne had taken up with."

D'Artagnon quirked his eyebrow. He had heard of the death of Anne's beau — trampled by his own horse, or so his father had led him to believe.

Old Tumas chuckled. "Not the story yer remember, young wolf? I assure yer, it was yer father that killed 'im. And with good reason, too. Was gonna spread the truth about the pack. He was not family, yer see. Given a job at the keep because Anne had fallen in love with him. Then he betrayed her and planned on betraying yer father. I tell yer no lie. Was not much left of him once yer father was done with 'im. An awful sight. But what I saw through that window that night..."

Old Tumas squeezed his eyes shut. "It still haunts me some nights. The blood, so much blood, comin' out of his ears, his eyes, his nose and his mouth. And old man Brun redder than a blacksmith's face working at his forge. Like somethin' had boiled him alive. *She* had boiled him alive."

The little healer's face paled, and she shivered beside him. Against his better judgment, he pressed closer, laying a paw across her knee. Like he had eased an arm around her waist as she had slept. He forced the images away. *Focus.*

She rested her hand on his paw, her thumb brushing across his fur. His body trembled. *Merde.* This woman tested his control.

"How did you know it was her?" Constance asked, snapping him out of his thoughts.

Tumas opened his eyes. "Old man Brun had argued with 'er that morn, then stormed off toward the keep. Perhaps to talk yer *grand-pére*. About what, no one ever found out. He never made it. They found his body that night. No one else in the village had cause to harm him. And I never saw the likes of an illness do that to a man. Have yer?" He speared a gaze at Constance.

She shook her head, tightening her hand on his paw.

Tumas poked at his stew. "Someone must have got word up to the keep, because yer *grand-pére* came down with half the pack at his back. Seems it put the wind up 'im, too. 'Twas only 'cause of the babe he banished her, instead of…" Tumas let his words hang in the air.

His *grand-pére* could have killed the witch. Should have killed the witch.

"What about the babe's father?" asked Constance.

Tumas shrugged. "She arrived in the village alone, her belly rounded with the babe. No one knows where she came from, or what trouble she was in."

"And where did she go?" pressed Constance.

Again, Tumas shrugged. "We never saw the likes of her again. Somethin' to be grateful for."

"I thought you said…at supper…" She paused, a spoonful of stew poised near her mouth. "So you have never had another witch—healer—in the village since?"

Something in the little healer's voice tugged at D'Artagnon. Disappointment? Resignation? He should pull away before he considered shifting so he might hold her hand in his.

There was a glint in Old Tumas' eyes. "Now I never said that, girlie. And it is a good thing yer asked. There was another healer—lovely lass by the name of Helene—who lived here for a time."

Constance gasped and dropped her spoon into her bowl. "Helene? My mother?"

Interesting. The witch, the one he had spied in the library the night Marie had arrived, had once lived in the d'Louncrais village. Not by the time his father had summoned her and little Constance. Yet still, his father had maintained the connection. That Helene, and now Constance, had a book full of information about the Wolves of Langeais spoke of how far back that connection had gone. His father had trusted Helene. His brother trusted Constance.

D'Artagnon shook out his fur and snatched his paw away. The woman had suggested binding him in silver. He should keep that in mind.

Tumas' face screwed up in a wily smile. "She was yer mother? I figured as much. Apart from those eyes of yours, yer have yer mother's look."

Constance raised her chin and met the old man's gaze head on. "Did you run *her* out of this village, too?"

Tumas set his spoon down and pointed a gnarled finger at her. "Yer have the wrong of it there, girlie. She was a good healer. A kind lass. Many of us hoped she would up and settle with one of the young lads 'ere. *We* did not run 'er out. Not Seigneur Jacques either. She left of 'er own accord, and no one truly knew why. But she had taken up with that good for nothin' stable hand, Didier. Cannot blame a woman for runnin' from him."

Didier?

Old Tumas nodded at him. "Yer father run 'im out of the village, too, like 'e did Cordelia. Never saw either of 'em again. As for Didier, good riddance, if yer ask me." He turned to Constance. "And before yer ask, yer mother ne'er had no little girl with 'er while she was 'ere."

Constance frowned, her shoulders sagging, and she stared at her bowl of half-eaten food. For a moment, she had brimmed with hope. At a connection to her mother? That she may have found her father? Only to sink into disappointment at Tumas' poor opinion of Didier. It tugged at him, at the man inside the wolf. The little healer, all alone against the world. The stink of her loneliness was so thick in the air, even Old Tumas with his rheumy eyes and grouchy demeanor could not fail to feel it, to be moved by it.

D'Artagnon huffed. He leaped off the seat and padded over to the door. Time to go. There was nothing more Old Tumas could tell them that would make sense of the coincidence of names. And if he were to stay here any longer, he might do something sentimental. Something stupid to lighten her mood. Like another uncontrolled shift.

He pushed the door open with his nose, and fresh air filled his lungs, but her scent, her heavy emotions, followed him. As did the woman herself, thanking Old Tumas and his daughter for the information, and for the meal. They headed back to the keep, side by side, in silence, Constance clutching that book to her chest as though it were the only friend she had in the world.

Chapter Thirteen

Constance trudged up the stairs to the bedchamber, her feet as heavy as her heart. Supper had come and gone, and she was tired, yet still her mind would not rest. Her mother *had* once lived here. In the d'Louncrais village. A place so accepting. A village that had wanted her to stay. Was hoping she would take up with one of their sons. And she had. This Didier.

But what had caused her to leave? Didier? Tumas had not spoken highly of him at all. Had she truly run from him? And if so, why? Could he be...? She paused on the steps leading to her bedchamber. She should have asked Tumas more about Didier. Constance shook her head. No. What point was there in wondering? Her mother was gone. Perhaps Didier, too.

Though Tumas still lived. As did Anne and Seigneur Gaharet's head steward. In a village where the seigneur took good care of his people, it was possible for peasants to live long lives. Perhaps Didier was also still alive. Constance might not have been born when her mother left the d'Louncrais village, but that did not mean Didier was not her father. Slovenly or not, if he lived, she would like to meet him.

She started back up the steps. Thankfully, the witch, Cordelia, was long gone. A shiver danced up her spine. She was no closer to knowing if there was a family connection, but in truth, Constance did not want to know. Not after what had happened in the village. It was possible Cordelia had done to Brun exactly what Old Tumas had said — boiled him alive. From the inside out.

Though Constance had never heard of a specific spell to boil a person's blood, she *did* know of one to boil liquid. It helped speed up the process of certain spells and was useful when a fire to bring fluids to boil was not prudent or possible. You need only to choose the liquid. A witch would have to have a black heart to use it on a person.

Constance stepped into her bedchamber — *Monsieur D'Artagnon's* bedchamber — with the black wolf on her heels. She had one more task to do. She shooed the young maid away and prepared herself for bed, laid her dress across the chest and washed her face. Then, as the black wolf sat, his keen eye fixed on her, she removed a small knife, a bowl and a few herbs from the collection she had brought with her. A pinch of each herb went into the bowl, then she pricked herself with the blade. Monsieur D'Artagnon stilled and slunk into a crouch as though ready to pounce.

Blood welled up on her finger. "Fear not, Monsieur D'Artagnon. I do not aim to boil you alive. I am merely casting a warding spell around the bed. It is something I have done every day of my life, and it has kept me safe. I do not plan to stop now."

Ignoring the black wolf, she let droplets of her blood drip into the bowl, and using the lit candle from the table, she set the herbs and her blood alight. Starting from the wall, she walked the bowl of smoldering herbs in a semi-circle around the bed, reciting her warding spell as she went. Monsieur D'Artagnon eased onto his haunches, his head cocked to the side.

Constance pinched her fingers together, stemming the bleeding, and set the smoldering bowl on the table beside the bed. "It is a simple spell to warn me should anyone approach the bed." She cleaned her knife and replaced it with her belongings. "If anyone were to cross it, I would feel a tingling across my body. It will not stop you from sleeping..." Heat rose up her neck. Constance swallowed. "I...I mean, I would not dare prevent you from sleeping on your own bed, Monsieur. If that is where you would like...you wish to..." Constance ducked her head, her voice trailing off.

Would he sleep on the bed again? Beside her? Despite the thread of longing that refused to be snuffed out, Constance dared not hope he would.

Monsieur D'Artagnon padded over and sniffed at her ward. Then he huffed and leaped onto the bed, the tingling of her skin not only from his crossing of her ward.

"Oh, well... hmm." Constance pressed her hands to her cheeks, willing the heat in them to subside. "Of course you wish to sleep on the bed. It *is* yours, and I imagine it is by far more comfortable than the floor." Yet she could not help the smile that tugged at her lips as she slipped beneath the covers and slid her feet down beside the black wolf.

Monsieur D'Artagnon circled on the spot at the end of the bed before curling up with his tail tucked around him and his blue gaze centered on her. She closed her eyes. Her heart was heavy with the things she had learned from Old Tumas, from things unresolved, but with the comforting presence of the black wolf at her feet, and the possibilities it presented, sleep and dreams of a one-eyed naked chevalier soon claimed her.

* * * *

Constance snuggled deeper into his warm embrace. With his chest flush to her back, his knees tucked behind her and his arm across her body, he pulled her in tight. Soft lips fluttered along the curve of her neck, sending a delicious shiver up her spine. His musky scent surrounded her, and she breathed it in as her body melted into his. A trail of open-mouthed kisses weaved their way up to her ear, and with a gentle brush of his teeth, he took her lobe between his lips. She arched, thrusting her hips back, and a tremulous moan escaped her parted lips. Something thick and hard prodded her bottom, sending a thrill up her spine and heat to her core.

She moaned again, giving another backward thrust of her hips.

"D'Artagnon," she whispered, and his grip about her waist tightened.

Thank the Fates this is only a dream. She would never dare to call him anything but Monsieur D'Artagnon whilst awake. But this was her dream, and it was a splendid, *splendid* dream.

She rolled over in his embrace, the soft glow of the brazier revealing his face — the puckered skin where his eye had once been, his full lips, his nose and jaw much like his brother's. His beard and hair a little wild, and desire shining in his eye. Desire for her.

Constance's eyelids fluttered closed again. This is how she imagined him — scarred but proud. Untamed. Beautiful. And in this moment, all hers. Only here, in her dreams, could she allow her vision, her fantasies, to take flight and become real. It was divine and fleeting, but she would hold on to it, enjoy it, until deep sleep or morning signaled its end.

He dropped a kiss on her nose, oh so gently, and she brushed her hands across his bare chest, curling her fingers in the soft hair. So fine, so real, as if he were truly there. A low, guttural growl rumbled in the back of his throat, sending shivers across her skin. Then his lips were on hers, a slide of his tongue along their seam, coaxing her to part them. She opened for him. She could not refuse him, wanting his attentions, his kisses, if only in her dreams.

His tongue, hot and demanding, took up her invitation, slipping into her mouth and, oh, the taste of him, the feel of him, the sheer mastery… *L'enfer.* She had never experienced the like of it. She doubted she ever would. But here, now, anything was possible.

He tugged at the covers, pulling them down to her waist and cool air brushed over her, but she was not cold. Nay, her body was on *fire*. From his kiss. From the slide of his hand across her back, urging her closer, and the press of his hard body against hers. Sensation burned through her and she curled her toes beneath the covers, wishing she were naked. That she was free of the covers and as close to him as was possible. That this was one of those dreams she could control and make it so.

Eager to explore, bolder than she would ever be in her waking life, she inched her hand lower, across abdominal muscles honed and taut. Further still, her yearning fingers seeking…

Blackness tugged at her, calling her from her dream. She fought it, clinging to D'Artagnon, but the pull of sleep was too strong and it dragged her under and he slipped away, lost. With a disappointed mewl, she let him go and succumbed to the darkness of a deep and dreamless sleep.

Merde.

D'Artagnon flung himself off the bed, his chest heaving, and stared down at his body. His naked *human* body. He had done it *again*. An uncontrolled, uncalled upon shift. In his sleep. *L'enfer*, he had done more than that. He had kissed her in his sleep. Kissed her in *her* sleep.

Merde.

If his father were alive, he would have had him flogged. His mother would have strung him up by his testicles. Even the thought of *that* did nothing to dampen his ardor. His stupid cock was hard and willing. More than willing. The way she had opened to him, moaning into his mouth and letting him… *L'enfer*. She had been but a fingertip away from taking him in her hand. His cock jerked at the memory, a bead of pre-cum glistening at its tip. He stifled a groan. *Merde*. He had wanted her hand on him. Craved it. Hungered for it even now.

Constance mumbled in her sleep, her words unintelligible even to his heightened hearing. A blessing. If she had whispered his name, it would have been his undoing. *Had* been his undoing.

Perhaps he should have stayed off the bed, slept by the fire, but the pretty flush of her embarrassment when she had mentioned him sleeping on the bed, the coy way she had ducked her head, biting her bottom lip, had been too much of a temptation to resist. Then, as he had slept, too close a proximity to her had vanquished his control.

She rolled to face him in her sleep, her golden tresses a mess about her head, her lips parted on a soft sigh. More blood flowed to his throbbing cock, and his wolf prowled in his mind.

A fine thing for you to prowl now. *To want to get out* now. *Where were you when I shifted?*

He had not had an uncontrolled shift since he was a young boy. Since he had competed with his brother for the attention of young she-wolves. That he had done so twice in his sleep unnerved him. That this female could undermine his defenses, honed over long years of exile, astonished him.

He should have stayed off the damn bed, pretty pink flush on her cheeks or no. Kept his distance and slept by the brazier. Perhaps then he would not have shifted. Thank the fates she had not awoken and caught him taking advantage of her lush body. He could only hope she would have no memory of it on the morn.

D'Artagnon closed his eye and willed his mind and body to relax, to ignore the heady scent of the little healer in the bed. In *his* bed.

Merde. Stop thinking *about her.*

He paced the floor, his agitation growing. At his inability to exert control over himself, and at the unfamiliar feel of walking on two legs. Every time she moved, or murmured soft words in her dream state, his damn body responded and his wolf evaded him. His heart pounded, his mouth went dry and his hands shook. He wanted, *needed* his wolf back.

He called on the discipline his father had instilled in him as a youth and tried to center himself and reestablish some measure of control over his body. It took a moment. More than a moment. Elusive and fleeting, it slipped from his grasp several times until, finally, D'Artagnon got his mind under control, if not his cock, and was able to call forth his wolf.

He heaved out a sigh and let the change flow through him, sinking to the floor on four legs, into the fur-covered form he had become more at home in, protected from the cold night air and from the world and all its dangers. He turned from the bed, shoving his raging need and the discomfort in his groin to the dark recesses of his mind, and curled up by the brazier. Here, with only the heat from the coals, there was nothing to tempt him. For he could no longer trust himself when he slept.

Chapter Fourteen

Constance groaned and snuggled deeper into the covers as the door opened and Anne swept into the room.

"Good morrow, child." The old cook bustled over to the shutters and banged them open. "Good morrow, D'Artagnon," said Anne, addressing a spot beyond the end of the bed.

Constance frowned, and kicked her leg out, encountering linens and bed covers but no wolf. She sat up and peered over the end of the bed. By the brazier. *Oh.* Disappointment burned the back of her throat.

At some point in the night, he must have slunk off the bed. Perhaps her dreaming had disturbed him. Heat rose over her chest and her nipples hardened at the memory. *Oh, no. Had I...? Did I...?* She flopped back against the pillow and stared at the ceiling. Could she have muttered his name in her sleep? Her eyes widened. Or worse, had she *reached* for him? She would not have. Surely? The accusation in Monsieur D'Artagnon's eye told a different story.

"Come, child. The ladies are all waiting for you downstairs. Erin is eager to assist you in your search for something to help D'Artagnon." An indulgent smile curled on Anne's lips. "Never have I seen a more curious girl than her."

Constance tucked away her embarrassment and climbed out of bed. She would simply pretend she had no recollection of it, as though it had never happened. But as she let Anne dress her, as Monsieur D'Artagnon's glare deepened, she suspected it might not be that simple. She may have — unintentionally — hardened his resistance to her. She needed Monsieur D'Artagnon willing. And with another morn she had slept late, this time keeping Dame Erin waiting, she had a lot of ground to make up. She might have skills the Langeais wolves required, and be their best hope of unlocking Monsieur D'Artagnon from his wolf, but she needed her connection with them more. This was *not* the way to impress them. Or convince Monsieur D'Artagnon to trust her.

She snatched up her grimoire and headed down the stairs to the hall, a subdued and wary Monsieur D'Artagnon following a few steps behind her.

Seated at the large table with all the men, Seigneur Gaharet looked up as she paused in the doorway. "Good morrow, Constance. The women are convening in the library this morn." He turned his attention to the black wolf beside her. "Will you join us, D'Artagnon?"

Monsieur D'Artagnon hesitated. He had barely left her side since her arrival, but this morn... Not waiting to see what he would choose, Constance curtsied to Seigneur Gaharet and made her way down the corridor. To Constance's surprise, Monsieur D'Artagnon followed. Mm, mayhap she had put too much stock in his expression. Perhaps it had naught to do with her. An uneasy night's sleep, maybe? If the fates were on her side for once.

With a lift in her shoulders, Constance entered the library and sprang back, hand clutched to her throat as a blade swished through the air, narrowly missing her. "Oh, my."

Beside her, Monsieur D'Artagnon growled, the hair on his ruff standing on end.

Dame Kathryn flounced away, stabbing and swinging a sword with reckless abandon. D'Artagnon whined and Constance, her heart pumping a little too fast, dropped her hand, reaching for the black wolf and running her fingers reassuringly through his thick fur. "Yes, she took me by surprise, too."

Dame Erin looked up from reading the journal and smiled. "Morning, Constance."

Constance eased into the cozy room lined with chests of books and scrolls, keeping a wary eye on Dame Kathryn. D'Artagnon slunk past her, and scooted under a chair, out of reach of Dame Kathryn's flailing.

Constance curtsied. "Good morrow, Mes Dames."

Dame Erin waved her off. "There's no need to stand on ceremony here, Constance. It's just Erin and Bek and Kathryn. Please. Calling me Dame makes me feel like an old woman."

"But...but Ma Dame, I am but a peasant, and you are—"

Erin laid the journal on the desk. "In my world, I had no title to speak of. And Bek worked in an alehouse. We're all friends here."

Friends? To be included in this select group of women, if only in this moment, warmed her.

Constance bobbed her head. "As you wish, Ma D—Erin." She dodged another swing of Kathryn's sword.

Erin rolled her eyes. "Kathryn, will you put that thing away? You're going to hurt someone if you're not careful."

Kathryn clutched her weapon with two hands and swung, beheading an imaginary foe. "Aimon gave it to me this morning," she said, puffing from her exertions. "He is going to teach me how to use it."

"Yeah, well, maybe should…you wait, then, before you…" Bek waved her hand at Kathryn's prancing about. Sprawled in a chair by the brazier, dressed in the finery of the nobility, she frowned. "Why you need…know how…a sword, anyway?" Bek's words were halting, muddled and difficult to comprehend, each word punctuated by intense concentration. "You werewolf. No need…fight with swords. We got"—she tapped at her mouth—"teeth"—she wiggled her fingers—"and claws now."

The last time Constance had met Bek she had not spoken Franceis. Women from the future were so quick to adapt.

"Werewolf blood has improved Bek's memory, and her ability to learn, but she still has a long way to go," said Erin. "She understands more than she can speak, though she is getting better. Sometimes it takes Kathryn and I a few moments to decipher what she's trying to say." She turned to Bek. "You need to work on your tenses and sentence structure. You're all over the place."

Bek jabbed her middle finger at Erin in some sort of rude gesture. In response, Erin poked her tongue out.

Both of them laughed, neither woman taking offense. *Quick to adapt and a little unusual.*

"The men are all werewolves, and they know how to use a sword." Kathryn twirled and stabbed, her flame-colored hair swinging about her shoulders as wildly as her sword. "Why should I not know, too?"

Constance settled herself in the chair Monsieur D'Artagnon hid beneath as Kathryn reluctantly lowered her sword and sheathed it in its scabbard.

Kathryn sat, hands clasped in her lap, the epitome of good breeding that had been absent but a moment ago. "Good morrow, Constance. I trust you slept well."

"Thank you, yes." Apart from her dream of kissing a naked and human Monsieur D'Artagnon. She glanced at the black wolf. His head poked out around her skirts and nestled on his paws. Or perhaps because of it.

"Right, down to business," said Erin. "After what you learned yesterday from Old Tumas, I've been searching Gaharet's father's journal to see what else I could find out about these Cordelias."

"I'm surprised...found time...you to read any, Erin," interrupted Bek. "You...hurling too much...doing."

Erin pressed her hand to her mouth. "Please don't mention it. It makes me want to do it more." Erin rubbed her face with her hands. "One more reason not to be happy about being pregnant."

"You are not happy about being with child? Why ever not?" asked Kathryn.

"It's not... Don't get me wrong, Kathryn. I love Gaharet, and yes, I want to have his babies, but... Well, for one, the timing is *awful*. We may not be in hiding anymore, or hunted by the comte, but things are far from safe. The traitor is still out there. He's already murdered numerous women and children. I don't think me being pregnant would stop him. In fact, I'm a two for one deal right now." She blew out a long breath. "Besides, I would have liked to have a little more time enjoying my relationship with Gaharet. He's not the only one missing the sex."

A vision of Erin laughing, wearing only her chemise, and a naked Seigneur Gaharet chasing her around the bedchamber, flashed into Constance's mind. She quickly banished it. Sometimes her visions were helpful, lifesaving even. Sometimes they were a warning. But others…others she regretted being privy to.

"There are a few herbs useful to ease the nausea of pregnancy," offered Constance. She tapped her grimoire. "I have some tinctures detailed in here."

Erin brightened. "Really? That would be wonderful. The ginger tea Anne prepares for me just isn't cutting it. Right." Erin slapped her hands down on the table. "Now that's settled, can we get back to the witches, these Cordelias, and what's in that book of yours?"

"I do not suppose…? If there is something in your book for Erin's problem" — eagerness shone in Kathryn's eyes — "could there be something in your book that could help with memory? My memory, specifically. If I could remember something more about my attack, we may be able to work out who the traitor is."

"That's not a bad idea," said Erin. "Kathryn was there when Gaharet's mother died, Constance. The murderer also attacked Kathryn, turning her. We believe it's the same werewolf that has turned traitor to the pack. But Kathryn can't remember much. If you could help her get her memories back… Well, then there would be no great urgency to get D'Artagnon to shift. That would make Gaharet happy. I think he'd rather not push his brother too hard in case he leaves."

D'Artagnon raised his head, catching her gaze, a steely glint in his eye. Constance frowned. It should please him there might be an alternative to him shifting. That sense she was missing something returned, hovering beyond reach. She let it go. It would come to her in its own time.

Constance considered Kathryn's request. She could think of a couple of herbs to aid memory. "I will need to use double the dosage, or maybe triple," she cautioned. "Most herbal potions have little to no effect on a werewolf. The herbs I used to ease Erin's and Bek's turnings were in high doses and had to be taken at regular intervals lest they wear off too soon. It is the way of werewolves. There are herbs that can kill a human that werewolves would survive."

Kathryn and Erin excitedly discussed the possibilities, but Constance was no longer listening, her mind whirling. *There are herbs that can kill a human that werewolves would survive.* Some of the most toxic plants were also the most powerful. She rubbed her hand absently over the binding of her grimoire, glancing at the furry head of the black wolf at her feet. Three in particular came to mind. Ones her ancestors had used in small quantities.

Would it work? Could a werewolf's immunity to poisons be the answer? She opened her grimoire, flicking through the pages until she found what she was looking for. A potion oft used by witches for purification, to enhance visions and to increase their power — mandrake root, henbane and deadly nightshade.

For most — for the inexperienced — deadly nightshade berries promised death. Her grimoire spoke only of their potential. In small quantities, in salves, they could ease pain and relax a patient. Mixed with henbane and mandrake root, it was a powerful potion. Powerful enough to relax a werewolf so he would shift? It might well be. If she raised the quantities.

She would have to be careful. The potion had some complications. Fantastic visions and sexual arousal. Tales of witches imbibing the potion and believing they could fly abounded, not forgetting the uninhibited sexual couplings of covens who used the combination for group gatherings.

Would it affect Monsieur D'Artagnon, a werewolf, in such a way? The memory of her dream surfaced, and she fidgeted in her seat. The black wolf raised his head and sniffed the air. Heat crept up her neck. Something shimmered in his eye. Then he blinked, and his lip curled. Perhaps not. And his werewolf blood would be sure to soften some of its effects. But would it work as she intended?

She would have to search for the plants she needed from the forest, make them into a potion and somehow slip it into Monsieur D'Artagnon's food, but... The old cook might know where she could find some.

She snapped her grimoire shut. "I have to see Anne. Kathryn, Erin, I will speak to her about some herbs for you, and..." Her gaze dropped to Monsieur D'Artagnon.

Erin grinned. "You've thought of something to help D'Artagnon, haven't you?"

"I..."

"Get back to us." Erin tapped the desk. "I'll be right here when you're done in the kitchen with Anne."

Constance rose. Yes, she might well have her answer to getting Monsieur D'Artagnon to shift.

Chapter Fifteen

Constance rushed from the library and D'Artagnon, swift on his paws, followed her. A plan was afoot, involving him, herbs and perhaps a spell from her book. A plan to make him shift. Uncontrolled shifts in his sleep were disturbing enough. Having Constance force him to shift sent ice slicing through his veins.

If she were going to attempt some sorcery on him, if she was going to solicit the aid of the canny old cook, he was going to do everything in his power to stop her. To stop them.

As soon as they entered the kitchen, memories and familiar smells assaulted D'Artagnon — smoke from the large wood fire, fresh baked bread wrapped on the shelves, herbs, cooking meat, laughter, squeals of pretend fright. Anne's bellowed curses as she chased him and his brother from the room, stolen treats clutched in their hands. The fond memories of his childhood before tragedy had struck. Before his life and its purpose had changed forever. Some of the tension eased from his body as he soaked in the warmth of the room and his memories.

"Constance?" Anne looked up from the pot over the fire. "To what do I owe the pleasure of your company?" She raised an eyebrow at him. "I see you still have your faithful shadow."

"I have need of some assistance with some preparations, Anne. If you would be so kind as to assist me."

"Of course, child. My kitchen is at your disposable."

"To begin with, Erin's ginger brew — add lemon to it, and substitute some of them with either a peppermint or raspberry leaf brew. That should help with her nausea a little. And I need to make one for Kathryn, and…" She cleared her throat. "And another I think could prove useful."

D'Artagnon snorted. Did she think he did not catch her side glances in his direction? That he could not smell the subtle hint of deceit in the air?

Wickedness glinted in the old cook's eyes. "What do you need?"

Constance flipped through the pages of her book until she found the one she was looking for. "I would like to create something to assist Kathryn with her forgotten memories." She smoothed the page. "It uses rosemary and balm, but some of the herbs I need come from a region further south. As Seigneur Gaharet is quite…um…wealthy, I had hoped you might have some savior plant in your larder. I will also need a particular root known for calming" — she caught his eye, before her gaze skittered away — "henbane and" — another side-eyed glance in his direction — "there is a little black berry. Perhaps you have seen it growing around here?"

"The herb garden here is quite extensive. I have some of the ingredients right here in the kitchen. The others you speak of can be found nearby in the forest." Anne pointed to the bunches of hanging herbs. "Do you need them fresh or will dried herbs suffice?"

Herbs that were used for cooking? How could they have any effect on a werewolf?

"Fresh is best."

"Then I will send out one of the kitchen hands to fetch *all* the ingredients you need."

Anne beckoned a young girl over, handed her a basket, gave her the list of what she needed, describing the items the girl was not familiar with.

"Do not mind if the root screams as you yank it from the soil," cautioned Anne.

Screams? Mandrake root. He had heard the tales. Mandrake root was not for a memory potion. He narrowed his eye on the little healer. And henbane. Plants used by witches. And what of these berries she was loath to name?

"You will not hear it scream," placated Constance. "I assure you. No human… It is a scream of the spirit. Human ears are not attuned to it."

The girl, wide eyed, turned to leave.

"Wait," Constance called out. "You will need to wear gloves when handling the berries."

Gloves? To handle berries? Did this plant have thorns? Or was there something about these black berries?

A little pale, the girl departed.

"Anything else you need, child?" asked Anne.

"Bowls."

Anne set three bowls on the bench.

Constance turned to the doorway. "I shall fetch my ceremonial knife from my…*the* bedchamber."

She was coming to consider his bedchamber as hers? The thought pleased him, though he could not think of a reason why.

Constance disappeared to fetch her blade, leaving D'Artagnon alone with Anne.

The old cook fixed him with a stare. "Now, young man. You are not going to make this more difficult than it is for the young lass, are you? I believe life has been harder than most for the girl, living alone in the forest as she does. Not much goes in her favor in the Langeais village neither, I would suspect. Not with those eyes of hers. The villagers there are not as accepting of the unusual as they are here."

He flattened his ears against his head. *Empathize* with the little healer? After she suggested using silver on him? And now hatched some nefarious plan involving black berries?

Anne planted her hands on her hips. "Mmm. I see. You have your mind set on thwarting her. Even though shifting is for your own good, and for the good of the pack. Harrumph. You always were a stubborn one. Well"—she leaned closer, and pointed a stubby finger at him—"I am warning you, I will not stand for it. I will help that child in any way I can." She stared him down. "And you know from experience, I am not one to be trifled with. That young girl deserves some happiness in her life, and I aim to see she gets it."

A growl rumbled in his chest. The old woman was as stubborn as he was. And she was right. She *was* a force to be reckoned with. She had been when he was younger and, it appeared, nothing had changed since then.

Anne had never cared much for rank and title, charging through accepted courtesies with all the subtlety of a battering ram. Even his father had trodden carefully around her. D'Artagnon would have to do the same. The villagers, the other servants, the chevaliers and his brother, all held her in such high regard. Were she to be disrespected, were harm to come to her at his hand, he would most likely find himself locked in the training room. His brother had made that clear.

And what does Constance's happiness have to do with me shifting?

Constance returning, followed by the servant girl, broke the standoff between them. Anne took the basket of herbs the kitchen hand had collected, shooed the girl away and sorted them into two piles on the bench. In one, he recognized common herbs for cooking and some sort of mint. For Kathryn's memory potion? In the other, foul smelling gray-green foliage, and a rosette of oval-shaped leaves attached to a root. Henbane and mandrake root?

Next to them, Anne placed a small linen bundle, opening it to reveal purple-black berries. He stilled. No wonder Constance had not named them. Had she thought he would not know them by sight? But he did. There was no mistaking the fruit of the deadly nightshade, ripe with poisonous promise. Nor the care with which Anne handled them.

These herbs — the berries, the root and the gray-green leaves — the little healer meant for him. Planned to slip them into his food or drink. His werewolf blood made him immune to the poisonous nature of the berries, but she believed they would have some effect on him and would precipitate his shift from wolf to man. She most likely had the right of it. Constance knew more of their kind than anyone beyond their pack. Perhaps even more than they did. He would have to watch her closely.

No. He would have to watch them *both* closely. Anne was her ally, not his. The old cook would not risk every human in the keep by putting anything in the cooking pot. She would have to put it in his food alone. With his sense of smell, that would be difficult, especially now he had the pungent scent of those leaves. He sat back on haunches. Thwarting their plan should be easy.

But as Constance mixed up her potions, pricking her finger and casting her spell, the significance of the *three* bowls became apparent. One bowl for Kathryn's memory concoction. Two bowls containing deadly nightshade berries.

Anne slid one bowl toward Constance. "Off you go, child. I will see Kathryn has her herbs. And this" — she picked up the second bowl containing the purple berries — "I will keep with me."

Constance gathered her book and the bowl. "Thank you, Anne. Are you coming, Monsieur D'Artagnon?"

D'Artagnon sat, unable to move. Both women had the deadly mixture. Anne, by far, was the more cunning of the two, but if he stayed in the kitchen, it would give Constance ample time to plant her portion. Perhaps somewhere he might not expect. Yet Anne had access to all the food in the keep. Unless he planned to hunt, he would need to eat the food she prepared. But that would leave Constance alone to plot and plan.

Constance shrugged and headed for the doorway. The pull to follow her was too strong. His instincts were telling him the little witch was the greater threat. D'Artagnon jumped off the stool, ignoring Anne's smug smile, and followed Constance from the room. He would have to rely on his nose to tell him if his food was tainted. He had survived in the wilds for nine long years, with only his werewolf instincts to keep him safe. Two human women could not outsmart him.

* * * *

Gaharet stepped into the room from the bailey, the smells of the kitchen enveloping him, but not enough to hide the foul-smelling henbane leaves, or the bitterness of the deadly nightshade berries. "How do you plan to get that into D'Artagnon's food without him smelling it?"

Anne wiped her hands on her apron, unsurprised by his sudden appearance. "Perhaps his sense of smell is not as good as you, or he, thinks. He did not catch a whiff of your presence."

Gaharet shrugged. "There is enough of a breeze to carry my scent away. And with Constance by his side, D'Artagnon is distracted."

"Mmm, maybe. But you are right, Gaharet. Getting that potion past a werewolf's nose will be nigh on impossible." She handed him the bowl. "Place that on that high shelf for me, will you? It will not do to have some fool think it is a new seasoning and add some of it to tonight's meal."

Gaharet blanched, and did as he was told, pushing the bowl to the back behind numerous pots of dried herbs.

Anne took up a ladle and shuffled to the pot over the fire. "All we need do is keep him close to that girl, and nature will take its course." She stirred the pot's contents. "Needs thickening." She motioned to the kitchen hand. "Go fetch some more potatoes from the store."

Gaharet crossed his arms and regarded the woman who had been a constant presence in his life since he was a boy. "You have come up with a plan, Anne?"

Anne set aside the ladle. "I believe I have." Mischief danced in the old cook's eyes. "Now that you and Erin are here, the farmer's cottage is empty. A perfect place for them to…well…do what mates will do given the opportunity. They would be close enough to keep an eye on, and yet have the privacy they need. And there is that lovely pond with the waterfall. I may have overheard that Ulrik and Rebekah used them both to great effect."

Mm. A good plan. It could work in more ways than one. Lothair's summons came to mind. At the bottom of the parchment were several lines he had not shared with the others.

Gaharet. The church has appointed Eveque Faucher to stand in Renaud's stead until such time as his whereabouts can be determined. I need not tell you of Faucher's reputation, but I must warn you, Faucher has been asking questions about you and your men. I will do what I can to keep him preoccupied here in Langeais, but I fear he may take it upon himself to visit your demesne unannounced.

Faucher, the witch hunter, in his keep? With D'Artagnon refusing to shift and a witch with eyes of different colors? D'Artagnon could slip away into the forest, but then he might never return. And Constance… Never was there a more vulnerable woman. And she, his brother's mate. Yes, sending them to the cottage could work well. "That is a truly excellent idea, Anne. How long do you need to prepare supplies for them?"

"A day at most."

"Good. They shall leave over-morrow."

Anne clasped her hands together. "I shall see it done."

Gaharet shook his head at his cook, smiling. "Remind me, Anne, never to cross you. For I do not think I would win."

Chapter Sixteen

D'Artagnon lay in the corridor beyond the library doorway, resting his head on his foreleg. From his position, both the conversation between the men and that of the women in the library were within earshot. A night and one full day had passed since Constance had made her potion. Two since he had shed his wolf in his sleep. He had followed her everywhere, listening into conversations and sniffing his food with extra caution.

Nothing. No mention, much to his relief, of his shifting at night. Nor of the kiss he had stolen as Constance had slept. No hint that either Anne or Constance had used the noxious concoction. The bowl Constance had taken from the kitchen sat untouched on the table beside the pitcher in his bedchamber. What were they waiting for?

"Are you truly teaching Kathryn how to use that sword you gifted her?" The rasp of Ulrik's voice, still so foreign, filtered to him from the hall.

D'Artagnon sniffed. If Aimon did not train her, someone would have to. He was in as much danger of being skewered by Kathryn and her sword as he was from Constance's potion.

"Of course," said Aimon. "I gave her my word I would teach her anything she wished."

The sincerity in Aimon's voice, the devotion, slid under his fur, and his thoughts, unbidden, turned to Constance. The flutter of her eyelashes against her sun-warmed cheeks as she slept, her blonde hair loose and tousled from sleep, the way she looked at him when she thought he was not paying attention. Full of wishful longing.

"She is a werewolf. She has teeth and claws," said Ulrik. "Personally, I would rather spend my time teaching my mate something else. Perhaps something a little more…intimate. If you need some ideas…"

The hint of curves beneath Constance's thin chemise. The feel of her body beneath him and the taste of her lips on his.

Someone choked on their wine. "That is my daughter you speak of, Ulrik."

"My apologies, Farren." Ulrik did not sound sorry.

"Given what has happened to her in the past, perhaps it gives Kathryn some comfort, having another means to defend herself," said his brother, backing the young chevalier.

Should Constance have another means to defend herself? Of all the women in the keep, she was the most vulnerable, especially when she returned to her forlorn little hut in the forest. Not so long ago, he had hidden in the shadows of the forest as tendrils of smoke filtered through the hole in the thatched roof of her humble little cottage. Had not the storm raged around them, it might have looked less small, less sad, but even on a sunny day the poorest cottage of any village would have outshone it. The thought of her leaving, returning there, did not please him at all. As it should. Rather, it lodged in his gut, a discomforting unease.

"You would not think to train your mate to defend herself, Ulrik?" Incredulity crept into Aimon's voice. "She is from another century. One where men do not wear chain mail, nor carry swords. It must be daunting, nay, frightening for her."

L'enfer. How had Constance survived out in the forest all alone? At the mercy of nature and the capriciousness of villagers.

Ulrik snorted. "Bek was dangerous when she had only her fists to defend herself with. The woman knows how to use them. Near broke a guard's nose when she first materialized in Lothair's godforsaken chamber. Now she is a werewolf. Trust me, Bek does not need lessons with a sword to be lethal."

Though, Constance was a witch. The berry potion in his bedchamber was testament to the fact she was not without means to defend herself. And she had her wards.

Gaharet chuckled. "Erin did a similar thing to Archeveque Renaud. She is also fairly handy with her knees and feet." His brother shifted in his chair, his discomfort sharp in the air. "I can attest to her ability to defend herself. It took everything I had to stay on my feet after she kneed me in the groin. That is *not* an experience I wish to repeat."

But still, knowing how to use a sword was an added layer of protection. Although, if Constance knew of spells like the one Cordelia had used on Brun, she would have no need of one. Constance might be more powerful than any of them realized.

"And yet," countered Aimon, "a mercenary stabbed Erin, and the keep guard captured Bek and threw her back into that underground chamber beneath Lothair's keep."

"That was before either of them were werewolves," refuted Ulrik.

D'Artagnon's heart did a little skip. Constance was not a werewolf. She did not have the healing abilities their blood afforded them.

"He does have a point. Gascon." His brother called out for his steward. "Speak to the blacksmith. We will need swords for both Erin and Bek. Given our current circumstances, we should not neglect anything that may keep our mates safe."

Constance was not one of their mates. He should speak... No. That would mean he would have to shift.

"Shall I ask the blacksmith to make a sword for Mademoiselle Constance as well, Mon Seigneur?" asked Gascon.

The ruff on D'Artagnon's neck prickled as his brother's gaze slid his way through the open doorway.

"Thank you, Gascon. Yes. Constance should have one, too."

D'Artagnon breathed easier. Yes, Constance should have a sword, too. *Thank you, brother.* Though why it was so important to him...

"If D'Artagnon does not come to his senses and shift, I will train Constance myself."

A growl rumbled up in D'Artagnon's throat, and he was almost on his paws before he realized. He eased back to the floor. A simple taunt from his brother should not goad him so.

D'Artagnon snarled at Gascon as he passed him in the corridor, and the conversation in the hall turned to preparations for their journey to Langeais Keep. D'Artagnon let their voices drift into the background. He swiveled an ear in the women's direction.

Erin passed by the library door, flipping through the pages of his father's journal. "Any luck with that memory spell that Constance and Anne made for you, Kathryn?"

The swishing of a sword through the air paused. "Not the kind of progress I was hoping for. And the herbs... My apologies, Constance, but they taste *awful*." Kathryn made a gagging sound.

Interesting. Should his nose fail him, his sense of taste should warn him if Anne or Constance had tainted his food.

A book slapped shut. "What progress?" asked Erin. "Anything could be helpful."

The swishing of the sword resumed. "Well..."

A footfall, a grunt. A lunge, perhaps. Kathryn's lessons were proceeding well, from what D'Artagnon could tell.

"I have been having nightmares, but not about the attack. More about what followed. My turning."

D'Artagnon breathed easier. If Kathryn remembered who her attacker was, D'Artagnon would need to leave before his brother took it upon himself to hunt him down.

"You're getting...well at using that sword, Kathryn," said Bek. "It looks fun."

"It is. You should try it. And your Franceis is getting so much better, Bek," praised Kathryn. "It must be all your practicing. You used the correct word for sword this time, too, instead of dagger."

"Thank you. Maybe I will ask Ulrik for a sword. Erin, what…think you? You want to learn to be a chevalier, too?"

He sniffed. Kathryn was a long way from being a chevalier, but Gaharet was right. All the women should have a sword. Including his…including Constance.

"Mmm, maybe not," replied Erin. "I was never really sporty. I'm more likely to cut off my own foot than do any harm to an enemy."

"Not if Gaharet teaches you properly…to use it," countered Bek.

"Maybe. Anyway, can we get back to Kathryn's memory? Constance, can you tweak the spell slash herbal mix you gave Kathryn?"

The whooshing of the blade stopped, and the slide of a sword being sheathed cut through the air. "Is there something that would make it work better? And taste better?" Kathryn's voice held hope. "Or maybe target specific memories, Constance?"

"I…well…yes. There are other herbs and things I could try that might work."

D'Artagnon turned both his ears toward the library. Constance rarely said anything unless directly spoken to. When she did speak, her words held weight. She knew things, had generations' worth of knowledge, and she had experienced a lot in her life. For all their incessant chatter about their mates, and how things were different in the future, the other women always paid attention when Constance spoke. As did D'Artagnon. She was a good healer. An asset to any community. Did the villagers in Langeais not realize how lucky they were to have her?

"You have experienced a traumatic event, Kathryn. Could it be you do not want to remember? That you are blocking it from your mind because it frightened you so?"

Agitated footsteps paced the room. "But I *do* want to remember. I *want* to help find who did this to me." Distress laced Kathryn's words. "Could I really be blocking my own memory?"

"It is possible," said Constance. "Fear is a powerful motivation, and it affects people in different ways. I will make a few changes to the herbs I have been giving you and perhaps change the wording of the spell. We will see if that helps. I am sorry this is resting all on you, Kathryn. I had hoped..."

The room fell silent. The ruff on his neck rose as they all stared at him through the open doorway.

Erin's green gaze met his as she laid a comforting hand on Constance's shoulder. "You'll get through to him. I have every faith in you."

D'Artagnon yawned, got to his feet and stretched. Beyond the large entrance doors, the sounds of the servants making their way up the hill for supper reached his ears. He turned his back on the women and padded into the hall. Mayhap this would be the meal Anne tried to slip the potion into his food.

Chapter Seventeen

Constance climbed the stairs to her bedchamber, her heart beating a little faster than it should. Had Anne laced Monsieur D'Artagnon's food with her potion? Anne's wink suggested she had. The black wolf sniffing and tasting his food, then eating it with gusto, implied she had not. As inconspicuously as she could, Constance had observed Anne serve Monsieur D'Artagnon's meal—slices of meat bloody and partially raw, chunks of bread lathered with butter and large helpings of the vegetable stew.

It would have to be in the stew. There was nowhere else to hide it. If the old cook had slipped anything into it, she had been fast. So fast Constance had not caught her. Perhaps living with werewolves her whole life gave her an advantage.

The following hours would tell if Anne had succeeded. Constance had never gotten the chance. Not with the black wolf's singular gaze following her every move. He had suspected she was planning something.

It had been hard to disguise. Had he recognized any of the plants she collected?

Anne had known, but would he? Monsieur D'Artagnon was a chevalier. In his youth, before he had sustained his injuries, he would have focused on his training. But there were years of his life not accounted for. Years where he had spent doing who knew what. Surviving, yes, but where? And with whom? There was no accounting for what he knew now, and Monsieur D'Artagnon was not talking.

As usual, Monsieur D'Artagnon followed her into the bedchamber. Constance, as she had every night she had been here, placed her grimoire beside her pillow and undid the braids in her hair. She removed her clothing but for her chemise, washed down her face and prepared her ward around the bed. She did not want him thinking this night was any different from any other.

Constance hopped into bed and pulled the covers up. "Goodnight, Monsieur. Pleasant dreams."

It would take time for the herbs to work. If she had the dosage correct. She snuggled into the soft mattress and closed her eyes. If not, she would try again on the morrow.

* * * *

Constance stirred and her eyes fluttered open. The coals in the brazier had burned down and the chill night air had seeped into the bedchamber. During the night, she had rolled onto her side and pulled the covers up under her chin, but something was different. Something had disturbed her sleep. A noise? Was her spell working?

She listened, not daring to move. *There.* A pop and crack, and a subtle change of weight at the foot of the bed. More pops and cracks.

Is he shifting?

For all her knowledge of werewolves, she had never witnessed one shift before. Dare she risk a peek?

The bed dipped, and a warm body, far too big to be a wolf, curled in behind her. A hot breath brushed against her cheek, and an all too human arm snaked over her and pulled her close. Constance's heart fluttered. She did not move. She yearned to turn over and look upon the man that was Monsieur D'Artagnon. If she gave in to her desire, he might startle and revert to wolf form. She could not risk it.

Soft lips dropped kisses against the bare skin of her neck. *Oh my.* Those oft spoke about consequences had made an appearance. Her spell was working *too* well. The hand about her waist dipped lower, holding her firmly in place as his hips ground into her bottom from behind. Despite the thickness of the covers between them, there was no mistaking the effect her potion was having on him.

Constance shivered, but her body flushed with heat. His warm lips moved up the column of her throat and, Mother help her, she arched her neck to give him greater access. A lick of her earlobe, and a nibble, just like in her...

Like in her dream.

Constance rolled over. The light from the coals was soft, but as her eyes adjusted, she got her first look at Monsieur D'Artagnon the man. No. Not her first look. She had seen this man before. Standing over her, watching her sleep, and again a few eves' past. That nose, the untamed beard, the puckered skin of his scar beneath a lock of black hair where his eye had once been. This was her dream D'Artagnon. Except...he was *not* a dream. He was here. Real. Shifted. And as she stared at his face, it was clear to her this was *not* the first time.

Constance opened her mouth, and he dove right in, stealing her words before she had the chance to utter them. With his mouth, with his tongue delving deep, speaking of all manner of carnal sins, he swept away all her thoughts, all her shock. She closed her eyes, overwhelmed by the solid feel of him, the heat of his skin, and the musky swirl of his scent that surrounded them both. Her hands, as though they knew their own mind, trailed over his shoulders, around his neck and she twirled her fingers in his hair.

She should not encourage him. She should *stop* him. He was not in control of his actions. Were it not for her potion... But she had not given him anything yestreen, and her dream... She tried to grasp hold of her thoughts, make sense of them, but when he rolled her under him, parted her thighs beneath the covers and slipped between them, she lost the fight. She let her concerns slide away, too caught up in what was happening to care. With a moan, she pressed her hips to his, seeking the delicious rub of his length against her core. Chasing the promise of her vision.

He tugged at the covers, pulling them down to her waist, and her nipples puckered, but not from the cool night air seeping through her thin chemise. His large hand cupped her breast, and she pushed against his palm, offering him her body. Never had she thought herself so brazen, so demanding. To forget who, what, she was. A mere peasant and an outcast. And he a d'Louncrais. She had taken such care when handling the berries and the herbs, but maybe, somehow, she had absorbed some of their properties through her skin.

He groaned against her mouth, pinching her nipple, and heat rippled through her, intense and far beyond anything she had experienced before. The whisper of his beard as he dropped kisses across her jawline, down to nuzzle at her neck only heightened the sensation. With a tug on the neckline of her thin chemise, he tore it, laying her bare from neck to hips. He stilled, and Constance held her breath, not daring to move lest he came to his senses. Not wanting this moment to end.

Oh, Constance. You are surely going to hell for this.

But would she? Had he not shifted yestreen? Had they not found themselves right here until sleep had claimed her? Taking advantage of Monsieur D'Artagnon when he was in this condition, while her potion influenced his actions was wrong, but...was she? Was this happening *only* because of her spell, or was something else at work? Something more in line with her vision?

It did not matter, because — Mother forgive her — she could not bring herself to make him stop.

Monsieur D'Artagnon stared down at her naked breasts, his chest heaving. Muted light from the coals in the fire bathed his face, and dark shadows shifted in his eye. With a rumble of sound, he dipped his head and sucked her nipple into his mouth. Constance grabbed hold of his shoulders and held on, arching her back and pressing her head deep into the downy pillow. She found it hard to breathe, her body a riot of sensations. Any thought of pushing him away scorched from her mind like the fog of a winter's morn burned away by the sun. She embraced the heat, her desire, and squirmed against him. Wanting more. *Needing* more.

Monsieur D'Artagnon growled around her nipple, and her whole body pulsed with pleasure, a persistent throbbing setting a steady beat between her thighs. She tilted her hips, wishing the barrier of the covers between them would disappear. That she had the strength of mind to compose a spell to make it so, but her thoughts skittered wildly as he laved her nipple with his tongue.

He must have had the same thought, for he lifted himself away from her and gave an impatient tug on the covers, dragging them down past her hips, the ripping of the remnants of her chemise bracketed only by their heavy breathing. Then his mouth was on hers, and his large palm pressing between her naked thighs.

Oh, the Fates, this is…

Monsieur D'Artagnon rubbed the heel of his hand against her mound, sliding his fingers through her slick folds, and she moaned. The tension between her thighs begged for release, and she chased his fingers. She might not have had much experience with sex, but she knew what this feeling was, what it led to, and she hungered for it with every fiber of her being.

Then he was wrenching himself from her arms and throwing himself off the bed. He backed away from her, staring down at his body, his chest heaving and his hands clenching and unclenching. A strangled noise erupted from his throat, neither human nor wolf, and he stared at her, his nostrils flaring and his mouth working, but no sound coming out.

Constance wanted to scream her frustration, but one look at his expression, at the sheer panic writ across his face, and her stuttering orgasm vanished.

She eased from the bed, ignoring her nakedness. "Monsieur D'Artagnon."

He squeezed his eye shut and thrashed his head from side to side. Even in distress, he was beautiful. Scarred, but strong. Troubled, damaged, but still proud. With the body of a seasoned chevalier. It made her mouth water. Had her longing to touch him, to run her hands through the dusting of dark hair on his chest. To trace the angry scar curling up over his rib cage and around his shoulder. Her gaze dipped lower. And yes — Mother help her — she wanted to touch him there, too. Take him into her body, lay with him.

Another guttural groan drew her gaze back to his face. The longing she saw there between the strands of his dark hair had her body tingling.

Is this because of my potion?

He clenched his fists at his side, the muscles in his shoulders and arms bunching. He let out an agonized cry that all but tore her heart open.

Shame flushed her cheeks. *What sort of person am I? The man is in* pain.

She took a step toward him, her hand outstretched. He straightened and reached for the door.

"Wait. Please." She pulled the pieces of her torn chemise together. "Stay. Talk to me. Please. Or…I can fetch Seigneur Gaharet?"

Another vigorous shake of his head.

"Then…tell me who betray — "

He snarled and flung the door open. It crashed against the wall as he disappeared down the darkened stairway. Constance raced after him, heedless of her nakedness, her torn chemise flapping against her sides. She followed the glimpses of his bare torso, ignoring the cold floor beneath her feet. If she did not catch him before he shifted back…

She burst into the kitchen, the door to the bailey hanging open. *Am I too late?* She skirted the kitchen table and peered out. By the keep wall, staring back at her, was the black wolf.

No. Constance's shoulders sagged.

Monsieur D'Artagnon turned and slunk away into the night.

She slumped against the door frame, the anguish in that guttural cry still ringing in her ears, burning into her memory. Monsieur D'Artagnon had shifted, whether by her interference or for some unknown reason, but at what cost to the man?

Chapter Eighteen

D'Artagnon sped through the gloom of the forest, his mind racing and the thud of his heart keeping time with the beat of his paws on the ground. He ran as though he could outrun what had happened, as if outrunning himself was truly possible. He had had another uncontrolled shift. Pulled the little healer into his arms, tore at her chemise and almost...

Merde, what is wrong with me?

Not once in all the years since his fellow wolf had cut him down had he shifted. From the moment he had crawled from the battleground and taken wolf form, he had remained so. Even when his body had healed and he had traveled so far northeast that he had run into them, he had not shifted. When they had accepted his presence and allowed him to stay on the fringes of their pack, still he had remained a wolf, though returning to human form would have been the honorable thing to do.

As a wolf encroaching on their territory, it was the *expected* thing to do. To reveal himself and announce his intentions. They could have demanded it, and forced him out when he did not. As an interloper, they could have killed him, but they had seemed to understand why he did not, perhaps more so than he did, and let him be.

If he were honest, shifting had never tempted him. Not in all those years. Now, in the last few days, he had shifted *three* times. Involuntarily. In his *sleep*.

She must think her mixture with the deadly nightshade was the reason, and it would be easy to lay the blame there. He knew differently. Oh, he had caught Anne's wink, and Constance's little catch of breath, but his food had been untainted.

D'Artagnon slowed to a halt in a clearing, his chest heaving. No. He had not shifted because of her potion, but because of *her*. Constance. The woman with the golden braids and unusual eyes. The way she looked at him with such…*empathy*. It echoed in every word she spoke, even if those words were about him. For him.

And, *merde*, she had felt good beneath him. Better than good. She had felt…right. As though his mouth on hers and his hand wedged between her thighs, sliding his fingers through her juices was exactly where he was meant to be. Her heady fragrance and her naked body flushed as she balanced on the edge of a climax etched forever in his memory.

Shame twisted in his chest like a solid entity. He had taken advantage of her. Again. Yet even then, when he had collected his wits and pulled himself off her, she had not been angry at him. Or cursed him for taking from her, nor failing to give her what her body desired, the release she needed. No. She had reached out to him. She had thought only of him and his pack. Not her own denied pleasure, nor her right to be angry at him for forcing himself on her while she slept.

He sat on his haunches, the familiar hint of pine, oak and the damp earth of the forest surrounding him, hoping for the calm it usually brought with it. But the forest held other spoors. Crisscrossing trails of his brother, Ulrik, Aimon and their mates. It served only to remind him of Constance, standing in the kitchen doorway, her chemise hanging at her sides and her beautiful body bathed in moonlight.

He lifted his muzzle to the sky and howled. It echoed through the forest, a mournful sound carrying all his frustration, his confusion and his longing.

An answering howl, close and familiar, echoed back. That voice did not belong here in *this* forest, but D'Artagnon made no move to rise. Instead, he waited, until a big wolf, larger than D'Artagnon, larger even than Gaharet, with gray peppering his muzzle and brow, padded into the clearing.

With a crack and pop of bone and muscle, the wolf's body distorted and changed. His spine elongated, his hips straightened and his paws became hands and feet. The gray wolf's snout shortened and his large canines disappeared, revealing a face D'Artagnon knew well. This was not his enemy, but his friend. His—dare he think it?—mentor. What was he doing here, so far from his home range?

Vladimir. A man in his seventh decade, yet still strong in a lean, wiry way. Perhaps stronger than any wolf he knew, despite the hard years of experience marked in the lines of his face.

Vladimir raised his bushy gray eyebrows. "You think I would not follow you? That I would leave you to hunt the one who cut you down alone?" The old wolf sighed. "Bratishka." The word a gentle chastisement.

Little brother. At a time when his body had healed but his heart and mind were broken, the old wolf had taken him in. Had spoken for him to the Rus pack when he could not, had chosen not to speak for himself.

D'Artagnon shook his head. The old wolf should not have come. This was not his fight.

"Your fight is our fight, Bratishka."

D'Artagnon huffed. He had not wanted to involve the Rus pack. They had done enough for him. For a wolf whose name and origins they may have suspected but for whom they had no confirmation.

"Another wolf has cut you down, with a blade, no less. Such a wolf is a danger to us all." Vladimir settled beside him on the forest floor, his back against the smooth bark of a beech tree. "You may not talk, Bratishka, but it was not difficult to determine what befell you. Why you had to leave your pack when you were injured so."

D'Artagnon stared out into the forest. It had seemed so simple when he had set out from Rus, his thirst for vengeance, for retribution, to acquit himself of his failures, a driving force. His anger at his betrayal, a thing of purity. Too long had he skulked around the border of the Rus wolves' territory, hiding himself away. He had thought himself restored. Ready to face his past. His uncontrolled shifting, and his panic when he had stood as a man, suggested otherwise.

With a single-minded focus he had tracked his nemesis, but the moment he had stepped into the d'Louncrais keep, surrounded by the walls of his childhood home steeped in memories, and stood before his newly mated brother who pleaded with him to stay, his determination had wavered. With Constance's arrival, things had become complicated, his path no longer clear cut, the edges of his control fraying, and the simplicity of his purpose compromised.

"You were ready, Bratishka. But coming home, facing the man who had done this to you, and being around your pack again was always going to test you." Vladimir raised his head and sniffed the air. "And there is something more." He sniffed again. "Female." Knowing eyes stared at him. "Her scent is all over you."

D'Artagnon tracked the flight path of a tawny owl before it disappeared in the gloom of the forest.

"You shifted?"

D'Artagnon hung his head.

"Good."

D'Artagnon bared his teeth. He understood why Vladimir would think so, but it was *not* good.

"Ah, you did not call upon the change."

Perhaps it was the way of wolves. Perhaps it was a consequence of Vladimir's long life, and a knowing that only came with age and experience, but Vladimir had never had any trouble understanding him.

"Then what made you shift, Bratishka? Is she your mate?"

D'Artagnon jerked his head up. His *mate*?

The old wolf smiled. "Even one as wounded as you has a mate. Perhaps fate has sent her to you when you need her most."

D'Artagnon flattened his ears against his skull. When he needed her most? Then why was Constance here now, and not when blood had poured from his shoulder and the slash across his face that had taken his eye? When, grievously injured as he was, he had had to keep his wits about him to evade his attacker. As he had slunk through the forest, barely able to stand, looking for a safe place to hide and heal, the skills of a healer would have helped him beyond measure.

Instead, here he was now, out in the forest, hiding from her, when he should be hunting his enemy.

And his *mate?* Fate was a cruel mistress if she thought to saddle some poor woman, Constance or any other, with him. He had not, for one moment in nigh on a decade, thought beyond his nemesis and his mission. To what he would do, where he would live. If he would live at all.

He stared out into the forest, the gloom beckoning, trying to envisage himself once again taking his place beside his brother, living in the keep as a man. As D'Artagnon. His stomach sank, heavier than the armor he had long since abandoned.

The life he had once lived was a thing of the past. The old D'Artagnon was gone. He did not belong here anymore. He did not belong in a keep, or around people. The only thing he knew, the one place he felt at home, was in the forest. A life Constance had lived her whole life through no choice of her own. No, Constance could not, *would* not, be his mate. He had nothing to offer her.

But he *would* track down the man who had betrayed him, and he would avenge his parents. Beyond that, D'Artagnon had no plans.

D'Artagnon had promised his brother a few days. He had fulfilled his promise. It was time to return to his hunt for the traitor. Alone. He would rid the world of this traitor, or he would die trying. Nothing would prevent him from that. Not even the call to mate.

Chapter Nineteen

Constance groaned, her eyes gritty from lack of sleep. Had her unsatisfied yearning of her body not kept her awake all night, the anguish on Monsieur D'Artagnon's face as he had fled the bedchamber would have. She rubbed her hands over her face. In all her years tending to people and what ailed them, not once had she doubted herself. Not once had her visions left her so bereft of guidance she did not know what to do, what course of action to take.

She rolled onto her side and met the blue-eyed gaze of the black wolf. She sat up.

Monsieur D'Artagnon? When had he come back?

Constance could have sworn she had not slept a wink, awaiting his return, the grip of guilt churning her stomach when he had not. But there he was, by the brazier, watching her, as though he had slept there all night.

Her bare skin prickled and — *L'enfer! Her chemise!* Constance clutched the covers to her chest, hiding her nakedness. Heat rose over her chest, neck and face. "I did not hear you come in. I…"

The one-eyed wolf fixed her with his haunted gaze. Could she do it? Force him to shift? It *could* be a good thing. Anne certainly believed so. As did Seigneur Gaharet. He would not wish his brother harm. Perhaps it was a kindness, a way to help him heal. The evidence of his injuries was impossible to ignore, but some scars were invisible—those written large across one's heart and soul. Constance suspected, for Monsieur D'Artagnon, those cut the deepest and had caused the most damage.

Her gaze skipped to the bowl on the table containing the deadly nightshade potion. She could be doing more harm than good.

Constance turned back the covers, careful to keep the torn edges of her chemise covering her nakedness, and slipped from the bed. She hunted around amongst the clothes Anne had left her and found a fresh chemise. With her back to Monsieur D'Artagnon, ignoring the prickle of his regard, she shrugged out of her ruined one and quickly dressed. Her old chemise, she bundled up and shoved beneath the mattress. She did not want anyone—Anne or any of the other servants—to think less of Monsieur D'Artagnon. To assume he had forced himself on her.

"Good morrow, child." The old cook ambled in, bustling over to the shutters and banging them open. "Good morrow, D'Artagnon. I see you are dressed already, Constance. Good. It is to be a busy day today," said Anne, prodding the coals in the brazier to life. "You will be taking up residence in the old farmer's cottage."

"The old farmer's cottage?"

Anne beamed. "Yes, child. It is a lovely little cottage in the woods. Just delightful."

"Oh." Constance banked her disappointment. She had been enjoying her time with Erin, Kathryn and Bek—the companionship, the way the women had included her in their conversations, asked her opinion.

"Nice and quiet. No one to bother you out there." Anne rubbed her hands together. "Just the two of you."

"Just the two of us?" Was that wise? After what had happened last eve?

"Why yes, child. You did not think we would send you out there all on your own. Tsk, tsk. *Of course* Monsieur D'Artagnon will be going with you. It is the perfect place for you"—Anne jerked her head at D'Artagnon—"to work on his furry self's little problem."

Constance swallowed. "I…" What could she say without revealing the happenings of last eve? Events Constance had been an active participant in.

"Come now, child." She gestured Constance to a seat, running a comb through her hair. "There is a cart and a man servant down in the bailey awaiting to take you."

Constance stared at the grand bed with its soft covers and divine mattress. It had been nice while it had lasted. An experience few peasants would ever have, sleeping in such a bed. Having servants wait on her, helping her dress, tend to her hair, cook her meals and stoke the fire.

"Now this cottage you are off to has a gorgeous little pond." Anne pinned her head veil in place. "I have heard told the young ones found it quite romantic. That they would go out there when the moon was full and do what lovers are wont to do." She heaved out a big sigh. "Oh, to be young again."

Constance risked a peek at Monsieur D'Artagnon, the feel of his mouth on her breast and his hand between her thighs fresh in her mind.

"He was a handsome lad, was our D'Artagnon," said Anne. "I imagine those scars of his would only add to his appeal." Anne leaned in close. "If I was young and slim like you, with a wolf like D'Artagnon sleeping in my bed…" Anne gave her wink and a sly smile. "That is not an opportunity to be wasting."

Constance gaped. Was Anne suggesting…? Had the old cook guessed what had happened last eve? Did she suspect Constance's deepest desires?

"Off you go now. Both of you." Anne made a shooing motion with her hands. "I have made sure you have all you need." Mischief twinkled in Anne's eyes. "For as long as you need. There is no cause for you and D'Artagnon to rush back."

The wolf's eyes narrowed. No, he did not like the idea one bit. Lord, had her potion, and the…incident last eve made things worse? Her stomach churned. Never as a healer had she set out to cause a patient pain.

Constance scooped up her things, and with one last look at the room and the luxury she would likely never experience again, she headed down the stairs, D'Artagnon trailing along behind her.

The hall was empty, save for Seigneur Gaharet, sitting by the fire. He looked up as she paused in the doorway.

"Good morrow, Constance. The women are in the library as usual. I believe they wanted to say goodbye before you leave." He turned to the black wolf. "D'Artagnon, a word."

Monsieur D'Artagnon pushed past her into the room, and Constance curtsied to Seigneur Gaharet before heading down the corridor. Alone in a cottage together. In the forest. Beneath her doubt, her confusion over what to do, and despite the guilt lodged in her chest, a thin tendril of hope curled its way into her heart.

Chapter Twenty

D'Artagnon sat on his haunches by the fire, waiting for his brother to speak. Was it Gaharet's plan to send Constance and D'Artagnon to the farmer's cottage, or Anne's? His brother wanted him to stay, wanted him to shift, and Anne, it seemed, had her own agenda. Perhaps they were working together, conspiring against him. It did not matter. He would not be going anywhere with Constance. Not after what he had done last eve. He would not be staying here either.

Gaharet leaned his elbows on his knees, his hands clasped in front of him and looked him square in the eye. "D'Artagnon, I want you to go to the farmer's cottage with Constance. I need you to keep watch over her." Gaharet held up a hand. "Now, before you decide to leave and disappear back to wherever you have been these last nine years, there are a few things you need to know."

Once again, his brother had guessed his intentions. D'Artagnon stared into the flickering flames. He never could hide things from his brother. *Let him talk.* He swiveled an ear in his brother's direction. He would listen, but nothing Gaharet could say would change his mind.

"As I told you when you first arrived, much has happened while you have been gone, but I have not told you of *all* our troubles. Thanks to Ulrik and his sword, Archeveque Renaud is no longer one of them, but there are more threats than the wolf who gave you those scars."

Gaharet paused, and the distant chatter of the women, and the deeper rumble of Ulrik and Aimon filled the space. Ulrik and Aimon were giving their mates a lesson on how to use a sword in the library.

"They will do anything to keep their mates safe." A wry smile tugged at the corner of Gaharet's mouth. "We all would. You will learn that in time."

D'Artagnon huffed.

The amusement in his brother's eyes dimmed, and his expression turned serious. "D'Artagnon, Lothair knows what we are."

D'Artagnon recoiled. *Lothair? Comte Lothair?* He flattened his ears against his skull and bared his teeth.

"I agree with you, brother. It is not an ideal situation, but one we must contend with all the same. As troubling as that is, this is not my immediate concern." Gaharet pulled something from beneath his tunic. The parchment from ere-yesterday, with Lothair's command for the pack to present themselves at Langeais Keep. "There is a new, perhaps greater threat in the county. Eveque Faucher has shown an interest in us. He has a reputation for routing out things the church deems as evil. People like us."

All the more reason he should leave, and not be seen anywhere near his brother, or any of his pack. Gaharet would see the wisdom of that. A wolf in the forest would draw little attention, but in a keep, a village…

Gaharet opened the parchment and held it out for him to read. At the top, the summons from Lothair that Gaharet had read out. At the bottom, a warning he had not. D'Artagnon read through it. *This Eveque Faucher could already be on his way here? To the keep?*

"They call this Eveque Faucher a witch hunter."

A witch hunter? D'Artagnon froze. *Constance.*

Fear like he had not experienced since the day his enemy had cut him down sliced through him. They could send her back to her cottage in the forest, but it would not take long before someone from Langeais told Faucher of a woman in the woods. One with two different colored eyes who used herbs to heal. Perhaps they already had. But she could not stay *here*. With the threat of this eveque making a surprise visit, the keep was not safe for Constance, either.

"We must protect her, D'Artagnon."

D'Artagnon chuffed his fervent agreement.

"Constance is precious to us. She is a skilled healer. She can make potions for us to ease the turning, and she has more knowledge of us than we do ourselves. It was her coven who created our amulets."

The amulets? Their connection with the pack was that old?

"We cannot let her fall into the hands of this Eveque Faucher."

D'Artagnon's shoulders bunched. His brother was right. They must protect Constance, but…

Gaharet's dark gaze pinned him in place. "I know you want to hunt this traitor, to be the one to take him down, D'Artagnon. It hangs over you like an autumn storm cloud — your anger, your thirst for vengeance — but some things are more important. No one but us knows you have returned. No one will notice your absence. And who better to keep Constance safe in the woods than you?"

D'Artagnon turned an ear toward the doorway and the library beyond. The lessons had stopped, and Constance was comforting Kathryn over her failure to remember. There was a melodious softness to her voice, a calm thoughtfulness, as though she chose her words with care, and a gentleness that would ease the fears of even the smallest of children. The woman cared for people, gave her time and her energy to help them heal, and what had she received in return?

Gaharet rose then crouched in front of him. "I give you my word, D'Artagnon. When we hunt down the one responsible for the death of our parents, we will do it together."

D'Artagnon did not move, torn between his wish to spare his brother and his desire to protect Constance.

"It will not be for long, D'Artagnon. When we go to renew our vows, I will meet this Eveque Faucher, and I will be better able to assess this threat. I will send for you when I think it is safe for Constance to return."

A growl rumbled in the back of his throat. He did not like the thought of his brother facing this witch hunter alone. And what of his nemesis? Would he be there? Renewing his vows also?

"I will not be alone, D'Artagnon. Ulrik and Aimon will be at my side, and the twins will have my back."

D'Artagnon huffed. The twins were formidable, and surrounded by loyal pack, out in the open, his brother would not be an easy target.

"Will you do this for me? Who else would I trust with this than mine own brother?"

D'Artagnon dipped his head. He would go to the cottage. He would protect Constance until his brother deemed it safe for her to return to the keep. Then he would go after the traitor. In truth, he would hunt better knowing she was safe.

Gaharet laid a hand on his shoulder. "Take care of her, D'Artagnon. We need her. *You* need her."

D'Artagnon sniffed, turned on his heel and trotted off to collect Constance. The pack may have need of her knowledge, but D'Artagnon had no use for her healer's skills. Not now, not ever.

Chapter Twenty-One

Lance closed the door on Godfrey's steward and surveyed the room. Though not as impressive as the d'Louncrais library, it was filled with many more tomes and scrolls than his own — stacked in chests, on side tables and on the desk. It had been years since he had set foot in the Lagarde's keep, but Godfrey, it appeared, had continued his father's pursuit of collecting knowledge.

A comfortable chair rested by the brazier. A few scrolls with their bindings loose, a journal and an empty goblet with dregs of wine sat on the table beside it, and the coals in the brazier had long since gone cold. On Godfrey's desk, unopened, were two folded parchments stamped with Comte Lothair's seal.

Lance had received a similar one yesterday. A summons. And an earlier one a sennight prior. Godfrey had not returned to open either of them. The steward, on Lance's arrival, had expressed his concern about Godfrey's unusual absence. No one had seen him for nearly a fortnight. It looked damning for the chevalier.

Lance eased himself into the chair by the brazier. What had Godfrey been reading? He unfurled one of the scrolls. The chevalier's agitation in the clearing when Kathryn had chosen Aimon as her mate, his visit to Lance's keep and his cryptic comment about secrets, suggested he was hiding something. It warranted further investigation.

He read through the scroll — an account of Victor's visit from Bretaigne and his taking of Marie as his mate — written in Godfrey's familiar, concise hand. There was nothing in it Lance did not already know. He had been there. Together with Godfrey, he had escorted the miscreant stable hand, Didier, off the d'Louncrais demesne. It had been a foolish move on Jacques' behalf, banishing Didier rather than killing him on the spot. Lance would not have shown such mercy. Or risked the secret of their existence by allowing Didier to walk free.

Had Godfrey thought to track Didier? See if he still lived? The stable hand would for certain have harbored resentment toward the d'Louncrais. He set the scroll aside. It was worth considering.

Lance picked up another scroll. The writing was more slanted, brisk. Written by Godfrey's father, if his memory served him. He skimmed the first few lines. Ah, the account of Ulrik's exile, and the punishment of Ulrik's family in his stead. A sorry business all round. At least now Ulrik appeared to have pulled his head out of the wine barrel. Finally. Finding your mate would do that to a wolf.

A flicker of resentment sparked in his chest. That Ulrik would be the one to find his mate, after all the problems he had caused the pack — exiled by his own parents, challenging Gaharet, spending years bedding every available and unavailable woman and imbibing more wine than was good for any man, werewolf or no—irked him. Both he and Godfrey had waited decades. He grunted. Fate was a fickle mistress.

Lance tossed the scroll back onto the table. With Ulrik now absolved of any wrongdoing, it was of no use. He unfurled another scroll. A recounting of a battle against the army of Blois. The battle where D'Artagnon had died. Lance paused in his reading.

They never found his body.

They had discussed this possibility—that D'Artagnon was their rogue wolf—and dismissed it. Lance had to agree with Edmond. D'Artagnon would never have killed his own mother. And, by Kathryn's account, the wolf who had attacked her and killed Gaharet's mother had had brown fur, which ruled out D'Artagnon. Why had Godfrey set aside this scroll? What was he searching for?

He read through it twice, but nothing struck him as being amiss. The battle had been ferocious, and many chevaliers on both sides had died before they had routed the enemy. There were several accounts of D'Artagnon crawling away into the forest, a deep slash to his face and a grievous injury to his side. Mortal injuries for a man, and possibly for a werewolf, too, if he were to bleed out before healing could begin. There was mention of others of the pack—his own name amongst them, and Godfrey's—fighting to get to the downed chevalier. None successful. Of the search for days afterward with no sign of D'Artagnon, living or dead.

Lance set the scroll aside. There was nothing in it to suggest anything other than D'Artagnon had crawled away from the battlefield and died from his wounds. His armor alone would have been cause for someone, whether peasant or enemy, to steal away his body.

He opened the leather-bound journal full of slanted scrawl. This was one of Godfrey's father's journals. Geoffroi Lagarde had been as prolific and as fastidious with keeping records as any monk. Perhaps more so. On the desk, and most likely in the chests lining the walls, were more journals like these. What made this one so important?

Lance flicked through the pages, searching for any sign of a section, a line, that had caught Godfrey's eye. He paused at a page close to the back of the book, his own name leaping out at him, circled in fresh ink. He read through the lines. Reread them again.

Merde.

There on the page, in the bold hand of Geoffroi Lagarde, was motive enough for a twisted jealous mind to have committed heinous acts — attacking a child, and killing his friend's, his alpha's, mate. And they pointed the finger squarely at him.

He read through them again.

I needs must write this down, for should it come to anything, this shall be my witness.

He swallowed. In his mind, Geoffroi's voice rang clear. A man long since fallen, but alive in these pages, in these words, as though speaking from beyond the grave.

As children, Elise, Lance and mine own son, Godfrey, were inseparable. A bond formed between them and remained through to adulthood, extending to Jacques d'Louncrais upon his claiming of Elise. But I fear that bond may soon be broken, for I have observed an unhealthy interest in Lance toward Elise. One that, on Lance's behalf, extends beyond friendship. Jacques and Elise appear to be unaware of Lance's infatuation. Lance has yet to act upon it, and may never do so, but I have, on more than one occasion, scented his dissatisfaction with Jacques. Though, in all honesty, I could not, without a doubt, attribute it to his feelings toward Elise.

This may amount to naught, for both my son and Lance have always had a fondness for Elise, and she them. Perhaps it is merely Lance's wish that he, too, had found his mate.

Lance snapped the journal shut. This was the secret Godfrey suspected him of harboring. It was damning if one considered the actions of an infatuated young man as evidence. Believed *him* to be the infatuated man Geoffroi had thought him, rather than a man envious of the happiness his childhood friend and his alpha had found.

Given what had recently come to light—Elise's death, and Kathryn's attack at the hands of one of their own—it would be an easy enough conclusion to come to. If one had not been there. Had not seen that Jacques' mate had been the object of desire for almost *every* man in the county. Elise was a beauty. A flame that burned so brightly, so hot. Sometimes too hot. She had set many a man's imagination on fire with her boldness, only to burn them to the ground with her temper. Jacques had succeeded where others had failed, taming her in some small way.

But for those who were not there, who had not witnessed the bond between them, Godfrey included, the words of Geoffroi could call his loyalty to Jacques, to the pack, into question.

He pushed himself to his feet, rubbing his hand across his face as he paced the room. What should he do with this? Should he bury it amongst the hundreds of tomes? He paused at the desk, eyeing the summons from Lothair. In a few days hence, he would attend

Langeais Keep with the rest of his pack. With Gaharet. He could confess he had found this. Lay it all bare for them in the interest of being honest. Or he could leave it and do nothing. He alone had been tasked with searching Godfrey's library. None would seek to follow in his footsteps. However, if he were to conceal it and Godfrey were to return, or Gaharet himself came to search for the missing chevalier, it would only point to his guilt.

Lance traced the Comte's seal. He had until then to decide what he should do. He tore the page out and tossed the book on the table where he had found it. Without a backward glance, he left the library, thanked Godfrey's steward and collected his horse. He stuffed the page beneath his armor. He could always burn it if there was a need.

Chapter Twenty-Two

The sun was well on its way to reaching its zenith as Constance stepped down from the cart and surveyed her surroundings. Nestled in the center of a small clearing, bathed in warm sunlight, was a small but sturdy cottage, more reminiscent of the huts in the village than her own.

As the servant unloaded the supplies, she turned her face to the sun and let its warmth soak into her skin, squinting up at the sky, breathing in the smells of the forest. Birds twittered, the last of the summer insects hummed and the whisper of a breeze caressed the treetops. She had missed this.

Constance took it all in — the space, the quiet, the fresh air. So familiar to her, it comforted her and soothed away the consistent hum of tension that had plagued her since she had arrived at the keep. The opulence of it, the constant noise of people — servants and the like — the busyness of it all, and the expectations resting on her shoulders as oppressive as the walls that had surrounded her. The muscles in her shoulders loosened. She had spent a good portion of her life alone in the forest, and while she was more than a half day's ride from her crude little cottage, this place felt like coming home.

Monsieur D'Artagnon emerged from the cottage. With a bark and a jerk of his head at the open door, the black wolf trotted off into the forest, his nose to the ground. She watched him go. Good. She needed time to think, to sort out her muddled feelings. Time without his constant presence.

Constance collected her things from the cart, turned her back on the forest and stepped inside to take stock. She unpinned her head veil and dropped it on the table beside her grimoire. In the not too recent past, someone had lived here. The pots of herbs, salt and honey were all full, and the bowls, platters and mugs were new. The pot hanging over the fire was so new it had yet to blacken with layers of soot.

She pushed aside the heavy drape over the bedding nook. One cot, barely wide enough for two people. It was, after all, a farmer's cottage, but whoever had spent their nights here were not mere farmers. The bed covers were thick and soft, and the mattress was of goose down, not straw.

She sat on the cot. Not as comfortable as the large bed in the keep, but close. Far more so than her own straw-filled mattress in her cottage. She ran her hand over the bedcovers. Would Monsieur D'Artagnon sleep at her feet as he had done in the keep? He had not glanced in her direction once the entire journey here.

The servant's appearance in the doorway jerked her from her musings. "That is the last of it, Ma Dame." He placed a basket full of vegetables by the wall. "I will be on my way."

She smiled at him. "Thank you." There was no point correcting him, telling him she was no more a dame than he was a monsieur.

He bowed and disappeared, the clop of horse's hooves and the creak of the cart wheels fading into the distance.

She grabbed a small basket from a hook beside the door and stepped out into the sun. She would gather a few herbs for a ward around the cottage. Now they were no longer within the fortified walls of the keep, something stronger, more akin to the one she maintained around her cottage was warranted. Many plants grew close to water. Spotting a trail she hoped would lead her to this pond Anne had spoken of, Constance set off through the forest.

She followed the trail, stopping to pick leaves for her ward as she found them, until the path opened into another clearing. She paused at the edge of the tree line. The morning sun glinted on a pond, and moss-covered rocks glistened under the gentle spray of a small waterfall. She swallowed. Such a beautiful place, and yet she carried the ugliness of her actions and the pain she had caused in her heart and mind. It threatened to bubble up and choke her.

Constance breathed through the sensation and stepped to the water's edge, dipping her fingers in and sending ripples across the water. Constance stared at her reflection, willing it to impart sage advice, to live up to the wisdom Anne saw in her eyes. She ran her fingers through her image. Despite the fancy dress she wore, it revealed nothing but the face of a peasant, an outcast healer.

A healer.

That is what I am. What she had dedicated her life to. *Healing.* She helped people. When they were in need and at their most vulnerable. As her mother before her had done. And her mother before her. Yet, from the moment Constance had stepped into the hall in the d'Louncrais keep, she had forgotten the most basic principle of her trade. The patient's needs took precedence over all else.

Had she worried that forcing D'Artagnon to shift might cause him harm? No. Had she considered his pain when she had suggested using silver? Also, no. Had she made any attempt to ease the suffering she could so clearly see in his eye? She heaved out a sigh. No. All she had thought about were her own needs. How the rekindling of her connection with the Langeais wolves would afford *her* protection. How, should she succeed in the task Seigneur Gaharet had set for her, she might ask for a permanent place for *her*self in the village.

And from the moment she had first laid eyes on the black wolf beneath his brother's hand, she had wondered if he might be the wolf from her vision. A wolf that would take *her* as his mate.

Not once had she considered the man beneath the wolf's fur. A man who was suffering—damaged, physically and emotionally. A man who had comforted her, supported her at her first supper in the keep. Had let her sleep in his bed. Had taken her to see Old Tumas, where she had learned more about her mother.

Constance closed her eyes, unable to face the disappointment mirrored in her reflection. D'Artagnon was right to mistrust her, to fear her. She had betrayed every healer and every one of her ancestors.

Constance would do better. She *must* do better. It might mean her own future would be less secure, and she could lose the Langeais' wolves protection. Her chance for a place in the village, for friends like

Georgette, might be beyond her reach. Her vision may never come to pass. But that was not for her to anticipate. She was a *healer,* and she would do what she was called to do. *Heal.*

As Kathryn's memory loss was best treated as a symptom of her fear, D'Artagnon's inability to shift had an emotional cause. Healing his pain might prompt him to shift, but *forcing* him to shift should *never* have been her focus. And it would not be moving forward.

Constance opened her eyes, her mind quieter and at peace with her decision, her heart lighter. She stepped back from the water's edge and glanced around at the forest. She was alone. Unlacing her dress, she stripped off her clothing and walked into the pond. When it lapped at her thighs, she sank beneath the cool water, cleansing herself of the past and of the mistakes she had made.

She dipped her head under and resurfaced near the waterfall. Wet leaves glimmered in the dappled sunlight, and the gentle splash of water muted the sounds of the forest. So beautiful, so serene. She could only imagine what it would be like on a moonlit night. A perfect place for lovers.

An image unbidden swept into her mind. Of her and Monsieur D'Artagnon. The two of them entwined in an embrace, naked, the pond all silvery and aglow. Her breath caught in her throat, the memory of his hand cupping her mound, his fingers —

A soft thud behind her had her spinning around. On the edge of the pond stood the black wolf. At his paws, a large hare.

"Monsieur D'Artagnon. You startled me. I thought to be alone."

He stared at her, a magnificent, scarred beast, his tongue sweeping out to lick his muzzle.

Her body came alive and her face heated, the memory of his tongue laving her nipple too recent. She wrapped her arms around herself. Could he scent her arousal? Read her thoughts?

"The water looked so inviting, I…" She swallowed.

A low rumble reverberated in his chest. She clenched her thighs together. Perhaps he was still suffering the effects of her potion. Or was something else happening here? As his shifting twice before, and the kiss she had thought but a dream, suggested?

She pushed away all memories of last eve. It did not matter. She had amends to make.

"I am going to come out now," she warned him. "We need to talk."

Monsieur D'Artagnon turned away and sat on his haunches, facing the forest. An ache formed in her chest. She did not merit such consideration after what she had done, yet still he had granted it to her.

Constance dressed, mindless of her chemise clinging to her wet body and the squelch of her wet feet in her boots. She kneeled in front of him. She would face this head on, let him know the truth, the sincerity of her words. "I deceived you." Her voice echoed across the whisper of the forest. "I imagine you know what I am talking about."

The black wolf snarled.

Constance firmed her resolve. "I made a potion from the leaves of the henbane plant, mandrake root and deadly nightshade berries, and Anne slipped it your food last eve."

He made no move toward her, but his snarl remained.

"What happened…between you and me…when you shifted…" She dropped her gaze to her boots, sucking in a few deep breaths, before facing him again.

She deserved his anger, the accusation in his eye. "You may not have been responsible for your actions. The potion is known to have that effect. And I made the potion strong." She had come this far, she would not stop now. "The berries were a mistake. *I* made a mistake, and I am sorry."

Dark shadows flitted within the blue of his iris, and his fur rippled.

She swallowed, then lifted her chin, never more sure of her decision than she was right now. "I know what Seigneur Gaharet has asked of me, but I will not force you to shift. Not anymore."

His eye narrowed, and he cocked his head.

"But I am going to help you."

He would be wary, and though he was a wolf, a predator who feared few things, he was a wounded one. Like any patient, to help him, she must first gain his trust. After last night, she had much catching up to do.

"I have a few more herbs to collect" — she held up her basket — "then I shall return to the cottage and prepare us a noon meal." She gathered up the hare. "This will make a lovely stew for supper."

She set off along the path, sweeping the forest with a practiced eye, searching for the plants she would need. Monsieur D'Artagnon made no move to stop her, but his eye — which saw too much — followed her every step. This time, Constance made no attempt to conceal her intentions.

Chapter Twenty-Three

D'Artagnon fought the urge to shift, clinging to his wolf as though his life depended on it. Mayhap it did, despite her heart-felt apology. But his wolf did not care. Not since the moment he had found her by the pond, naked, her back to him, her clothes in a pile at her feet.

He had tried to block the images swirling in his mind. Of them together in the water, of him laying her naked in the shallows, his human body nestled between her pale thighs, but they had persisted as she had swum in the pond. Had his dropping of the hare not startled her, had she not turned around, he feared he would have shifted, intent on living out his imaginings.

He gnashed his teeth and shook himself, drawing on every ounce of control he had fostered over his long years in exile. He must resist her, as beguiling as she was. Now was not the time to let his base instincts reign. He knew this for a certainty when she knelt by a bush and plucked a few of its leaves.

What had prompted her change of mind, he could not fathom, but he was wary of trusting it. This could be a ruse, though he sensed no lie in her words. She appeared to genuinely regret making the deadly nightshade potion. She also, much to his consternation, remained steadfast in her determination to help him. What that entailed, what the herbs would do, given she had professed she would no longer attempt to force him to shift, he could not fathom.

"A simple ward for around the cottage," she explained, tucking the leaves into the basket.

He raised his eyebrow. *A ward? For the cottage?*

"Yes, Monsieur, I will ward the cottage. I have done so with every cottage I have ever lived in, and I have lived in many in my lifetime. I have warded my hut in the forest since the first day it became my home, though in my absence, its power will be waning." A sadness descended over her like a thick blanket of winter snow. "It takes little for people's gratitude for your healing abilities to change into anger and fear. Milk that turns sour, a hen that no longer lays eggs, a young boy taken by illness despite all your best efforts. It does not matter that you do not live in their village." She raised her hand and swept it in an arc, taking in the forest. "Or that we appear to be far from the notice of anyone."

D'Artagnon eyed her warily. Her body was loose and relaxed, and she maintained eye contact. More than any other human, Constance had knowledge of them. Pages of it in her precious grimoire. Information she could use to counter the advantage of his heightened senses. Was she using that knowledge now? Couching a lie amongst the truth?

Constance collected her basket and veered further off the trail, stopping at another plant. "Villagers are superstitious, and fear is a powerful emotion. My eyes have always caused concern and have made me a target more than most. The d'Louncrais village is the only one I have ever been in where people did not stare, or point fingers and whisper as I walked past."

She kneeled, plucked a few leaves and added them to her collection. "It surprised me that day we visited Tumas and his daughter. Here I was, a stranger with two different colored eyes—no doubt rumors of me being a witch had already spread—and beside me, a big black wolf. You cannot imagine the furor, the panic had we walked into Langeais village like that. Yet nothing but greetings and smiles from the villagers." Constance stood and regained the trail. "It would be a nice village to live in, the d'Louncrais village. The people are friendly, the cottages are sturdy. Seigneur Gaharet is as benevolent a seigneur as I have ever seen. It would be a good life."

D'Artagnon did not need his wolf senses to hear the thoughts, the dashed hopes that Constance left unsaid. Anne was right. Life had not been kind to Constance. No woman would choose to live alone in the forest so far from people, had she any other choice. How long had she lived there? The only occupant of that rundown, sad little building deep in the woods? By the air of loneliness that followed her around like a fog— long enough.

She halted at the edge of the clearing, the cottage awaiting them. "I do not know why my mother left the d'Louncrais village," she said. "And perhaps I may never have the answer. With her and your father gone, I have no one left to ask."

Constance crossed the clearing and ducked through the doorway of the cottage, leaving him standing outside. An ache pressed against his sternum. Such simple dreams she had. A sturdy cottage, acceptance, to understand why it had all been denied her. The urge to comfort her surged within him, pressing against the barrier of his wolf, the man inside clamoring to get out, to be set free. His poor little healer.

He dug his claws into the dirt. Since when had *the* little healer become *his* little healer? Since Vladimir had suggested she was his mate? A growl rumbled in his chest. She had crept in where she did not belong. That he was here, protecting her instead of hunting down his betrayer, was proof enough. No. She would not deter him. She would not defeat him. When his brother called for their return, he would still be a wolf.

Grateful for the concealment his wolf's fur gave him, he buried his feelings deep. When he had his wayward impulses under control, he entered the cottage.

D'Artagnon followed every move Constance made as she emptied the contents of the basket onto the table.

She grabbed a knife with an elaborate handle and a bowl. "Watch me make my preparations." She lined up three items from her collection. "These herbs will go in a bundle I shall hang over the door. It will infuse the cottage, and both you *and* I shall feel its effects." She pointed to the first item, a cluster of pink and white flowers with a root attached. "This is the all heal plant. It has many uses, but I have chosen it for its ability to quieten emotions."

D'Artagnon leaned in and sniffed at the root. He wrinkled his nose, wishing he had not. The inside of his old boots smelled better.

Constance grinned at him. "An unpleasant smell, but a very useful plant. It will represent the water element of my spell."

Her finger hovered over three heart-shaped leaves. He did not need an introduction to recognize burn nettle. A careless romp in the woods as a pup, a tussle with his brother and a lack of awareness of their surroundings had seen them both land within its stinging clutches. The leaves looked innocent enough, but the fine, needle-like hairs created a burn he had not soon forgotten.

D'Artagnon snarled at the leaves and kept his nose a respectful distance away from them.

Constance smiled. "I see you have knowledge of the burn nettle leaf. Painful to touch, but good for dispelling darkness and fear, and it will aid healing. This will represent fire."

The final element, delicate green leaves, she held out to him. He pulled back. The first herb was unpleasant, the second could burn. What would this one do? She waited, her hand outstretched. He inched closer, and she rubbed the leaves between her fingers, releasing their aroma. He sniffed, then sneezed. Shaking his head, he sneezed again. He scrunched up his nose, bared his teeth, and sneezed again.

D'Artagnon jumped off the seat and rubbed his muzzle along the dirt floor, desperate to be rid of the bitter scent that coated the inside of his nostrils.

Her laugh filled the cottage, a joyous sound that washed over him, and like her voice, it sank deep. D'Artagnon huffed and shook himself, casting off the warmth before it could take hold. She had tricked him again. He sneezed once more and glared at the leaves in her palm.

Constance pressed her hand to her mouth, hiding her smile. "I am sorry, Monsieur. I should not laugh, but I did not expect it to make you sneeze. It is but wormwood." She set the leaves back on the table. "It represents the earth and is helpful in removing anger."

D'Artagnon half sneezed, half snorted. Herbs to quieten his emotions, to dispel fear, to remove anger?

He sniffed again and shook himself. A bunch of herbs and an incantation or two would not wash away the darkness, anger and grief that swirled inside him, so deep there seemed no end to it. Emotions that had only grown and solidified during the icy winters of his time with the Rus wolves.

Constance stooped before the baskets of supplies stacked against the wall and began digging through them. "I need one more ingredient and I am hoping Anne has packed it, for it is not something I can forage for in the forest." She selected a pot, lifted the lid and sniffed. Then put it back, selecting another and another before she smiled, triumphant. She held it out for him to see. "Savior plant. For grief, loss, purification and healing. It will represent air for this herb bundle."

She set the pot beside the other three ingredients. "All spells require a balance of wind, earth, fire and water, corresponding to the east, north, south and west. Everything in nature has balance." She selected a bowl and picked up the knife. "Summer and winter, autumn and spring, light and dark, night and day, body and spirit. If one element is missing, the spell is unbalanced and has less chance of being successful, or working in the way we intend it to."

D'Artagnon jumped up onto the seat again and surveyed the table. Set aside were four more ingredients. He planted his paw beside the little pile, careful not to touch it. He met her gaze.

"What are these for? These are the herbs I will use to ward the cottage." Constance used her knife to separate them. "Mugwort represents the earth and is for strength, protection and to amplify my magic and my second sight. Angelica is for wind and is a powerful protection herb. It also aids visions. Pine needles are for fire, offering protection and for divination, and the root from the mallow plant is for water. It also enhances protection."

Hm. The herbs were not for him alone.

Constance selected and cut the herbs, and placed them in the bowl, taking care with the burn nettle leaves. "This is a spell my mother taught me when I was very young. It is one of the first spells I learned. My *grand-mére* taught her, and her mother taught her. It is a very old spell."

Constance paused her grinding of the herbs. "There was a time when there were many of us in our coven, when the rituals performed included a score of witches — men and women. That was long before I was born. When villagers revered the knowledge and the skills our coven had."

Constance took up her ceremonial knife and nicked her finger, holding her hand over the bowl so her blood dripped onto the ingredients. "Things have changed since then. Are changing still. Now people seek help from the church, from the monks." One, two, three drops. She set aside the knife and pinched her fingers to stem the bleeding.

"I harbor no ill will to the monks, nor the church." Her smile carried a tinge of sadness. "Sadly, the church does not feel the same way toward people like me. Miracles of healing come only from God, they say. All else is a heathen act, not born of the sanctity of heaven and is discouraged or punished if the witch is not repentant." She screwed up her nose. "The monks use the same herbs I do."

D'Artagnon had never been one for wagers, but he would bet a purse full of *livres* the monks did not use their blood as part of their preparations. Nor chanted spells. No, the church did not view people like Constance kindly. Especially not churchman like this

Eveque Faucher. It was why they were hiding here in the farmer's cottage. To keep Constance safe.

D'Artagnon huffed. He would do as his brother asked. Protect her from Faucher, though she insisted on attempting to heal him. He would do so, until his brother deemed it safe for her to return.

D'Artagnon eyed the little witch, the confident way she mixed the herbs, the little frown of concentration on her brow. He could only hope his brother did not tarry. One slip of his control, one too many glimpses of her smile, and D'Artagnon feared he would not be able to hold himself back.

Chapter Twenty-Four

Constance placed her hands over the bowl, closed her eyes, took a deep breath in, then released it on a long, steady sigh. She centered herself, a sense of calm washing over her, the words of the spell rising within her mind. Words of healing, release and renewal.

Constance focused her intent on the bowl of ingredients.

"Pain and sorrow, guilt and shame.
Lay at the feet of him to blame
Release from heavy mind and heart
Anger and vengeance doth both depart
Set free that which keeps him bound
So peace and healing can be found."

When she opened her eyes, D'Artagnon had not moved. Good. It was a beginning. She used her knife to cut a square of cloth from a fresh linen, bound the herbs in a bundle then reached up and shoved it in amongst the thatching above the door. He made no move to stop her.

Constance wiped the bowl clean and began preparing the other herbs — tearing apart the leaves and cutting the root and pine needles into small pieces. She paused. "It is not as though the church does not have good cause to distrust us, unfortunately. Not all of us use our skills, our power for good. Cordelia, the witch from your village, for one."

She resumed her chopping, then scraped up the pieces and dropped them into the bowl. She cut another slice in her finger, squeezed a few drops of blood over them, and stirred the contents of the bowl, coating them. "It is witches like her who deserve to be hunted down by the church."

An icy shiver ran up her spine, and she stumbled against the table as a vision hit her. One of her hands bound before her, begging, pleading. Of a man in black robes with a young, almost angelic face standing over her, a fervor in his eyes.

For a moment, Constance was there, trapped in the body of her future self. Her fear, her certainty she was going to die as real as the small cottage she stood in. She clutched at her chest and slumped onto the seat. The tickle of coarse hair beneath her palm snapped her from her vision, bringing her back to the present. Monsieur D'Artagnon had leaped over the table and pushed his muzzle into her hand.

Her breathing shallow, she ran her fingers through the wolf's ruff, seeking comfort. That he should offer it to her warmed her heart and eased some of her fear. Constance had no sense of how this would come to pass but, if her vision were to be believed, soon she would become the prisoner of a priest.

D'Artagnon stared at a pale-faced Constance, her eyes bright with unshed tears. What was happening? Was it a vision? When she had sucked in her breath and slumped to the seat, her eyes glazing over, he was on the table, nudging his head beneath her palm, comforting her without giving his actions a single thought. His entire body and soul, wolf and man, cared only that she was in pain. Something in her vision had caused this pain, and he could not resist his need to console her. He fought his urge to rend and tear apart that which would provoke the emotions rolling off her, clogging up the air in the little cottage. He could barely breathe with it.

She took a shaky breath and brushed away her tears. "More blood," she muttered, taking up her knife, slicing it across her palm this time.

The coppery scent flooded the cottage, and a growl rumbled in his chest. He did not like it when she cut herself so. She ignored him, squeezing her hand into a fist, letting the blood drip into the bowl. With her uninjured hand, she pulled her grimoire closer and frantically searched through the pages before settling on one.

The flowing script of their amulets mocked him. A ward of some kind. Until he unlocked the secret of the language, he could only presume.

Constance read through it several times, then grabbed the flint, striking it. She blew on the little sparks it created, coaxing a flame in the herbs. A swirl of pungent smoke curled in the air, and she gathered up the bowl and raced from the cottage. D'Artagnon leaped from the table and followed her, skidding to a halt in the doorway. Constance had set aside the bowl and was shucking her boots.

What is she doing?

She tore at the laces of her dress, wrenched it off and cast it aside. Her underdress followed. "For the spell to be more effective, to be the strongest it can be, I must have a connection with the earth." She wiggled her bare toes. "I must be at one with my surroundings. Nothing should stand between my body and the elements." With her back to him and a nervous shake of her hands, she slipped out of her chemise.

Merde. Constance was...*naked.* Again. Twice in one day was beyond his forbearance. For a moment, staring at her bare body—the gentle flare of her hips, her smooth skin, the dimples on either side of her spine, the soft curves of her cheeks—D'Artagnon forgot how to breathe.

With impatient fingers, she unpinned her braids, shaking out her hair so it flowed over her shoulders and down her back, glinting in the sun like a river of pale gold.

Beautiful.

He wanted to reach for her. Put his hands on her like he had last eve. Press his lips to her bare shoulder, run his nose along the curve of her throat. Hold her body flush to his and rub his scent all over so all would know she was—

He shook his head and focused on the grass beneath his paws.

"I need to set the ward. *Please* do not cross the circle until I have completed it."

She spoke with purpose, but the tremble in her voice betrayed her. It called to him, wrapped its fingers around his heart. The muscles in his shoulders bunched in his effort to stay where he was, to remain wolf. Her soft footfalls moved away. She paused, and he glanced up.

Facing due north, her back to him, she offered her bowl to the sky. She invoked the earth, whispering her incantation, before circling the cottage until she faced east. Here she called upon the wind. Words of protection, of warding. She continued her circle, disappearing out of sight, and he tracked her with his ears. She paused twice more — to the south and to the west. He did as she had asked, and did not move.

Constance completed her circle and stood staring out at the forest. "This is a strong ward, but, as with any ward, I will need to replenish it every day. The more layers it has, the stronger it will be."

Every day? The words settled in his mind, heavy and full of promise. And temptation. She would bare her body to his hungry eye. Every. Day. The desire to bring forth the change was intense, yet... His gut clenched at the thought of shifting. Of making the deliberate choice to return to human form. To stand once again as a man, vulnerable in his human skin.

D'Artagnon gritted his teeth. He could simply stay within the cottage. Or patrol the forest. There was no need for him to watch as long as he remained within or without the circle of her ward. Yet he knew, like bees drawn to the flowers of a meadow in springtime, he would not be able to resist.

Her shoulders sagged, and she turned to face him, so lost in her thoughts she had, perhaps, forgotten her nakedness. It took everything he had to lock his gaze on her face. To ignore the gentle curve of her breasts and the soft pink of her peaked nipples in the periphery of his vision.

"I had a vision. I think…maybe…" She stared down at the bowl clasped in her hands, dried blood smeared on her fingertips. "There is a priest. He may come for me. Soon. Perhaps." She scrunched up her face. "I…I am not sure."

D'Artagnon shook himself and focused on her words. *A priest? Eveque Faucher?* She had seen this. But… He cocked his head. Was her vision not clear? She had told Erin the way of her second sight could be vague, but…

She threw her head back and stared up at the autumn sky. "I saw myself bound, pleading. There was a clergyman there. I sensed…"

When she dropped her gaze to meet his, the pain in her eyes sliced through his heart sharper than the blade that had cleaved open his shoulder. The need to scoop her into his arms, to comfort her and promise to protect her so powerful he all but shifted right then and there. For a moment he hovered, the change but a breath away.

She broke their connection and stared out into the forest. "I do not have visions of myself often. In truth, there have only been two others. One which foretold of my mother's death and another…" An embarrassed flush stained her cheeks. She pursed her lips. "When it comes to ourselves, visions can be— Our own desires and fears can cloud them and…and as such, they are not always…not always accurate. I cannot rely on them."

Her eyes shimmered with her uncertainty. "I cannot know if what I saw will come to pass, but I *cannot* ignore it. I have strengthened the ward. If anyone should come here with ill intent in their hearts, I will know."

The scent of her fear lay thick on the air. "Can you...? Can I ask you to guard me?" She glanced nervously around at the forest. "While we are here, beyond the walls of your keep? If he comes...would you...would you protect me?"

A naked Constance trembled before him, pleading with him, so heart-wrenchingly vulnerable, he could not hold back the force of the change. It ripped through him, caring naught for his fears. His bones were contorting, and his fur receding before he could stop them. He did not want to stop them.

His paws shifted to hands and feet, his spine elongated and he was striding toward her, shaking off the last vestiges of his canine muzzle as he pulled her into his embrace, bare skin against bare skin. He gave in to temptation and ran his nose along the curve of her throat, breathing in her heady scent. His chest rumbled, and in his mind, his wolf purred.

Yes, Constance, I will protect you. No one will harm you. Not while I have breath.

She clung to him, leaning her head on his chest and tucking herself into his embrace, and he reveled in the warmth of her body and the softness of her skin. In the way she sought shelter in *his* arms and comfort from *his* strength. A lazy afternoon breeze whispered across his skin, a sensation he had not experienced in years, and he did something he had not done in a long time. He smiled.

"You...you shifted?"

Her words, mumbled against his chest, snapped him out of his stupor and he dropped his arms, stepping away from her.

A hesitant smile flickered across her lips. "Monsieur D'Artagnon, you shifted."

He swallowed, and he dipped his head so his hair fell across his face, hiding his damaged face and missing eye. He had shifted. They stood there, the both of them naked, and — he frowned — he found himself in no rush to shift back. Then his gaze dipped, unbidden, and a pretty pink flush wound its way up Constance's chest and neck.

"I should probably dress now," said Constance, breaking the spell and darting toward her clothes. Clutching them to her chest, she disappeared into the cottage. "Hopefully, Anne has packed something for you to wear," she called out from inside.

D'Artagnon listened to the rustle of fabric as Constance dressed. Right now, in the forest with Constance a bare few paces away, his previous panic at being human was little more than a low hum in the back of his mind.

"Oh, good. You are still human." Constance stood in the doorway, a pile of clothing in her hands. "Anne had confidence in you." She held garments out to him, her chin lifted and her gaze fixed on his face. "Breeches and a tunic."

He took them and jerked his head toward the pond.

"Yes, yes, of course you would want to bathe. I will…" She gestured toward the interior of the cottage. "I have things to do."

Constance disappeared inside the cottage once more and, on legs wobbly and unsure, D'Artagnon made his way down the trail to the pond. He had a need to cleanse himself. To wash away the years of living as a wolf, and to reconnect to the man he had once been. And though he tried to convince himself it had nothing to do with how good she had felt in his arms, or any desire for her to see him as a man, the smugness of his wolf within his mind confirmed the lie. Vladimir had spoken true. Constance was his mate. What he planned to do about it now he was human again, he really did not know.

Chapter Twenty-Five

Constance eyed the man sitting at the table. He had returned from the pond, hair wet and dripping and his lean, muscled body covered in tunic and breeches. Anne's confidence Monsieur D'Artagnon would shift was something to be grateful for, but the image of him naked in the bright sunlight would remain forever imprinted on her mind. As would the feel of him as he had crushed her in his embrace. The hardened planes of his torso, his muscled arms banded around her, the soft hair of his chest flush against her breasts. The line of his spine between his broad shoulders she followed to the taut globes of his cheeks as he had stumbled away from her toward the pond.

But what tugged at her heart and made her long for her childhood vision to be true more than anything was how he had comforted her when she had needed it most. Taken her up in his arms and surrounded her with his strength, telling her in a way words never could, he would protect her. Reassuring her he was there for her.

He had shifted. For her. When it pained him so much to do so. And he had remained so, as the afternoon sun had dipped below the horizon and darkness had crept in.

Now, with his beard and hair trimmed, he sat at the table, reading page after page of her grimoire. Aside from a quick jaunt to the pond to fetch water, he had not moved all afternoon. He turned another page, smoothing it down with his large hand. She licked her dry lips. Not so long ago, last eve, his hand had been —

Monsieur D'Artagnon glanced up, shadows shifting in his eye. As with every time he caught her staring, he let a lock of dark hair flop over his face, obscuring his scar.

She cleared her throat. "Perhaps, on the morrow, we should make the journey back to the d'Louncrais Keep."

She would feel safer at the d'Louncrais Keep, after what she had seen in her vision. And now he had shifted — and remained so — there was no need for them to stay out here in the forest. Despite her ward and Monsieur D'Artagnon's reassuring presence, she was still a little off kilter, and a lot unnerved. She calmed the tremor in her body.

Her greatest fear, one she had harbored through her childhood and into adult life, was that one day the villagers, or the local aumônier, would do more than move them on. Being forced from their cottages to wander from village to village, seeking a permanent home that would never eventuate until they finally settled in the forest, had been hard, but it was far preferable than the alternative.

He glowered at her, a rumble rising from deep within his chest.

Constance pursed her lips. There it was again. The sense there was more. Something she could not quite see that hovered in the corner of her eye. That he felt betrayed, angry, that he grieved was unquestionable. That his scars bothered him, obvious by the way he hid the one on his face with his hair.

Constance calmed her mind, pushing out all thought of herself, her fears and her hopes, and focused in on Monsieur D'Artagnon, trusting her ability, the power of her herbs and the spell she had woven to guide her, to give her the answers she was seeking.

Pain flowed from the black wolf, its suffocating presence filling the cottage, and it hit her with sudden conviction. Shame, and a dark, insidious thread of guilt. He had stayed away for so many winters because he was ashamed. Not for the way he looked — though it served as an uncomfortable reminder, a visible manifestation — but for how he had *failed*. His parents, his brother. It would be easy to assign his sense of failure to not prevailing against the traitor, the werewolf who had killed both of his parents, but Constance sensed something more, something deeper that continued to dance beyond her understanding.

As a wolf, she had sensed the damage in him. As a man, those emotions were bigger, carved into his soul as clear as his physical scars marked his body. Her heart broke for him, and she longed to reach out and comfort him.

She took a step toward him. He growled, and she retreated.

"Did you...want to talk about what happened to you? Tell me who did this to you?"

He grunted, coarse dark hair sprouting across the back of his hand and along his jaw.

"Or not," she rushed out, and his wolf retreated once more. "Well, then." She smoothed her hands down the front of her dress, resisting the temptation to reach for him again. "Perhaps you are right. A few more days is neither here nor there." She hoped. Seigneur Gaharet would not be expecting them to be back so soon. That Monsieur D'Artagnon had shifted on their first day here was something no one, least of all Constance, had anticipated. She reached for the flint on the shelf. "I will light the fire and prepare a meal."

Monsieur D'Artagnon loomed behind her, his movements so sudden, so fast, she gasped. His body flush against her back, he laid a large hand over hers, slipping the flint from her nerveless fingers. Her stomach fluttered, and the urge to sink back into the warmth of his body was almost too strong to resist. Then he was gone, snatching up kindling from the pile stacked against the wall and kneeling before the fire pit.

Constance turned away, hiding her breathlessness, and rooted through their supplies for some vegetables for a stew. The fire lit, he rose, dipped his chin at her and returned to the table, and to reading her grimoire.

Constance filled the large pot hanging over the fire with water and dropped pieces of butchered hare in. Her gaze slid over his shoulder to the sleeping nook and the single cot, barely big enough for two. Heat swirled in her stomach, sliding lower. Last eve he had… She had almost… She swallowed.

He looked up, his nostrils flaring and his eye boring into her.

"I... I..." *L'enfer.* Was she a stuttering fool? Best to speak what was on her mind. She heaved in a quick, shaky breath. "Will you sleep in the cot this eve?"

He glanced over his shoulder at the cot before turning that intense, singular gaze on her, dark shadows flickering in its depths. His eyebrow rose.

Did he think she was asking him into her bed? Was she? After what had happened yestreen, she would not deny him if he so chose.

He continued to stare at her. Her skin prickled. Moisture pooled between her thighs. She had not missed the weight of his stare as she called on the directions and the elements, the heat in his eye when she had stood before him, naked and vulnerable. Perhaps some of her herbal potion remained in his system still. Perhaps he feared he would succumb to its influence once more. Maybe it had little to do with her potion.

His steady gaze did not waver.

Or mayhap... A different kind of heat flushed her face, and she shut her eyes, mortified. "My apologies, Monsieur D'Artagnon. Of course you will sleep on the cot." She opened her eyes, but kept her gaze fixed on the table, on chopping the vegetables. "I will sleep on the floor."

Monsieur D'Artagnon growled, drawing her attention. He lifted his chin at her and jerked it at the cot.

"Oh no, Monsieur D'Artagnon. It would not be right for me to take the cot. I am but a poor —"

He snarled, repeating the gesture.

The fire in her core rekindled. Did he mean...? Was he asking her to join...?

He stood, turned his back and slipped his tunic over his head. He shucked his breeches next, and before Constance had a chance to take in the expanse of his naked back, buttocks and muscular thighs, he had shifted. The black wolf turned to face her, leaping up on the seat. He blinked. Blinked again and nodded, seeming satisfied with his solution.

A wave of conflicting emotions washed over her. Consternation he was once again wolf, with no guarantee he would return to his human form, and disappointment, thick and sharp.

Ever since she was little, the black wolf had enticed her. From the story in her grimoire of the first black wolf, to her vision and her childhood dreams. Those feelings, those hopes, had rested on an idea. Something vague and undefined. Monsieur D'Artagnon, in the flesh — man or wolf — was none of those things. He was as solid and real as the table beneath her hands, and the roof over her head. Yet here, with him a mere few paces from her, he had never been further away.

Chapter Twenty-Six

Gaharet stood on the ramparts overlooking the bailey, Lothair by his side. The morn had gone as well as he could have expected. Every peasant, every merchant, every chevalier within a day's journey had been there to bear witness to his and his men's public humiliation as Lothair had forced them to renew their vows like stripling lads, all legs and beardless chins. His men had chaffed at it, but it had been necessary. Though he doubted Lothair trusted him entirely, the spectacle in the hall had ensured they were no longer on opposing sides.

Beside Lothair had stood Renaud's replacement, Eveque Faucher. It was difficult to reconcile his reputation with the baby-faced youth, but there was a hunger in this new eveque. A thirst for power and a dark thread of obsession that wound through his scent, coating it like oily scum on an untended moat. Faucher either had not the experience to conceal it, or did not care to. A man who had no cause to hide his ambitions or his intentions was one to watch.

"This new eveque could pose more of a threat than Renaud," said Gaharet as Faucher, black robes billowing about his legs, made his way across the bailey to the chapel.

Careful to remain hidden amongst the bustle of servants, chevaliers and merchants, a little beggar boy trailed behind him. Edmond's habit of rescuing strays might well prove useful.

"Faucher has high connections," cautioned Lothair.

"And a reputation as a witch hunter."

"Do you think he knows?" Lothair turned to Gaharet. "That werewolves exist? Here? In Langeais?"

"Oh, I know so." Gaharet pointed at the beggar boy. "I believe we have our young spy to thank for that." Gaharet leaned his elbows on the stone ramparts. "Renaud gave Faucher a name. The name of the werewolf he was working with."

"The traitor?" Lothair snorted. "Typical of Renaud to double cross his accomplice. Godfrey? It did not escape my notice that he, once again, did not respond to my summons. I recall demanding *all* your men renew their vows."

Gaharet ignored the hint of steel in Lothair's voice. "If I knew where Godfrey was, I would have ensured he was here."

"Godfrey is missing? In hiding, fearing your wrath, or missing like Renaud?"

Gaharet watched his men make their way to the stables to collect their horses. Was it Godfrey? Is that why he was missing? Or had he fallen afoul of someone?

"I do not know. But he is not missing by Faucher's hand." The eveque did not have Renaud's accomplice in custody. Of that, Gaharet was sure. Nor had he killed him. "Werewolf musk is unmistakable. I caught no hint of it on Faucher, nor the certainty that came with one who believes himself victorious."

Lothair's eyebrows rose. "Your senses are that good? Interesting."

Gaharet did not deign to reply.

Lothair paced. "Faucher is not subtle. If it were Lance, he would have denounced him the moment he entered the hall this morn."

"Or," said Gaharet, "Faucher, seeing us all together, seeing the differences between us and Farren, recognized Lance is not the *only* werewolf in your county. It would take a brave and foolish man to proclaim six of your highest-ranking chevaliers as werewolves in such a public manner. He is young, he is greedy, but he does have a reputation for getting results. That does not come about by being foolish or rash."

His gaze slid to Lance, and to the jewel on the pommel of his sword. Unanswered questions hung over his friend and confidant.

"So, Lance then?"

"As yet, I cannot be certain," Gaharet admitted. "Renaud was cautious in giving Faucher the identity of his accomplice, refusing to speak it aloud. The boy has yet to get us that name."

If fortune favored them, Constance's presence and their time alone together would have an impact on D'Artagnon, and they would have their answer soon enough. If his brother proved too stubborn, perhaps

Kathryn would remember something, or Faucher would lead Edmond's spy straight to their betrayer.

Lance halted and turned, scanning the bailey. He raised his nose to the air. They were all on edge. It was only natural he would sense when he was being watched. He searched the bailey, then raised his gaze to meet Gaharet's. His body stiffened and his nostrils flared and for a long moment they stared at each other, then Lance tipped his chin at Gaharet, turned away and caught up with the others.

"Lance or Godfrey. It keeps coming back to those two." Lothair leaned against the ramparts, his arms folded across his chest. "I want this traitor, Gaharet. We cannot let Faucher get to him first."

"I want him as much as you do, Lothair. Perhaps more." Gaharet straightened, the ache in his chest as fresh as when he had first discovered the truth. "He murdered my parents. Cut them both down. For that alone, I would rip out his throat. But his crimes against our pack did not stop there. He attacked a child, Kathryn, and left her to die. It is by the grace of whatever God you believe in, she survived."

Lothair's eyes lit up. "But she *survived*. A *child* survived the turning. I am stronger than a child."

Gaharet grimaced. There it was. Confirmation this was not only about Lothair creating a supernatural army. The comte wanted to become a werewolf himself. "Children are resilient. Aimon was young, too, when I turned him. While you do not have the advanced years of Renaud, you have almost a score years on Aimon."

Gaharet was not going to tell Lothair they now had a means of tempering the pain of a turning. The last thing Gaharet—or the pack—needed was Lothair as a werewolf. The pack already had an alpha. It did not need another, and there was no doubt in Gaharet's mind Lothair would be anything less.

Lothair's gaze slid past Gaharet's shoulder, and his face flattened of all expression. A sickly miasma of pungent floral fragrance underscored by a dark note of deceit hit Gaharet's nose. He did not need to turn to know Lothair's wife, Marguerite, and her entourage of maids had appeared on the ramparts.

"You know what I want, Gaharet. And perhaps, at another time, we might discuss why I want it. *Need* it. For now, I have a *wife* to attend to." He clapped Gaharet on the shoulder. "Take care of your betrothed. If Kathryn and Aimon are anything to go by, she is devoted to you. Not every man is that lucky."

Chapter Twenty-Seven

Constance stacked the clean plates from supper on the shelf as D'Artagnon kneeled by the fire and stocked it with enough wood to burn through the night. Four more nights they had spent in the cottage. Four nights, and every eve after their meal, D'Artagnon would remove his clothes, giving her tantalizing glimpses of his body, and shift back into the black wolf. He would leap onto the cot and curl up on the end and Constance would climb beneath the covers, thoughts of the night he had shifted, of the feel of him pressed between her thighs swirling through her mind and stirring her hopes.

Each morning she would awake to find him outside sitting on a fallen log, once again human, watching over the cottage. She had not woken once in the night to a shifted and naked man, nor to his bare arm snaking over her to pull her into his embrace. Her potion had worn off. It no longer flowed through his veins, altering his behavior. Whatever had prompted him to shift before that had disappeared too, melting away faster than summer hail. The familiar heaviness in her chest was once again her constant companion. She should have listened to her mother.

Constance reached for two mugs. "Have you given any thought to returning to your brother's keep?"

Over the past four days, they had developed a routine. Him patrolling the forest, collecting water and wood for the fire, her collecting herbs and replenishing her ward. She would talk—about her life, about the forest, stories about the villagers she had treated, sometimes about her mother. He would read her grimoire. On occasion, he would slide it across the table toward her with a quirk of his eyebrow, and she would explain a process the grimoire detailed.

He never spoke, but he listened to every word she said.

"Your brother must be anxious for your return." He had to feel the urgency. Time was marching away from them. This pleasant repose could not last forever. The wolf who had struck him down and had done so much to endanger his pack would not remain idle for long. "This betrayer of your pack must be caught and held to account for his crimes. With your brother's mate with child—"

Hissed air exploded from between his clenched teeth. Monsieur D'Artagnon was healing. Her herbs and spells appeared to be working, but he had a long way to go.

She set the mugs on the table. "You do not want to tell him, do you?" She filled the mugs with mead. "Your brother. You do not want to tell him who the traitor is."

Monsieur D'Artagnon refused to meet her eyes, his shoulders stiff and taut with tension as he poked at the fire.

"Monsieur D'Artagnon, keeping this inside you is not helping anyone. Least of all you."

He snarled, a wicked canine punching through his gum.

Constance did not let that dissuade her. "Are you protecting him?"

He snatched up her grimoire, snapped it closed, and dropped it in front of her. Mead slopped onto the table.

Constance shifted the book away from the puddle of deep red. "No. There is no treatment, no spell, other than what I have already done that will aid you. I am sorry, Monsieur, but healing will only come if you face your fears and your pain. Talking about it may help you. If not to me, then let us return to the keep so you may talk with your brother."

Often healing was unpleasant, sometimes painful. A wound not thoroughly cleansed could putrefy. A broken bone would not heal right if first not set straight. Revealing his deepest thoughts, dealing with the sorrow and grief and the fears he held deep inside would not come easy. Made all that much more difficult because of his unwillingness to talk, but she had never given up on a person in need. She would not give up on him.

D'Artagnon reached over and flipped her grimoire open, turning pages until the remedies in Latin changed to the secret language of the wolves. He rapped his fingers on the book.

"You think I might find the answer in here?"

He shook his head and pointed at the lines of script.

Puzzled, she drew the book closer to her. He tapped the page, then his temple, then pointed to her lips.

"You want to know what it says? You want me to read it to you?"

A sharp jerk of his chin. A firm yes.

She recognized it for what it was. A distraction to stop her from pushing too hard and delving too deep. The curling script flowed across the page, hiding the secrets of the Langeais wolves. Of their origins and of their connection to Constance's coven, long forgotten. Things the pack *should* know, but did not. Perhaps, if she granted his wish and revealed the truth behind their existence, it might go some way to getting him to trust her with *his* truth.

"Monsieur D'Artagnon—"

He growled and made a slashing motion with his hand.

She stepped back, confused. "I..."

His brows dipped into a frown, as much as his scar would allow. "Not Monsieur. Only D'Artagnon." He pointed at her. "To you." His voice was husky from lack of use as he forced out the words.

Constance blinked, her mouth dropping open. "Oh." She ducked her head, hiding her surprise, her delight. The first words he had spoken in the Fates knew how many years and they were to tell her she need only use his name. As if he were not a nobleman, and she not a peasant. As though, over the last few days, she might have come to mean more to him than a healer. Perhaps a friend, or —

She cut the thought off. "Thank you, Mon—" She raised her chin. "Thank you, D'Artagnon. You honor me. Please." She gestured to the seat as she turned the grimoire up the right way. "Would you like me to read to you the story of how the first Black Wolf, your ancestor, came to be?"

Another nod. D'Artagnon, his hair flopped over his face, sat and curled his hands around his mug of mead and waited.

Constance slid into a seat and turned the pages until she found what she was looking for. "I loved this story as a little girl. It is possible I could recite it by heart."

D'Artagnon leaned forward, an eagerness, a hunger in his eyes.

She smoothed out the page. "There lived in the small village of Louncrais, a stable master by the name of Alexandre." Constance skimmed her fingers beneath the lines of script, translating as she read. "Alexandre was a kindly man, a good neighbor, loved by all in his village, a hard worker and an exceptional trainer of horses. It was said he could take the most difficult and wildest of horses and tame them to be ridden, to be obedient and gentle."

Constance paused. To this day, the d'Louncrais were renowned horse trainers. They had to be. A chevalier without a horse was nothing more than a foot soldier. And a horse not trained by the d'Louncrais would be of no use to a werewolf.

D'Artagnon grunted, taking a sip of his mead.

"Over the years, Alexandre's reputation with horses spread across the land, and he gained much recognition. He was but a humble man, and though he took great pride in his work, his newfound acclaim did not change him. Only the horses mattered."

As when she was a child reading this story, Constance pictured the crude little village with its simple mud huts, the stables, the wild horses, and the man they would come to call the Black Wolf.

"He was a handsome man, with dark hair, dark eyes and a strong nose, and he set many a young woman's heart aflutter. None caught his eye, so dedicated was he to his horses and his work. Until one day, a Vicomte came to see him about a horse. With the Vicomte came Genevieve, a daughter of uncommon beauty and willful nature. So wild and stubborn was she, refusing to behave as a woman of her station should, the Vicomte despaired of finding her a suitable husband."

It was not lost on Constance that the mates of Seigneurs Gaharet and Ulrik and Monsieur Aimon shared similar traits to Genevieve. Was it naïve of her to presume she would be a suitable match for any Langeais wolf, and a Black Wolf, no less? A direct descendant of the first Black Wolf?

"Intrigued by Genevieve, Alexandre admired the untamed quality of her character. Surprised Alexandre enjoyed her company, Genevieve challenged him with wilder, more willful behavior. It only made him want her more, and the two soon fell in love."

It was easy to see now how, as a child, Constance had been so enraptured with this story. How it could have fueled her fantasies. A woman who did not fit with society's expectations, a woman shunned by men and despairing of finding a match that was accepting of who she was, was something young Constance had felt in the depths of her soul. As though the story could be her own. But Constance was neither wild nor willful. Nor did she have one ounce of noble blood. That had not stopped her from dreaming of being plucked from her humble existence by a dashing black wolf. Neither did it dim the longing now.

"The Vicomte was upset his daughter wished to marry a commoner, but such was his desperation to see her married, he prevailed upon the King to grant Alexandre a title so Genevieve could marry a man equal to her station. Because of Alexandre's reputation, the King agreed. On one condition. Alexandre must commit to training all the King's horses. Alexandre accepted, and a wedding was planned."

Constance turned the page, flicking a glance in D'Artagnon's direction. His elbows on the table, his chin resting on his hands, he stared into his mug of mead. If learning his family descended not from nobility but from a hardworking stable master surprised him, he did not show it.

"Not everybody in the village rejoiced at the good fortune of Alexandre. There was a woman, a fair beauty despite..."

The words clogged in Constance's throat, and she dragged a trembling finger back across the page. There was no mistaking the translation. How had she missed it? How many times had she read this, recounting the origins of the Langeais wolves, and yet...never connected...?

Long before she had learned the secret language, her mother would read her this story. Over and over again, with the book on her lap, Constance snuggled into her side as the fire crackled and the wind whispered through the gaps in their straw roof. Even as she read it now, her mother's sing-song voice as she recounted the tale echoed in her mind. Could her mother have omitted these few words deliberately? Fearing Constance might identify with this woman? Think herself doomed?

That did not explain how she herself had not noticed this. Had she recited it more from memory than translated it word for word? Saw only what she wanted to see?

D'Artagnon shifted in his seat. "Constance?"

"I... My apologies." Constance cleared her throat, though it did little to ease the tightness lodged there. "There was a woman, a fair beauty despite" — she glanced up, gauging his reaction — "having eyes of two different colors, and she had set her heart on Alexandre."

An uncanny stillness settled over D'Artagnon, and those dark shadows danced in his eye. His wolf hovered close. The inked characters swirled on the page, and Constance blinked them straight. What other secrets would this story reveal?

She dragged in a fortifying breath. "The villagers had warned Alexandre about this woman. That despite her knowledge of herbs, she used her skills more oft to harm than heal. An evil witch. All those who crossed her had befallen serious misfortune, but Alexandre scoffed at their superstitions and would hear naught said against — "

Always before, there had been a smudge of symbols. Through age, or a deliberate scrubbing out of the name, Constance had never been certain. Names held power. But a spot of mead had splashed on the edge of the page. With careful fingers she blotted at it, the mead stinging one of the small cuts from her ward preparation. With each press, the symbols untangled and became clearer, revealing the word they concealed.

Constance gasped and stared at the name on the page.

D'Artagnon leaned forward and placed his hand over hers, startling her. His head cocked, he gave her hand a gentle squeeze, brushing his thumb over her knuckles.

"I…" Constance leaned away from her grimoire, but she did not pull her hand free from D'Artagnon's warm grasp. What did this mean? This could not possibly be a coincidence.

D'Artagnon's squeeze of her hand, more insistent this time.

Constance reread the name. There in ink, bold and unmistakable.

Constance placed her hand on her brow. "I do not know how this happened. I have never been able to read this word before." She stared at her cut finger. "It must have something to do with my blood, because the name is now clear, and… The woman responsible for creating the first werewolf, your ancestor, was a woman by the name of…" She met his gaze. "Cordoylla."

Chapter Twenty-Eight

Cordoylla. Were he in wolf form, his hackles would have risen. Cordelia. Cordoylla. Too similar to be a coincidence. Three women across time. Two with the same defining characteristic of two different colored eyes. And perhaps the third, too, though his ancestor had made no mention of it. All three connected to the d'Louncrais — and not in a good way.

His gaze dropped to Constance's hand, still in his. He had not questioned his instinct to reach for it. Nor his need to keep hold of it, the rightness of it — her small hand in his much larger one. She made no effort to pull away. Nay, she held tighter, as though she feared *he* would pull away. He gave her another gentle squeeze, urging her to continue with the story.

With a nod and purse of her lips, she turned her attention back to the curling script and the secrets it held.

"The evil witch attempted to seduce Alexandre away from his beloved. In a fury at Alexandre's rejection, she swore vengeance. The villagers were right about her. She had an uncommon power, and she cursed Alexandre."

Could a name in itself carry evil? This Cordoylla was no less malicious than the Cordelia who had terrified Old Tumas and killed farmer Brun.

"That night, a terrible pain struck Alexandre. His body burned with fever and shivered with chills. For three days he suffered, before falling into a deep sleep that lasted for a week."

The turning. D'Artagnon had not experienced it, but he had heard the tales.

"When he awoke, he was no longer a man but a large, black wolf."

The skin on the back of his neck prickled. This was how it had all started. With a scorned woman. A witch. And yet, D'Artagnon could dredge up little resentment. Never had he seen being a werewolf as a curse. More a blessing. It made them stronger and gave them abilities humans did not have. It had kept him alive.

"Keep reading," he said, his voice rustier than old iron. He sensed there was more of the story to be told.

Constance nodded and dropped her gaze to her grimoire. "But the evil witch had not counted on Alexandre's ability with animals, nor his love for Genevieve. He soon mastered the wolf, taking control of his mind, if not his form. Genevieve remained by Alexandre's side as they searched for a cure."

D'Artagnon could guess what came next, but he did not stop Constance.

"There were whispers of those who had a power to match the evil witch, who used their powers for good.

They found such a one in the small settlement of Langeais by the river Loire."

Constance's ancestors.

"The good witch agreed to help them but warned them she had not the power to undo the curse of another. No one did. But she could alter it, allowing Alexandre to be both man and wolf, though she cautioned him of its limitations."

D'Artagnon cocked an eyebrow over his good eye.

"It would be impossible to repress the beast forever and live only as a man, for this would surely drive him mad. As it would be impossible for him to remain a wolf, least he lose his humanity. He must spend time as a man and time as a wolf."

Constance's breath hitched, and she glanced up at him. Time as a man, *and* time as a wolf. For nearly a decade he had remained as a wolf, not once shifting to human. Had he been standing on the precipice of losing himself?

Constance squeezed *his* hand. Expecting pity, he saw nothing but kindness in her eyes.

She dropped her gaze to the text and pressed on. "Alexandre and Genevieve would rather be together half the time than not at all, and the witch used her power to alter the curse."

Constance paused, halting her finger beneath the last character she had read. It was but halfway down the page. There was more.

"But a curse is never a simple thing. The true horror of what the evil witch had done soon became clear. As a werewolf, Alexandre's body could heal itself far beyond that of a man. He was resistant to disease and he would live longer than his peers and his beloved Genevieve. He would live to watch her age and die."

A tightness squeezed in his chest. Living without his mate had all but killed his father, that he suspected someone had murdered her, the only thing that had kept him from taking his own life.

"They pleaded with the good witch to do something. Unwilling to disturb the flow of nature, she gave them one option. She would devise a spell to allow Alexandre's bite to turn his beloved into a werewolf. Mindful of the pain of his turning, Alexandre begged her to ease the transition. Fearful of unleashing werewolves on the world in ever greater numbers, she would not relent."

D'Artagnon had heard the tales. Of those succumbing to the pain, their hearts giving out. Others thrust to the brink of madness by it. It was no small thing to undergo a turning, and something rarely sanctioned. He had never experienced one.

Constance looked up from her grimoire. "My ancestors did develop a potion to ease the turning, but it was many, many years later. At the same time, and for the same reason, we created the amulets. But that is a story for another day." Constance turned the page. "Such was his love for Genevieve, Alexandre refused to have her suffer. He fled, disappearing into the forest." Constance sighed. "I always found that part of the story so sad."

"It did not end there."

Constance's face brightened with a smile. "No, it did not. That you are sitting here now is proof of that. Genevieve was not about to let her beloved roam the forest alone. For him, she was willing to suffer the turning, and nothing would dissuade her."

"With the good witch's potion, her courage, and hired hunters, she tracked Alexandre through the forest, and cast the witch's spell. Though she pleaded with him to bite her, Alexandre refused. Counting on a werewolf's ability to heal, she snatched up a hunter's knife and plunged it into her heart. If Alexandre would not bite her to save her life, she would rather die than live without him."

Such courage. Such love that she would risk death to be with her beloved. "She was an exceptional woman."

Constance's lips pressed into a thin line, the corners turning down. "Yes, she was. Those who are the mates of the Langeais wolves all appear to have that in common." She closed her grimoire, retracted her hand from within his grasp, and got to her feet.

"You have not finished the tale." D'Artagnon did not know what he had said, but something had changed.

Constance pasted a smile on her face that belied the despondency in her eyes. "Alexandre bit Genevieve and she became a werewolf like her beloved." She shrugged. "And that is the story of the Black Wolf and how Alexandre became the first *Lous Garous*, the first werewolf."

Chapter Twenty-Nine

Constance busied herself prepping the herbs for her ward, tearing at the leaves of the angelica plant. It had been a shock to discover the name Cordoylla. And to learn the woman responsible for the Langeais wolves had the same curse — two different colored eyes — as she *and* Cordelia, the witch the villagers had cast from the d'Louncrais village. But the greater impact had come from D'Artagnon. He thought Genevieve exceptional. She had been. There was no denying it. She had braved death to be with the man she loved.

She focused on her hands, aware of D'Artagnon's regard and conscious of the sting of tears that threatened. Erin had forsaken her life in the future for Gaharet. Chosen not to pursue finding a way back to her century. As had Rebekah. Kathryn had lived a life in hiding for years. Now she was learning how to wield a sword. Each one of them was exceptional in their own way. She was a peasant, an outcast, no one special, and here she was, over the last few days, imagining...

A chair scraped along the floor, then he was behind her, placing gentle hands on her shoulders. "Constance?"

The deep growl as he spoke her name, sent shivers down her spine. She wiped away a stray tear with the heel of her hand. "I am sorry, D'Artagnon, I... It was a foolish notion, something from my childhood."

"What notion?"

Mother help her, the man had spoken more words tonight than in the past five days, nay the past nine years, and it would be her undoing.

"The other vision you spoke of?" His warm breath whispered across her temple.

She rolled her lips together and tracked the trail of smoke as it swirled out of the roof hole, caught between her sorrow and her shame. Of course he remembered. Made the connection. He may have been silent, but his eyes, his hearing, and his mind were sharp. He had listened to every word, followed every gesture and had watched over her with a diligence bordering on obsession. He missed nothing.

D'Artagnon rubbed his hands down her arms and back up again. Perhaps he meant to comfort her, but goosebumps prickled across her skin and her stomach did a little flip, which served only to increase the depth of her misery.

"Tell me."

Constance hung her head. "I..."

With gentle insistence, he turned her to face him. He hooked a finger beneath her chin and tilted her head up to meet his gaze. "Tell me."

Soft words, a mere whisper of sound, but they tore at her resistance. "The day the villagers forced my mother and I to leave our village for the cottage in the forest, I had a vision about my future. At least, I believed I had."

She turned her head away and his hand dropped from her chin to her shoulder. Constance sucked in a deep breath, aware of the closeness of their bodies and the subtle rise and fall of his chest.

"I was untrained in the ways of my second sight. My mother did not have it, so she could not teach me. But she knew enough to caution me about visions I had of myself. To be wary of influencing them with my own desires. That they may not reveal the future at all, but rather my hopes and fears."

Silence stretched between them. She glanced up. With the patience of a wolf hunting prey, he waited for her to continue, to bare her soul to him.

Constance's lip trembled. "What I saw that day… I… There was a cottage in a clearing, and a woman. A woman with blonde hair. She was there with a black wolf, her mate, and a little girl. I believed…" Her breath hitched. "I knew the Black Wolf would come to me in the forest. And he did. Your brother *did* come. I believed, I hoped, the Black Wolf would come for *me*, but I was wrong. So wrong. The woman in my vision was Erin, and the little girl, the child now growing in her womb."

His blue gaze bored into her, and it was all she could do to continue.

"I had resigned myself to that, to the truth of my mother's words, but then your brother called me to the d'Louncrais keep, and there *you* were…"

Constance closed her eyes, unable to look at him, to stare into the depths of his eye at the derision and rejection she would find there. "That night, when you shifted and…and I realized I had seen your face before…that you *had* shifted before, while I was sleeping, while *you* were sleeping…" She shook her head. "It may have only been the potion I had prepared, but it gave me hope there was a man who would see past what I am, ignore my eyes, and see me as a woman. That mayhap what I'd seen as a child *was* a vision and not a little girl's fantasy. That it *was* me in that clearing, with the black wolf and the little girl."

His hands dropped from her shoulders, and she hung her head, waiting for him to back away. She had bared her soul and her foolish hopes. Constance braced herself, waiting for the inevitable — to be spurned as Tristan had spurned her all those years ago. But while Tristan's betrayal had burned, her feelings for D'Artagnon ran deeper.

It would not be so easy to put him behind her. Not after their days here at the cottage, where she had glimpsed beyond the black wolf, beyond his pain and his scars, to the man beneath. The man who comforted her in her distress. Who patrolled the forest every day, protecting her. Fetched water and collected wood for the fire. Sat in silent company while they ate meals together. She wanted, with all her heart, for one precious moment, to be seen as desirable by *this* man.

Large, warm hands cupped her face, and she gasped. The soft brush of his lips on hers stole her breath away. Then deeper, firmer, taking her mouth with his. Hope, and a desire so fierce, ripped through her body. He pulled her into his arms, engulfed her in his embrace and all the promise of her childhood vision came alive, more potent reality and less an impossible dream.

D'Artagnon reveled in the feel of his little healer in his arms. Too long had he resisted this. Too long had he avoided the cottage as naked she had replenished her protection ward. Shifted to wolf and slept at the foot of the cot, watching over her as she had slept, denying his body and his soul that which he needed. *Her*. His brother had been right. Had seen the truth of it during those few days at the keep. D'Artagnon *needed* Constance. Like his wolf needed the forest. Perhaps more.

He had fought against it. What did he have to offer her? With his enemy alive and yet to pay for his crimes, D'Artagnon's craving for vengeance still flowed through his veins like molten steel. He could not be the mate she desired. The mate she *deserved*. He could not offer her much, but he could give her this. Give himself this, and maybe, when the trials of his pack were over...

He coaxed her mouth open and slid his tongue in, tasting her. Wanting to be a part of her in every way possible. Craving her sweetness, her gentleness to smooth over the rough edges of the darkness inside him. Perhaps *this* was Constance's true power, not her second sight. Her empathy and her quiet persistence.

She was the most resilient woman he had ever met. Against all the hardships she had faced in her life, she was still willing to give of herself to aid others. And him. After all those villages she had fled, forced out by superstitious and ungrateful people, having lived half her life alone in that forlorn, rickety little hut, seeing his brother with his mate and believing she had misinterpreted her vision, she was still capable of hope. The woman was... He sucked her scent deep into his lungs, into his soul.... Extraordinary.

Constance moaned into his mouth, her small, calloused hands clutching at his tunic.

Merde.

That little sound, that little puff of breath, shot straight to his cock. He needed her naked. *Now.* But he cautioned himself to be gentle, to not frighten her. To take his time and be as patient as she had been with him. To worship her and treat her like the goddess she was.

Her eyes flew open as he dropped his arms and stepped away from her, the resignation in them all but breaking his heart. D'Artagnon ripped his tunic over his head and dropped it to the floor, satisfied when the flicker of surprise shifted to heat as her gaze fell on his naked chest. He kicked off his boots and peeled down his breeches. Tossing them aside, he stood before her and let all his desire, his *need* for her, show.

She swallowed and reached for the stays of her dress. He closed the distance between them, his hand covering hers, stilling her fingers.

"I do not understand. I thought…"

D'Artagnon tilted her head, forcing her to look at him. Beautiful blue and green eyes searched his face. That she had seen the evidence of his arousal and had any doubt at all he wanted her saddened him.

He dropped a gentle kiss on her forehead and another on her nose. She gasped when he sank to his knees before her and unlaced first one boot, then the other. Taking her hand in his, he placed it on his shoulder and lifted her leg. She leaned on him as he slipped her boot from her foot. Unlike her calloused palms, the skin of her foot was smooth and pale, and he dipped his head, pressing his lips to her delicate arch. Her toes curled.

He met her gaze and dropped another kiss on the top of her foot, one at her ankle and, sliding the hem of her dress higher, one on her shin. Her body trembled and her eyes glazed over. D'Artagnon set her foot down and lifted the other, repeating his actions, never once releasing her heated gaze. He would show her, prove to her that which she doubted — that he desired her. With everything he had.

D'Artagnon rose. With gentle hands, he wrapped her arms around his neck, and she curled her fingers in his hair as he worked at the laces of her dress. First one side, then the other, his fingers as impatient as the rest of his body. He ran his hands down over the gentle flare of her hips and, bunching the fabric of her dress in his fists, he slowly dragged it up over her head. He cast it aside. She stared up at him with hooded eyes and parted lips.

L'enfer, she was everything he had dreamed of as a boy. Everything he could have asked for. And she had been right there, in the forest outside Langeais all this time. Had his father not been murdered, the connection between Constance's coven and the Langeais wolves would have remained intact. Had one of their own not attacked him, their bond would have been stronger. The younger D'Artagnon, the one who had yet to know betrayal and exile, would have claimed her as his mate. Without hesitation.

He dropped his head to the crook of her neck and ran his nose along the column of her throat, breathing in her scent as though he could hold it in his lungs forever. With an arch of her neck, she gave him greater access, and his canines punched through his gums. His wolf wanted her. To bite, claim, and make her one of them. Every instinct he had screamed at him to do it. To make her his.

D'Artagnon forced his canines to retract, his gums throbbing and his chest heaving with the effort. Regret lodged in his throat. As much as he wanted to, he could not offer her that. Not yet. Maybe not ever.

Instead, he dropped soft, open-mouthed kisses on the fast-beating thread of her pulse, his tongue flicking out to taste her. She shivered, and he delighted in her response. He would have her writhing beneath him soon. Devote this whole night to her as though they had no cares in this world.

He slipped her underdress over her head and let it fall to the floor. Only her chemise remained. So many nights he had tormented himself with the shadow of her form beneath the thin material. No more. He eased it off her, and it joined the rest of their garments.

With fingers that shook, he unpinned her braids and removed the ties. The rise and fall of her chest, the heady fragrance of her filling his nostrils, tested his control, and his willingness to be patient. He fought against the urge to swoop her up in his arms, to let loose the beast inside and plunder the delights of her body. Instead, he ran his fingers through the lengths of spun gold, teasing them out so they hung over her shoulders and across her breasts. Delicate pink nipples peeked out between the strands, taunting him. He would have them in his hands, in his mouth, many times before the night was through.

A growl rumbled deep in his chest. She was the most beautiful woman he had ever seen. If he had to suffer all his years in exile, the bite of the blade in his shoulder and the slash of steel across his face again in order to be here with her now, he would not hesitate. He would do it all again. For her.

The memories of his betrayal, the agony of his injuries, and his need for vengeance slipped away. Here in the cottage, in this moment, with the promise of tonight hanging thick in the air between them, nothing could touch them. Not their past, nor their future. There was only now.

Chapter Thirty

Constance trembled, teetering on the precipice of all her hopes and dreams, all her fantasies, coming to life. Not a night had gone past since they had arrived at the cottage had Constance not fallen asleep with images of her and D'Artagnon, naked and entwined on the humble cot, weaving through her dreams. Standing before him, both of them naked, a riot of emotions swirled through her as turbulent as the heat and the sensations storming through her body.

He was every bit the warrior, chiseled and shaped by the life he had lived, as a man and as a wolf. Her fingers itched to curl in the faint dusting of dark hair on his chest and trail over the taut muscles of his stomach. To trace the scar that curved around his ribcage. Absorb and wash away the pain of it and quiet any lingering memories. Her gaze dipped lower, and she sucked in a breath. There was no hiding the evidence of his need.

Still, the voice of reason threatened to sour this moment, whispering *he is a man, and I am but the first woman he has encountered after so long as a wolf.* But when he reached for her, when he picked her up, carried her to the cot and sat her upon it as though she were something precious, something fragile, all logic fled.

D'Artagnon dropped to his knees, parting her thighs and pressing between them. The heat of his body so close to hers, his large hands on her thighs, his thumbs stroking her sensitized skin, banished all thought, centering all her focus on him.

Constance gave into temptation and raised her hands to his chest, savoring his jagged breathing and the thudding of his heart beneath her palm. Up his chest, over his shoulders she traversed, cupping his bearded chin in hands drawn higher by some inexplicable force. With gentle fingers, she brushed aside the lock of dark hair to reveal the scar hidden beneath.

D'Artagnon grasped her hands and tugged them away from his face, kissing first one palm, then the other, then looping her arms around his neck. He silenced any protest with his mouth, before pressing soft, moist kisses along her jaw, down the column of her throat and across her collarbone. Her breasts heavy, her sex clenching, Constance let her head fall back, his scar forgotten.

Strong arms encircled her, supporting her as he arched her over the cot and dipped his mouth lower. The scrape of his beard, the soft press of his lips, the hot, wet lick of his tongue had Constance gasping for breath. And when he took her nipple in his mouth, grazed it with his teeth and laved it with his tongue, in one fell swoop he wiped away all the disappointments she had borne.

Constance sank her fingers into his long black hair and held on tight. Desperate for more, she squirmed against him. If D'Artagnon noted her sense of urgency, the clenching of her thighs about his hips, or the scoring of her nails against his scalp, he gave no sign, continuing his patient onslaught of first one breast then the other with a devotion both divine and tortuous.

He laid her back on the cot, and dipped his hand between her thighs, a gentle, light touch, teasing her little nub and sliding through her slick folds. Constance thrust her hips at him, wanting more. *Needing* more. She moaned, and his deep, throaty chuckle, his hot breath across her damp nipple, set her core clenching on air. Then his finger was at her entrance, and her whole body quivered, hanging on a knife's edge.

He slid inside her, pushing deep. She gasped, and he took her mouth in his with a slow, languorous kiss as he slid his finger out, then pressed back in. And again. This time with two fingers, stretching her and creating a delicious friction that sizzled up her spine. He set up a rhythm, purposeful and determined, not swayed by her gasps, her entreaties for more, nor the impatient thrusts of her hips.

"D'Artagnon."

The word slipped out on a moan, and a growl rumbled deep in his chest, vibrating through her body and engulfing her.

"Come for me, Constance," he murmured against her mouth. Then he hooked his fingers inside her and pressed his thumb on her little nub and she crested the wave of her pleasure, arching her back and shuddering around his hand.

With his breathing jagged and harsh in the quietness of the cottage, and his cock as hard as stone, D'Artagnon held his savage thirst for the woman beneath him in check by the barest of threads. She lay on the down-filled mattress, her head thrown back, her eyes closed and her pussy still fluttering. The sight of his hand between her thighs, his fingers disappearing inside her… *Merde.* His cock throbbed, leaking pre-cum from the tip. He needed inside her. Now. If he did not, he might spill his seed like an inexperienced lad. All over her delectable breasts.

His wolf pushed forward in his mind, primitive, and guided only by instinct. *Mark. Claim. Rub his scent all over her.* D'Artagnon clenched his free hand into a fist. He could make no promises beyond this moment. He slid his fingers free of her to a delightful little mewl of protest. But he would not deny himself, or her, what their bodies were crying out for.

He nudged her thighs further apart with his knee and settled between them, taking his weight on his elbows, a low groan rumbling up from deep within him as he slid his length through her slippery folds.

With his cock primed and coated in her juices, he prodded her entrance. "Open your eyes, Constance."

One blue eye and one green locked on his, and with infinite slowness, his breath held, he pushed inside her, inch by incredible inch.

"Constance." He let her name out on an explosive breath. "*Merde.*"

The exquisite sensation of being seated to the hilt, of her pussy around his cock, the rightness of it, took his breath away and made his heart pound. Chest to breasts, his arms beside her face, his fingers curling in her hair, their panted breaths mingling and their gazes locked, he began to move. Unhurried and measured, one long thrust then withdraw. Then another. And another. Teasing her, taunting himself, testing every bit of his control. Then faster, rocking into her with a desperation he could not hide nor rein in.

Constance threw her legs around his hips, her heels pressing into his cheeks, and urged him on. Those beautiful eyes of hers remained open, fixed on his, as they stared deep into his soul, seeing everything, taking *all* of him. The two of them connected in every way possible. The loneliness, the boundless emptiness, slipped away with every thrust of his cock and every clench of her pussy. She did not shrink from him, nor turn away. She embraced him, and the intensity of it shook him to his core, broke him down and rebuilt him.

Pleasure ripped up his spine, and he could hold back no longer. "Constance."

Her mouth dropped open, her channel spasmed around him, and he let go, roaring his release, not once relinquishing her gaze, taking her with him over the edge into ecstasy. As he spilled his seed inside her, her childhood vision—Constance with a black wolf and a little girl—flashed across his mind. It burrowed deep, encircling his heart like a tight fist, and for the first time since his near death on the battlefield, D'Artagnon hungered for something other than vengeance.

Chapter Thirty-One

Remi slipped into the cool silence of the chapel, following on the heels of Eveque Faucher. Not too close, mind, for he did not want to be caught. The big chevalier with the twin brother paid well, but not so well he would risk a quick, short drop at the end of a rope. Comte Lothair liked his public executions, and one word from the eveque and Remi's days of running the streets would be over.

He blinked, his eyes adjusting to the dim light of the nave. Empty. Careful not to make a sound, he crept past the pews, sweeping a practiced eye over them should luck favor him with a left behind coat, a fancy trinket, or a coin slipped from a purse. He had once found a bejeweled broach belonging to a baron. Too fancy to sell, he had returned it to its owner, pretending innocence, as though doing his civic duty. In front of the aumônier, of course. He had accepted his tidy reward with much bowing and scraping. Today, he found nothing.

He checked the nave again, peering into the pockets of shadows created by the flickering oil lamps in case he had missed someone, head bowed in prayer. Or worse, the eveque sneaking up behind him. Satisfied it was empty, he skirted the altar, resisting the temptation to snatch one of the gold candle holders, and headed for the sacristy.

Remi pressed himself against the wall and listened. The soft murmur of voices floated up, too far away to be in the next room. He edged the door open, cringing at the creak of hinges. The voices continued, louder now, but still indecipherable. He needed to get closer. Remi had never lived so well since the big chevalier had caught him trying to slit his purse, then put him to work as a spy. If the chevalier wanted information, then information he would get.

He slipped inside the sacristy. Robes belonging to the aumônier and the eveque hung on hooks, two chests stood along the wall, a table with a pitcher and bowl and fresh linens, but otherwise the room was empty. Through the open doorway at the back of the room, a conversation echoed unabated. Beyond it a lit corridor, also empty.

He had ventured this far into the church once before, when spying on Archeveque Renaud. Perhaps this time he would get a name. The one Renaud had passed onto this new eveque, the witch hunter. The name of a man claiming to be a werewolf.

Remi rolled his eyes. Werewolves? Witch hunters? Were the nobles so bored with their rich and fancy lives they chased mythical beasts to entertain themselves? If they had to scrounge for every meal, or for a warm place to sleep like he did, they would be too busy for such nonsense. Then they might realize there were enough real monsters in the world without searching for imaginary ones.

He shrugged. The big chevalier wanted that name, and he would pay double for it. Remi was going to get him what he wanted. Then he could get himself a thicker coat for the coming winter. Maybe a blanket, too. That was all he cared about. The important stuff.

He eyed the hanging robes of the priests. No. Too conspicuous. Too many people would recognize them for what they were. With some regret, he left the robes untouched and made his way toward the voices, to a room at the end of the corridor.

Two voices. Aumônier Touissant and Eveque Faucher. No Archeveque Renaud. Odd that no one had seen Renaud for a while now. Several days ago, Eveque Faucher had taken Renaud's place beside Comte Lothair when d'Louncrais and his men, the big chevalier and his twin included, had renewed their vows. Remi had asked around. Now no one seemed to know where Renaud had gone. At least, no one willing to talk about it.

Remi did not believe the rumors whispered about the hall, that Renaud was off living a life of luxury, recalled by Rome. No. He suspected the archeveque had met a grisly end. The question was — by whose hand? Comte Lothair? This new eveque with his pretty face, soft hands and zealous, fiery sermons about the devil and the evil that walked amongst them? Or had one of the big chevaliers who paid Remi to watch the clergyman taken care of him? He could well believe it of them. Especially Aubert, the growly one.

Remi shrugged. The nobles could butcher each other until the streets ran with blood and still he would not care. He had more important things to consider. Like where he would sleep this eve. And, if he gave the twins what they wanted, could he demand enough coin for his new coat, a blanket *and* a good meal? Or maybe two?

Remi pressed himself flat to the wall outside the room and listened.

"I promise you, Aumônier Touissant, I will personally look into the disappearance of Archeveque Renaud. It grieves me as much as you that something may have befallen him."

Remi muffled a snort. This Faucher was as big a liar as Renaud.

"I am currently looking into the possibility d'Louncrais and his men may have been involved."

"Seigneur d'Louncrais?" asked the aumônier. "You don't think—"

A chair creaked, and Remi could imagine the saintly aumônier's discomfort. So humble and willing to see the good in everyone.

"Why, he is the commander of Comte Lothair's army, his closest adviser. I could not imagine he would—"

"And yet he vanished for a time only to return and re-avow his allegiance to the comte," said the eveque. "Him, and all his men forced to kneel before their comte again, as though they were little more than squires."

That must have chaffed. The twins had not looked happy. None of d'Louncrais' men had.

"Well, yes," agreed the aumônier, "but does that not signify their loyalty to the comte?"

"Mmm, perhaps," said Faucher. "What do you know of d'Louncrais and his men, Touissant? Do they join you for service at all? Have you had any dealings with them? Do you not notice how different they are from other men? Other chevaliers?"

"I… What do you mean, different?"

The eveque had a point. Remi had witnessed d'Louncrais and his vassals kneeling before the comte. Six of them big men, warriors. Yet the seventh man had stood out. Not because he was not a chevalier, or of noble birth, but because he was smaller, less…*other*. What did that mean? Could it be… Remi scowled at his scuffed boots. *Am I really thinking werewolves could exist?*

"Well," said Aumônier Touissant, "they are all accomplished chevaliers and high-ranking nobles. Wealthy men, many of them from well-known and respected families. I confess I have not had cause to associate with them. Most have their own chapels and their own aumôniers on their estates." There was a baited pause before the aumônier continued. "The Montagne twins have been in the chapel for service a few times of late, which is unusual. Sometimes Edmond, sometimes Aubert."

"You can tell them apart?"

Remi scrunched up his nose. How could you not? Were fancy eveques blind? Edmond was the twin who had pressed him into spying for them. He kept his beard neater, and there was almost always a hint of a smile hovering on his lips. Aubert, who always looked as though someone had stolen his favorite horse, had a small scar cutting his left eyebrow in half and was a hair-breadth taller. Remi had the ceremony in the hall to thank for now having names to put to their faces, but he had always been able to tell them apart.

"Seigneur Edmond has a wicked sense of humor and often helps those less fortunate," said Aumônier Touissant. "He rescues the strays — animals and children—and has been very generous to this chapel. Seigneur Aubert rarely speaks, but he feels things most deeply. You need only look into his eyes to see the extent of his emotions."

Remi scowled. Did Edmond think of him as a stray to be rescued? He had survived on the streets long before the big chevalier had come along. He would survive once he was gone. With more coin in his pocket if he stayed. Remi would be stupid not to take advantage of Edmond's *charity*. Did the aumônier know Edmond used the strays to do his spying? Doubtful.

"Tell me, Aumônier Touissant, what do you know of d'Louncrais' vassal Lance Vautour?"

Lance? The older one with the graying beard? The one with the strange crest—a rooster's head and the body of a winged serpent. Could he be the one Archeveque Renaud had spoken of?

"Seigneur Lance? He is much like the other vassals. Older, of course. He served as a vassal to Seigneur Gaharet's father, too, I believe. As did Seigneur Godfrey. Strange that Seigneur Godfrey was absent from the investiture ceremony."

L'enfer. Two names. *Which is the important one? The one I need?*

"Odd, yes, but it is not Godfrey Lagarde I am interested in. I have reason to believe Lance Vautour worked closely with Archeveque Renaud before he disappeared."

Remi pumped his fist in the air. *Yes!*

"What was that noise?"

A chair scraped against the floor, and footsteps crossed the room.

Merde. Remi pushed off the wall to race down the corridor, but a strong hand, the eveque's hand, grabbed hold of his arm and dragged him into the room.

Two faces stared at him — one surprised, the other angry.

Remi turned to the aumônier, his eyes wide, all fake innocence. "Aumônier Touissant, I was looking for you."

The eveque gripped him tighter and gave him a violent shake. "Spying, were you, boy? I take great offense to little beggar boys involving themselves in things that are not their business."

Remi ducked his head in feigned deference. "Forgive me, your graciousness. I was but looking for the aumônier." He did not get caught often, but when he did, most times he could talk himself out of trouble. "He is often in the chapel. When I did not find him, I looked for him further. It is a matter of importance."

"Lies." The pretty face of the eveque twisted into a gruesome scowl.

Now here was a true monster, hiding behind his soft hands and black robes. One worth the fear that sliced through him and turned his stomach to water.

"You were either spying or stealing."

The eveque patted down Remi's clothing. Did the eveque think he was stupid? Anything in the church worth stealing — the gold cross, the chalices — he would never be able to sell. Too identifiable.

"No, your graciousness," Remi gushed, pushing as much submission and awe into his voice as he could. The rise in pitch, the tremble, he did not have to fake. "I vow to you I was not."

The eveque finished his search. "Hmm. Not a thief. A spy then. I should cut off your ears."

Aumônier Touissant was on his feet. "With all due respect, Eveque Faucher, should we not first hear what the boy claims he came for before we make such conclusions? Before we take such dire actions?" Aumônier Touissant turned his kindly eyes on Remi. "You were looking for me, child?"

"Yes, Aumônier, I vow I was." Remi clapped his free hand over one of his ears. "Please do not cut off my ears." His heart pounded and his mind raced. He had never been so close to panic in his life. Not even when he first found himself on the streets. By the clenching of his hand, the eveque was itching to do as he threatened. No amount of money was worth getting his ears cut off. "A big chevalier asked me to come fetch you. Something about a donation to the chapel."

He had the name he needed. If Edmond Montagne wanted it, Edmond Montagne could pay for it. Remi could only hope the big chevalier's charity extended to keeping his ears firmly attached to his head.

Chapter Thirty-Two

Lance Vautour heaved himself off the cot and tucked his cock back into his breeches. The woman moaned and slumped to the mattress, her copper hair splayed across the pillow. He had chosen her because…well, because she had looked like *her*. In the dim light of the pleasure house, his vision clouded with lust, he could imagine — if but for a moment — it *was* her. The woman he had coveted and was meant to be his. He pulled his padded gambeson on. The woman he had killed in a fit of rage when she had rejected him and laughed in his face.

The *puterelle* on the bed curled into a ball, the welts on her back an angry red and the skin broken where he had clawed her, bleeding. She was but a poor imitation. Her skin not as pale or smooth, her eyes not the blue he remembered, and she lacked the spirit, the defiance of *her*. Elise. His love, his mate, stolen from him by Jacques d'Louncrais.

Anger boiled in his veins, not at all eased by his release, nor the imprint of his grip on the woman's thighs and hips. She would have bruises by the morn. He pulled on his hauberk, the familiar weight of its steel links settling on his shoulders. It did not matter. He paid the madam handsomely to overlook his predilection for violence and his rough treatment of her girls.

"Leave," he growled at her, and the woman's head snapped up, her face puffy and mottled from her crying and terror in her eyes. She snatched up her shredded chemise, clutching it to her chest, and hobbled from the room as quickly as her abused body would allow.

He buckled his sword to his waist. Of late, he had succumbed to the need to be battle ready at all times, his skin itching if ever he remained unarmed too long. With Gaharet certain one of the pack had betrayed them and that witch hunter, Eveque Faucher, knowing his name, he all but slept in his armor, his sword by his side. Damn Renaud. If the archeveque were not dead already, he would rip out his throat.

"She seems like she might be a bit of fun."

Lance glared at the man leaning against the open door, lank hair, more gray than brown now, flopping over his eyes as he leered after the woman stumbling down the corridor. Didier, disgraced stable hand and petty schemer, was useful to him in many ways. Intellectual conversation was not one of them. "What news have you of the d'Louncrais?"

Didier slouched into the room, shutting the door on the sounds of sex coming from down the hall. "Three days ago, a cart left the d'Louncrais keep and headed out into the forest. Not to the village, not to Langeais."

"Heading east?"

"Yes."

Lance grunted. The old farmer's cottage. So that was where Gaharet had hidden out. He remembered it well from his youth. He had once planned to take Elise there until... He gnashed his teeth... Until Jacques had staked his claim.

"There was a servant, and a woman, and enough supplies to last for a few weeks, maybe more." He paused, a cunning gleam in his eyes.

If Didier thought he could outwit him, then he was stupider than Lance had surmised. His resentment toward the d'Louncrais had been easy to twist to fit his own plans, but it was a singular connection Didier brought with him that had proved more beneficial than anything Didier could accomplish, weak, puny human that he was. He would tolerate a thousand Didiers to have the witch and her spells at his disposal. That woman, she had a darker heart than he, and had already proved useful. How a woman so powerful could beget a miscreant son like Didier confounded him.

Lance reached for his purse and pulled out a handful of coins. Didier eyed the coins, licking his lips, the scent of his greed so strong it overpowered the miasma of sex, stale and recent, that clung to everything in the chamber.

"There was a black wolf with them."

"Gaharet?"

Didier shrugged. "I could not get close enough to tell for certain, but who else would it be? He is the only black wolf left."

Who else, indeed? But why would Gaharet take his mate to the old farmer's cottage now? Gaharet had reconciled with Lothair. He had no need to hide anymore, and the keep was far more defensible than a lone cottage in the woods. *Could it be…?* Lance scowled. *D'Artagnon.*

He tossed the coins at Didier. They bounced off his chest and scattered. Didier cursed him but dropped to his knees and scrambled around on the floor, collecting every last one.

Lance stood over the groveling man. "Go back to the d'Louncrais keep. Find this black wolf. I want to know for certain it is Gaharet."

Resentment brimming in his eyes, Didier pulled himself to his feet and performed an exaggerated bow. "Yes, *Mon Seigneur.*"

Lance ignored the slur. There would come a time when he would end Didier, but for now, while he was not free to roam about, he needed Didier to run his errands and to do his spying for him. The madam provided him some information, but her reach did not extend as far as the d'Louncrais. For all that Gaharet shared the secret of his existence with his entire estate, not a one would betray him.

He slammed the door on Didier's retreating back, fighting the urge to release his wolf. He grabbed the table, with its pitcher of wine and goblets, and threw it across the room. It crashed into the wall with a cracking of timber, cheap wine running down the mud brick like blood. He picked up a chair, and it suffered a similar fate. Then another. He curled his fingers, his claws punching into his palms and coarse brown fur prickling across his knuckles.

Nothing, *nothing,* had gone to plan. D'Artagnon's death should have destroyed Gaharet. Like Elise's had destroyed Jacques. It should have left the leadership of the pack open to him. He picked up the cot and tossed it over, sex and blood-stained covers spewing across the room. His chest heaved as he fought for control. After all he had done, after all the schemes he had set in motion, Gaharet had remained strong.

Everything the d'Louncrais had should be *his*. He closed his eyes, sucking in deep lungfuls of rank air. It would be his. He would prevail.

A soft footfall in the corridor, and a tentative knock on the door had him snapping his eyes open.

"Mon Seigneur, is everything well?"

He flung open the door to the calculating eye of the madam.

She peered past him to the ruins of the chamber. "Are my girls not keeping you satisfied, Mon Seigneur?"

"I will need another room. And another girl. No. Two girls. I will pay you double our agreed price."

The madam smiled. "Of course, Mon Seigneur. It is always a pleasure doing business with you. Come with me."

He followed the madam down the corridor, his dark needs twisting within his chest. Once he had sated his fury and cleared his mind, then he would make his plans. He would not stay hidden forever. The time would come for him to take his rightful place as the alpha of the Langeais wolves. Nothing, not Gaharet, not this Eveque Faucher, nor the comte of this wretched county, would stop him. And if D'Artagnon lived, if he had survived his attack, Lance would soon rectify that mistake. This time, he would make certain he was dead. He would take his head.

Chapter Thirty-Three

D'Artagnon awoke to mid-morning light streaming through the smoke hole and the trill of birdsong beyond the cottage walls. Strewn across the floor were their clothes. Tucked in his embrace, her back to his chest and the lush curve of her ass snug against him, lay Constance.

He breathed in the heady scent of her, of sex, and a deep, contented rumble started up in his chest. She moaned in her sleep, pushing back into him, much to the delight of his already hard cock.

D'Artagnon skimmed his hand across her hip, reveling in the smoothness of her skin. He could not stop touching her. It was all he could do not to drag her onto her back and thrust his cock into her wet heat. Again. How many times had he taken her? He could not remember. A few. He had a lot of years to make up for. Years where he could have had Constance in his bed, and as his mate.

He tempered himself. She would be tender. The last thing he wanted to do was hurt her. But he could still give her pleasure. He slid his hand down to her inner thigh and her body responded, her legs parting, granting him access. She arched her neck, and he nuzzled at the soft juncture of her shoulder, careful to keep his canines leashed. His gums throbbed anew, his wolf aching to claim that which was his.

He brushed his fingers over her folds, seeking and finding the center of her pleasure. She gasped and her eyes fluttered open, capturing him, binding him. He rubbed his fingers over her nub—a gentle glide, circling, the occasional firm press—her needy whimpers a delight to his ears. He ground his hips, crushing his hard, hot length between them, then slipped his finger gently inside her. With every slide of his finger, he thrust his hips, his cock rubbing along the cleft of her buttocks.

Her fingernails dug into his forearm as she matched him thrust for thrust. A soft gasp slipped between her parted lips and it sank into his testicles, sending sparks up his spine. He was going to come already. So soon. That's what she did to him, his little healer. Stripped him of any control. He latched onto her shoulder and sucked hard—no teeth—and she jerked, spasming around his fingers.

His release hit him, and he was too far gone, too caught up in the wet heat of her channel squeezing around his fingers, and her breathy little moans he could not stop it, could not prolong his, or her pleasure. He exploded over her hot skin, emptying his testicles of every drop of his seed. Unable to hold his wolf back, he pulled her tight against him and howled his triumph, his claim—to the morn, the sun, the forest and its creatures, to all who would listen.

He collapsed back onto the cot, panting, his own essence thick on the air, coating his tongue. His wolf's smugness echoed in his mind. He tried to dredge up the familiar burn of his hunger for vengeance, the sting of betrayal that had been his constant companion, and his grief, but his heart and mind refused. It no longer filled all the empty spaces in his heart. She did.

But the fact remained. Lance still lived. And he continued to plot against his pack. Justice must be served. With his reluctance to involve his brother and risk his unborn pup, it left D'Artagnon with one option. He must hunt Lance down alone. Challenge him. Kill him. Or die trying.

With gentle hands, he used the covers to wipe his release from Constance's back. His wolf wanted to leave it there, smear it across her skin and mark her with his scent. The man in him understood she would find such a thing distasteful.

Constance threw her leg across his and stared up at him, a hint of sorrow in their depths. Did she know? Did she suspect? That he must leave her. That he might never come back. She reached her hand out, smoothing the lock of hair away from his scar. This time he did not flinch, nor pull away. With a gentle touch, she traced his scar across his cheek, dipping where his eye once was, and up over his forehead.

She straddled him, and leaned forward, the long strands of her hair brushing his shoulders, and touched her lips first to his cheek at the base of his scar, then to his forehead at the very tip. Without hesitation, she pressed her lips to his damaged eye socket.

"You are more than your scars, D'Artagnon. Much more. You need not hide them from me."

He closed his good eye, heaving in a ragged breath. This woman… She slayed him with her kindness and her acceptance. He wrapped his arms around her and held her close. If only they could stay like this forever. Her in his arms, his scent all over her, but they could not.

His brother would have returned from Langeais. Perhaps he had news. Or Kathryn might have remembered something more. The longer he lingered here, the greater the risk. He had thought, once he was gone, once no one was digging into the circumstances around his mother's death, that would be the end of things. How wrong he had been. And now, despite the long years he had spent in exile, an urgency pressed at him. He stared into Constance's beautiful eyes. Perhaps because now, more than ever, he had a reason to finish this.

D'Artagnon levered himself up from the cot, taking her with him. She wrapped her legs around his hips, and he strode from the cottage, heedless of their nakedness, and took the path to the pond and the little waterfall. He would give himself this morn, and maybe one more. Bathe with her, care for her, take her as many times as her body could bear. Imprint her on his body and his soul.

He could never slake his desire for Constance, not if he spent a score years—no, five score years— discovering her body and all its secrets. The sensitive hollows that responded to his kisses. Where she liked a firm touch, or a gentle caress. Or where he best use his tongue to lave her to a quick release. He would never tire of seeing her preparing herbs for her ward, sitting across the table from him sharing a meal, or the way she talked to him, sharing her stories, her life, though he never spoke a word, never shared his truth with her.

D'Artagnon was not free to have those things. He had made a promise to his father to avenge his mother's death. He had failed the first time, skulked from the battlefield beaten and cowed. His failure to fulfill his oath swirled in his gut, battered by his fear he might prove unsuccessful yet again.

He clutched Constance tighter to him as he broke through the trees into the clearing, the pond glistening in the morning sun. He must conquer his fears, face his enemy. She had said as much. That he would not heal unless he did so.

But what of this Eveque Faucher? Was it safe for Constance to return to the keep?

He did not pause at the pond's edge, stalking into the cool water. First, he would take care of Constance, then he would decide what action he must take.

Chapter Thirty-Four

Constance squealed as the cold water lapped at her bare bottom, her heart swelling at D'Artagnon's throaty chuckle. She clutched at him as the water rose across her stomach and over her ribs, her nipples pebbling. They weren't the only things that were hard. Trapped between them, his cock made its presence known. Again. The man was insatiable. She wiggled against him, clamping down on a moan when her over-sensitized nub rubbed against his hot, hard length.

Another chuckle. "Wash first, Constance." He dropped a kiss on the top of her head. "I promise I will not leave you wanting."

He pressed into the pond until all but her head and neck were above the water, her hair splayed out behind on the surface.

"Take a breath."

Constance did as she was told, and he dunked them both beneath the surface. She came up grinning, a matching smile on his face. By the Fates, it was a glorious sight, D'Artagnon smiling.

He walked them to the edge of the pond and laid her down in the shallows. Slowly, with gentle hands and a reverence fit for a queen, he cleaned her body. From her shoulders and arms, down her breasts and stomach, over her thighs, her knees, and to the tips of her toes, he washed her. No, he worshiped her, and Constance reveled in his ministrations.

With every pass of his hands, every tender caress, wrapped in the cocoon of water and his devotion to her care, she was unspooling in his arms. That such a big, scarred warrior could be so gentle. That a man so wounded could be so giving. She blinked at the prick of tears. That she could experience this. At his hands.

The images of her vision filled her mind — the black wolf, the child dancing about, and the woman smiling, happy. She remembered it as though it were but 'ere-yesterday. She had carried it around in her heart like a protection charm, warding her against the harshness of her existence. With every tender touch, with every brush of D'Artagnon's fingers, hope solidified in her chest. Could she be...?

D'Artagnon's hands left her body. For a heart's beat, their absence left her bereft, until he nestled between her thighs, his arms bracketing her shoulders. His face hovered above hers, full lips parted and a mere breath away.

He touched his lips to hers. "Beautiful."

A lump formed in her throat. He thought her —

He rolled his hips between her thighs and slanted his mouth across hers, and all thoughts of what might be, what her future might hold melted away, and she lost herself to the feel of him, and to the bliss he wrung from her body like a skilled master.

Constance lay on top of D'Artagnon, her head on his chest, the water cool against her thighs and his heart a steady thrum beneath her cheek. If only they could stay here until the end of time, in this moment, in this peaceful place, the two of them alone in the forest. It could not be. As the sun rose higher in the sky, so did the tension in D'Artagnon's body. Constance sensed it — his need for action and the heavy weight of change bearing down on them.

He let her go as she slid off him, sluicing her body clean and stepping out of the pond. In silence, he followed her. On the edge of the forest, he stopped and tilted his head to the breeze. He snarled and pulled her into the circle of his arms, surrounding her with his body.

Her throat tight, she searched the clearing. "What is it? Is someone there?"

Then she saw it, at the head of the waterfall. A wolf — big and grizzled with age. Her heart thumped loud in her chest, and she clutched at D'Artagnon. Another werewolf. He was too other not to be, but she sensed a foreignness about this one. As though he did not belong here, nor with the Langeais wolves. Was he friend or foe?

D'Artagnon turned her away, giving the intruder his back and hiding her, but his body no longer vibrated with his anger. "Do not fear, Constance. He is a friend. From my time away."

The gray wolf cocked his head and lifted his nose to the breeze. D'Artagnon did the same, listening for things her human ears could not possibly catch.

D'Artagnon nodded. "I was" — he grinned over his shoulder at the wolf — "distracted." He dropped a kiss on the top of her head. "Come, Constance. Aimon approaches."

They left the gray wolf behind and hurried along the path, back to the cottage. Constance may know Aimon, but she was not eager to greet him naked. D'Artagnon appeared to feel the same way, thrusting her clothes at her as soon as they cleared the doorway.

She dressed as quickly as she could, and was lacing on her boots as hoof beats skidded to a halt outside the cottage.

"Constance? D'Artagnon?" There was a note of hesitancy in Aimon's voice. "It is I, Aimon."

Constance followed D'Artagnon from the cottage. Aimon stood at the edge of the clearing, the reins of two horses in his hand.

Aimon's eyebrows shot up. "D'Artagnon. You've shifted?"

D'Artagnon pulled her to his side and ran his nose along the curve of her throat. He bared his teeth at Aimon, dark hair sprouting across his cheek. The heavy, musky scent of his wolf surrounded them. The horses stomped about and tugged at their reins, their whites of their eyes revealed. Aimon kept a firm grip on the reins and backed away.

Constance held her breath, her heart racing. Would Aimon move to defend her, not knowing D'Artagnon meant her no harm?

Aimon held up his hand and backed up further, keeping his gaze fixed on D'Artagnon. "Easy, D'Artagnon. I am a mated male. Remember. My mate Kathryn, your cousin, is back at the keep."

The air crackled with the potential for bloodshed.

D'Artagnon ran his nose along the curve of her neck again, as though the action reassured him, but he kept her held tight against his side. As the fur receded from D'Artagnon's cheeks and his wolf's scent faded, the horses settled, and some of the tension eased from Aimon's face. Constance released her pent-up breath.

Aimon lowered his hand slowly. "I come with news, D'Artagnon. Will you hear me out?" He took a step forward.

D'Artagnon growled.

Aimon hastily retreated. "Edmond and Aubert arrived at the keep this morn. We know who the traitor is."

Chapter Thirty-Five

D'Artagnon eyed Aimon and the two horses, his path clear before him. His brother had sent Aimon to fetch him, as promised. As soon as they returned to the keep, Gaharet would set out for the Vautour estate to confront the man who had murdered their parents. He clutched Constance close to his side. As much as it pained him to leave her, and entrust her into the care of another male, even a mated one, he must.

"Had I known you had shifted, I would have brought an extra horse." Aimon turned to one horse and lifted the saddle flap to get to the buckle beneath. "But we will make do. I will leave the saddle here and Constance can ride with you."

D'Artagnon shook his head. "No."

Constance jerked her head up.

"I will not ride," he said, softening his tone. He steeled himself for what he must do.

"I guess you have been wolf for so long it is more familiar than being on horseback." Aimon shrugged. "I can lead Constance's horse while you run along beside us."

D'Artagnon eased Constance out of his embrace.

Constance shriveled before his eyes. She understood. She knew. "You are not going back to the keep, are you?"

The deep well of hurt reflected in her eyes, all but bringing him to his knees. He dug deep, recalling his oath to his father.

Her voice dropped to barely above a whisper. "You are afraid if your brother goes after the traitor, he may not come back."

He cupped her face, her eyes bright with unshed tears, and brushed his thumb across her trembling bottom lip. "You were right, Constance. To heal, I must face my fears."

Constance placed her hands over his and squeezed. A tear slid down her cheek.

D'Artagnon pulled her into his arms and kissed the top of her head. "I have to do this. I have to go." He released her and stepped back, turning to Aimon. "Protect her with your life."

Aimon stepped forward, his young face earnest and his blue eyes troubled. "Do not do this, D'Artagnon. Gaharet awaits you at the keep. We are stronger together."

D'Artagnon backed away from them, turning to face the forest, and pulled his tunic over his head. Leaving Constance was going to be one of the hardest, nay, *the* hardest thing he had ever done in his life.

"That which you think you want was never meant to be yours."

D'Artagnon stilled. Those words. She had spoken them once before. In her sleep. He turned. Constance stood, a small, sad figure, her desolation wrapped around her as surely as her arms, but her eyes had glazed over. She was caught in the throes of a vision. He had once thought her words nothing more than part of her dream. He had been wrong. Her words had been meant for him.

His chest squeezed painfully tight. What he wanted was Constance, more than he wanted almost anything. Fate, it seemed, had other plans for him.

Had he not fallen on that battlefield, were he not faced with this nigh impossible choice, this beautiful, kind, giving, extraordinary woman would have been his. His *mate*. But he had, and he was, and he had another purpose, and a duty to fulfill. One he would most likely not survive.

"What *is* meant for you is far greater reward, if you have but the courage and the room in your heart to make the right choice."

D'Artagnon swallowed. He had found his courage. Thanks to her. He would have his vengeance and complete his vow. He would protect his brother and ensure the continuation of the d'Louncrais line. But looking at Constance—her golden tresses wet from their time in the pond, her upturned nose, her unique eyes—it did not feel like the reward he wanted it to be. Yet Constance's words confirmed what he knew deep down to be true.

She was not meant to be his.

He dropped his tunic, strode to her and, snatching her up in his arms, he took her mouth in his. One last kiss, one last moment. She melted into him and his wolf howled in the silence of his mind. It did not want to leave her either.

He set her down, pleased with her flushed cheeks and her parted lips. An image he would cherish until his dying breath. "It was never your potion, Constance."

Confusion flickered across her face.

"The deadly nightshade berries, the leaves and the roots. Anne deceived you. She did not slip it into my food. I would have scented it had she tried."

"It was not—"

He shook his head. "What happened between us that night was not because of some...potion. It happened because I wanted it to." He had not spoken so many words since before his exile, but it was important she did not doubt *anything* that had happened between them. "Constance, I have wanted you from the moment I skulked in the grass near your cottage, watching you through the storm."

He dropped his arms and stepped away from her. Before Aimon could say anything more, before he could change his mind, D'Artagnon shifted. His heart aching, but his mind clear, he went in search of Lance Vautour.

His words buzzing around in her mind, Constance tracked the black wolf until he disappeared into the forest. He had wanted her. From the moment he had... The presence she had sensed in the rain-drenched forest the night Seigneur Ulrik had stumbled into her cottage. It had been him. He had wanted her, and now he was gone. Despite her words, her prediction.

The shadow, the vision, that had hovered on the edge of her sight had come to her. And as the meaning became clear, that deceitful thread of hope had wound around her heart, before it had snapped as easily as the first thin film of ice on a pond in winter. It had not mattered her words' true intent. D'Artagnon had made his choice. To hunt down the traitor on his own.

Mayhap he would not return. She stared at the forest, the black wolf no longer visible. He had gone to spare his brother, but every bit of her second sight told her D'Artagnon believed *he* would not survive this.

Aimon stepped up beside her. "Come, Constance. We need to get back to the keep. Gaharet will want to go after him."

Constance nodded. "I shall fetch my grimoire."

Inside the cottage, the evidence of their days together remained, the covers on the cot rumpled from their night of passion. Constance blinked back the sting of tears. The healer in her understood he had to leave. That he would not rest until he sated his need for vengeance that roiled within him. That his need to protect his brother and his pack came first.

The woman in her mourned he had not chosen her. That his grief and his anger were too big, too all-encompassing she had not been able to reach him. That their time together, their night spent in each other's arms, had not swayed him from his path. There had been a chance for them, for a mate bond to form, but he had not been able to let his feelings of betrayal go. Perhaps he never would.

A hollowness settled in her chest. Constance closed her eyes, holding in the tears. She would keep the memory of these days in the forest close, cherish it. It may well be all that sustained her through the years ahead.

"Constance?"

Aimon's voice snapped her from her misery. She left the cottage, her grimoire cradled to her chest, her hopes and dreams, her childhood vision, no more than the burned ash and blackened coals of last eve's fire.

Chapter Thirty-Six

The ride back to the keep passed in a blur. Aimon pushed the horses hard, forcing Constance to focus on holding on to the horse, leaving her little time to dwell on her thoughts. The bailey bustled with activity as they rode up the hill to the keep — stable hands bringing out horses and groomsmen rushing around to saddle them.

In the hall, the scene was no less chaotic. Servants rushed about doing Constance knew not what, with Gascon and Anne directing them. Erin, Kathryn and Bek helped Seigneurs Gaharet, Farren and Ulrik into their armor. Another two huge men, twins, already armored, stood with them planning strategy. After the quiet of the cottage, the noise, the busyness, the people — too many people — grated against the frayed edges of her emotions.

Constance stood in the doorway, tempted to run and return to the forest hut. Or perhaps back to her own humble cottage, where memories of D'Artagnon would not assault her bruised heart.

Seigneur Gaharet raised his head as Aimon rushed over. "Good. You have returned." He peered over Aimon's shoulder at Constance and beyond to the empty doorway. "Where is D'Artagnon?"

Aimon pressed his lips together. "When I got there, he was in human form." Aimon shook his head. "But once I told him we knew who the traitor was, he shifted back. He has gone after Lance on his own."

"*Merde.*"

Seigneur Gaharet's dark gaze met hers. She saw no judgment there, only pity.

He turned to his men. "We ride out now for the Vautour estate. I will not have D'Artagnon face this threat alone. Anne, Gascon, I leave it to you to see to it our mates are safe. Organize the men to man the walls. And lower the portcullis when we leave. Lance will not know we are coming for him. He is most likely lying low with Eveque Faucher hunting him, but I will not take unnecessary risks."

Constance's blood chilled. Eveque Faucher? Was he the priest of her vision?

Erin, lacing up Seigneur Gaharet's vambrace, scrunched up her face. "If Lance *is* lying low, then he probably won't remain at his estate, will he?"

"No, you are right, Erin," admitted Seigneur Gaharet. "But where would he go? Where would he hide?"

Ulrik pulled his hauberk over his head and growled. "I know where he will be. There is a pleasure house in Langeais…" He avoided looking at his mate, his expression uncharacteristically bashful.

Bek crossed her arms over her chest, quirked an eyebrow and tapped her foot on the floor. "Go on."

"I have not left your side since we met, Rebekah, but..." Ulrik sighed. "It *is* a place I once frequented. A lot. *Before* I met you. I have seen Lance there many a time over the years."

Bek appeared mollified.

"I know the place," said Seigneur Gaharet. "Those women keep more secrets than the priests taking confessional. It is the perfect place to hide." He strapped his sword to his waist. "We ride to Langeais. If we are lucky, it will take D'Artagnon some time to track Lance from his estate to Langeais. If he has gone wolf, let us hope he will not risk entering the village."

Some of the tightness loosened in Constance's chest. She forced her emotions to calm so she could bring forth her second sight. To be of some help. Could she get a clear vision of D'Artagnon? Of Seigneur Gaharet finding him before he confronted Lance? A sense, a knowing D'Artagnon would survive? Her gift, her curse, remained stubbornly silent.

"You know, the house you talk of has a back entrance."

The hall fell silent, and all eyes turned to a boy Constance had not noticed before. The boy picked up a goblet, his eyes gleaming as he admired the inset gems.

One of the twins cuffed him across his head. "Put the cup down, lad. I did not bring you here to steal the dinnerware. I have already paid out more coin than I intended." He shook his head. "Donation to the chapel, indeed. You should not have gotten caught."

The boy scowled, then offered the big man an impish grin.

"Tell us what you know of this house," said the twin.

The boy shrugged. "I know it is more than a pleasure house." He put the cup back on the table and picked up an elaborately carved knife.

The twin snatched the knife out of the boy's fingers and tossed it on the table. "Explain."

The boy's eyes narrowed. "What is worth to you?"

The twin growled. An uncharacteristic wave of frustration surged through Constance's chest. They did not have time to waste. D'Artagnon was on his way to confront the enemy. Alone. Could they not hurry? Move faster?

The boy shrugged. "A person has to eat."

"They do, indeed," said Seigneur Gaharet. "We will compensate you well for your troubles, boy. A position on one of our estates? Edmond?"

The twin nodded.

The boy raised his eyebrows. "Like a stable hand, or kitchen boy or something?"

"Or something," growled Edmond.

The boy flicked shrewd eyes around the group. "Did you say this D'Artagnon has gone...*wolf*?" The boy tapped a finger to his chin. "Mm, I do recall Eveque Faucher —"

Edmond raised an eyebrow at him. "The eveque who was going to cut off your ears? I will not offer again, boy. A position on our estate, a place to sleep and plenty of food to eat, or you can see how much money you can squeeze out of the eveque. *If* you keep your ears."

Vulnerability flashed across the boy's face, then he raised his chin. "And a blanket and a warm coat? Winter is coming, you know."

Constance took a step toward the boy, then halted. It was not her place, but must they stand around talking? Bargaining with the boy? Give him what he wanted. She silently pleaded for Seigneur Gaharet to take his men and hurry after his brother. D'Artagnon needed him.

Seigneur Gaharet sliced his hand through the air. "Enough." The hall fell silent. "You will accept Edmond's offer and help us, or I will shake the answer out of you. Make your choice."

Constance did not believe Seigneur Gaharet would harm the boy, but in the face of an alpha losing patience, the boy's courage would surely crumble. It was a good offer — a place on an estate. The boy would be foolish not to accept.

The boy gave an elaborate bow. "Remi at your service."

"Good," said Seigneur Gaharet. "Now tell us about this pleasure house and its back entrance."

"Of course. The madam takes advantage of her location against the village wall. For a few coins, she will provide an escape route over it, should you find a need to leave in a hurry. You know, for those who cannot leave through the gate."

Edmond fisted his hands on his hips. "How is that supposed to help us?"

Remi rolled his eyes. "The route works both ways. If you want to get back into the village unseen, you only have to know how it works and have a few coins in your purse." He picked up the bejeweled goblet again. "A few coins should not be a problem for any of you, and I know how to get you through."

Seigneur Gaharet snatched the goblet from his hands and placed it on the table. "It looks like you are going to prove very useful after all." He turned to the old cook. "Anne, do you have the armor, sword and clothes for D'Artagnon I requested?"

"Already in a pack on a spare horse, Gaharet."

"Excellent. We ride for Langeais. Ulrik, Aimon, you go through the gate and approach the pleasure house from the front door. The rest of us and Remi will approach from outside the walls. D'Artagnon has a head start on us. Let us hope we get to Lance before he does."

With a thud of boots and a clinking of steel, the men left the hall.

As he passed her, Seigneur Gaharet halted. "I will find him, Constance. I will bring him back to you. That I promise you." With a gentle squeeze of her arm, he followed his men.

Constance stared after his retreating back, his broad shoulders and dark hair so like his brother's. And when, *if*, D'Artagnon returned? What then? The grand hall mocked her and her shoulders sagged. She was no Genevieve. Nor an Erin. The Black Wolf had made his choice, and once again, it was not her.

A gentle hand touched her shoulder, and she turned to meet Erin's sympathetic gaze. "Gaharet will find him, Constance. He wants his brother back as much as you want your mate."

Constance choked on the lump in her throat. "I cannot be D'Artagnon's mate."

"Really?" Erin's face expressed her doubt. "Are you sure about that?"

It was tempting to believe the certainty in Erin's voice. "Wishing it so does not make it real." She sighed. "I have done what Seigneur Gaharet called me here to do. I should return home."

Though the thought of returning to her lonely hut in the forest only deepened her misery.

"I've seen the way he followed you around, the way he looked at you," said Erin. "He was so protective of you. He might have been a wolf, but it was pretty hard to miss."

Kathryn and Bek gathered around her, nodding.

"Gaharet believes it," said Erin. "And he's not been wrong yet."

Constance shook her head. "You do not understand. Monsieur D'Artagnon is a black wolf. Descended from a long line of black wolves. From the *original* black wolf. Strong wolves with strong mates. I am not like any of the mates of the black wolves of the past. Nor am I like either of you. There is nothing special about me."

"Special? Me?" Bek chortled. "I worked in an alehouse. A lousy one at that."

"I"—Kathryn tapped her chest—"was the subject of gossip at court for my unladylike behavior."

Erin held up her hands. "Don't look at me as though I'm anything grand. I may have been an archeologist, but my own mother didn't consider me high on her list of priorities. If anything, Constance, you are more special than all of us."

Bek and Kathryn nodded their agreement.

What was Erin talking about?

Erin laid a hand on Constance's grimoire. "Constance, you are the keeper of all this knowledge. You know the lore of the Langeais wolves better than anyone. And you are a healer. A good one. In the future, healers are some of the *highest* paid professionals. You have the gift of foresight, and I bet you are a powerful witch in your own right."

"But—"

"There's no but about it, Constance. We all see it in you. And so does D'Artagnon, even if he won't admit it yet."

"No. You are wrong. D'Artagnon has no room in his heart for me. If he did he…" She stared at the doorway. "He would have chosen me."

Erin heaved out a sigh. "He has gone to face Lance on his own to protect Gaharet, hasn't he?" She rolled her eyes. "Men. If only they would talk about what they're thinking, we could disabuse them of their stupid notions and set things right." Erin gently guided her to a seat by the fire. "You are not alone in this, Constance. We've all come up against a stubborn wolf that can't see what's right in front of his nose." She pointed at Bek. "Ulrik believed Bek wouldn't want him because of his past." She shifted her finger to Kathryn. "Aimon thought other wolves would be a better mate for Kathryn because he was only three years turned. And me? Gaharet was willing to sacrifice his own happiness because he believed it served his pack best. All of them were wrong."

When Erin explained it like that… Now that she thought about it, Alexandre had fled from Genevieve, not wishing her to suffer the turning. Maybe…

Bek sat down beside her. "Erin's right, Constance. D'Artagnon's no different to all our mates."

"Give him a chance to get it right," said Erin. "At least wait until the men return."

"If he does not come to his senses, we can always enlist Anne's help," suggested Kathryn. "She helped me force Aimon's hand."

"She tried to force Gaharet's, too. In fact, I suspect," Erin chuckled, "Anne's meddling was the real reason you and D'Artagnon went to the farmer's cottage. She has been rather eloquent about the benefits of a certain pond with a waterfall of late."

Constance flushed.

"By the look on your face, I'd say it worked, too, just as Anne planned it."

Constance put a hand to her hot cheek.

"I have fond memories of that pond," said Bek.

"What are you saying about me meddling?" Anne plonked a plate of food down on the table behind them. "I only ever give things a little nudge in the right direction."

Erin's smile was full of fondness. "Of course, Anne. Things wouldn't have worked out so well if you hadn't."

Anne snorted. "Balderdash. Those boys know their mates when they see them, if it does take a while for them to acknowledge what they are feeling. All I do is hasten things along a bit."

Constance still had her doubts. "But—"

Anne fisted her hands on her hips. "Now you listen to what old Anne has to say, child. D'Artagnon is no different from his brother. Or Ulrik and Aimon. Or many other wolves who have taken a mate. The wolf inside knows. So do I, and there is no doubt in my mind you are D'Artagnon's mate. Make no mistake, he *will* come back for you."

"Told you," said Erin. To Anne, she said, "Constance was thinking of returning to her home."

"What? D'Artagnon will expect you to be here when he returns. And you will be. I aim to see to that. I promised Gaharet I would keep you all safe within these walls." Anne smoothed out her apron. "Now, there will be no more talk of leaving. Here, I have brought you a bite to eat. The men are not likely to return until after nightfall. Best we go on about our day as normal as we can."

From their pinched expressions, neither Bek, Kathryn, nor Erin would find it any easier to view this as a normal day than she would. She twisted her hands in her lap. She could almost convince herself the fluttering in her stomach was concern for D'Artagnon's wellbeing, his safety, and not a rekindling of hope. Her desire to remain rooted in the potential need for her healing skills upon the return of the men. Almost. She would be here when D'Artagnon returned. *If* he returned. Then they would see if Anne was right. Or wrong.

Chapter Thirty-Seven

D'Artagnon, his stomach pressed to the ground, peered out of the forest at the walls of Langeais. Beside him, Vladimir. He had barely left Constance behind when he had sensed the familiar presence shadowing him. It should not have surprised him. In truth, he was grateful for the older wolf's company and his support.

The steady beat of the blacksmith's hammer ceased and the heavy tread of boots along the streets slowed. Night would soon fall and darkness would creep through the streets of the village. The beginnings of a busy night echoed through the still air, but this part of the village had yet to come alive. When it did, it would with a furtiveness that would suit D'Artagnon's purpose well. Soon he would make his move.

Lance had not been at his estate. It had taken D'Artagnon some time to establish the chevalier's absence, skulking around the edges of the Vautour village until he had found an empty hut with some clothes they could steal, before sneaking into the keep.

The traitor's scent had been everywhere, but there had been no sign of Lance. A captured conversation between two maids confirmed what he had suspected. They would not find his nemesis there. They had wasted more time listening to the gossip of the kitchen staff, the guards on the wall and the stable hands, hoping to glean where Lance would have gone, to no avail.

Their noses were of no help. Many a horse had left through the Vautour gates. Anyone of them could have carried Lance. In desperation, he had turned to Langeais, and it was there, at the base of the wall, backing onto a pleasure house, they had found Lance's scent. Somehow, his enemy had gone over the wall.

He eyed the darkening sky. Gaharet would have made the same mistake, presuming Lance to be holed up in his keep. The most obvious place, but also the most defensible. He had time yet.

Vladimir rose, his ears pricked and his nose tilted to the breeze. With a soft chuff, he slunk away into the forest. D'Artagnon tensed, and sniffed the air. Coming toward him, the soft clop of horses' hooves and the unmistakable musk of werewolves.

Merde. How did my brother get here so fast?

They rode out of the gloom — his brother, followed closely by Farren, Aubert, Edmond and a…a *boy?*

Gaharet dismounted, his nose twitching, eyeing the flattened patch of grass beside him. He circled D'Artagnon, scanning the forest. D'Artagnon ignored the question in his brother's eyes. Vladimir was too wily to be found unless he wanted to be.

Gaharet shrugged and squatted in front of him. "Did you really think I would leave you to face Lance without me, brother?"

D'Artagnon huffed.

Gaharet dropped a sack in front of him that reeked of steel and sweat. "Will you shift, D'Artagnon? Shall we hunt him down together? Side by side." He glanced over his shoulder as the others dismounted, gathering behind him. "They have lost loved ones, too, because of Lance's treachery. Because of his alliance with Renaud. Vengeance belongs to all of us, do you not think?"

"He *does know* he is talking to a wolf, right?" whispered the boy, sidling up to Edmond.

Gaharet ignored the boy and opened the sack, revealing breeches, a tunic, boots and his armor. "Come fight with us, D'Artagnon, like you once did. As a man."

D'Artagnon eyed the hauberk, the vambraces and greaves, the padded gambeson. He had not worn such things since the day Lance had cut him down. Would he even remember how to use a sword?

The walls beckoned, his enemy's scent lingering. Langeais was not like the Vautour village. Sneaking in as a wolf would be difficult, and any hope of confronting Lance on his own was long gone now Gaharet was here. The only way he could protect his brother was to fight beside him.

D'Artagnon closed his eye and called forth the change. He stood before his brother, eye to eye, man to man, for the first time in nine years.

Dark shadows shifted in his brother's eyes. Then he was pulling D'Artagnon into a rough embrace. "Welcome home, brother."

Emotion threatened to choke him. He was home. Truly home.

Edmond gripped his shoulder. "Welcome back, D'Artagnon." He turned to the boy. "Come, Remi. Now is your chance to prove your usefulness."

The boy's eyes were wide, and he backed away from them. "I had thought you lot insane, but…but…" He eyed them all warily. "Are you *all* werewolves?"

Edmond snagged the boy's arm before he could back away too far. "Not so fast. We brought you here to do a job, remember?"

"Or what?" Remi's face paled. "You will eat me? Or turn me into one of you?" Remi stopped pulling against Edmond's hold, and his expression turned cunning. "You know, being a man who can turn into a wolf could be interesting. Can you smell better and hear —"

Edmond growled. "I am not turning you."

Remi's gaze turned on him as D'Artagnon slipped into his clothes and armor. "He might?"

D'Artagnon snorted. The boy was bold. D'Artagnon liked him. Gaharet handed him a sword, and he tested its weight, the grip settling into his palm as though he had handled it only 'ere-yesterday. He returned it to the scabbard and buckled around his waist.

Edmond cuffed Remi. "Nobody is turning you, Remi, and nobody is going to eat you, but I might consider thrashing you if you do not tell us this secret way of getting across the wall."

Remi pouted. "The least you could do is consider it." He shrugged and faced the wall. "You might change your mind one day. About the turning part, not the eating part."

Edmond growled.

Remi held up his hands. "Do not get your hauberk all twisted. I will tell you." He grinned. "I kind of like the idea of being part of a werewolf pack. I could get up to all sorts of mischief knowing I have you lot at my back."

Edmond rolled his eyes. "I have created a monster."

Remi winked. "Not yet, but maybe one day."

D'Artagnon growled. They were wasting time. The sky had darkened, and for the first time in a long time, D'Artagnon was eager for battle.

Remi turned to Aubert. "He is grumpier than you are."

D'Artagnon snarled, baring his teeth at Remi.

Remi swallowed and backed up a little further. "No need to get testy. To get over the wall, you throw three rocks at the pleasure house roof. Someone inside will throw a plank across to the wall, then a rope will drop. And you will need some coin to pay passage."

D'Artagnon slid his sword out a little, revealing the blade.

"Oh, you have coin. Of sorts." Remi glanced around at the group. "Are you going to be able to climb up a rope wearing all that steel?"

D'Artagnon slammed his sword back into his scabbard. If his enemy was in this pleasure house, no madam, or any of her henchmen, were going to stop him, coin or no.

He scooped up three rocks. One by one, he threw them, hitting the roof of the pleasure house. Shutters banged open and the scrape of timber against stone echoed in the night air. The end of a plank jutted across the wall and a rope dropped to the ground.

Gaharet stepped forward. D'Artagnon placed a hand on his brother's chest, halting him, and growled. Gaharet may be alpha, but D'Artagnon had not come this far, sacrificed so much, to let him walk head-first into danger.

D'Artagnon strode out of the forest and across the open ground. His brother, Edmond, Aubert, Farren and Remi, followed him. He grabbed the rope and, using the knots tied along it at intervals, climbed to the top of the wall. Crouched low, he unsheathed his sword and crossed the board to the open window. The smell of sex, stale sweat and rotten meadowsweet rushes coated the back of his throat, but beneath it all, the one scent he was hoping for. Lance.

D'Artagnon slipped inside. A burly man with small, squinty eyes in a battered face barred his way.

The man took in his armor and sword and grinned, holding out his meaty hand. "Four *Sol.*"

Gaharet stepped into the room behind him.

"For each person."

"That is outrageous!" said Remi, climbing through the window. "The price last week was four *denier.*"

The man scowled. "Keep yer mouth shut, boy, or the price will go up to four *livre.*"

D'Artagnon stepped forward, his sword raised.

Gaharet put a hand on his arm. "Would you kill a man for doing what he is paid to do, D'Artagnon?"

Remi spluttered. "But…but…the price…"

Gaharet held out five gold coins and one silver. "One *sol* per man, and a *denier* for the boy. Take it. It is more than fair." He jerked his head in D'Artagnon's direction. "Or I let my brother pay. His way."

D'Artagnon rested the tip of his sword at the base of the man's thick neck.

The man blanched and grabbed the coins. "Thank you, Mon Seigneur." He backed away into the corner of the room.

D'Artagnon pushed through the doorway and rushed down the hall, following his nose. His brother cursed behind him, but he did not slow. He would take his enemy down. He would spare his brother.

At the end of the corridor, he encountered Ulrik and Aimon. If they were here, who was watching over Constance? His wolf pushed forward.

Ulrik grasped his shoulder and leaned close. "She is safe, D'Artagnon," he whispered in his ear. "Protected along with all our mates."

The tightness in his chest eased a little.

Ulrik jerked his head toward a closed door, Lance's scent heavy on the air. And something else. Blood. And fear. No more. This ended today. The traitor would haunt his family no longer. D'Artagnon would avenge his mother's death. And his father's. Today Lance Vautour would die.

He kicked the door open and stalked into the room.

Chapter Thirty-Eight

D'Artagnon's eyes narrowed, and his nostrils flared at the scene before him. Two naked women cowered in the corner, raised welts and bloody claw marks across their backs and thighs. They huddled together, whimpering. Fully armored, Lance faced him. His sense of smell was as strong as theirs. He had known they were coming.

"Well, well, well." Lance drew his sword. "Look who is back from the dead." His gaze slid past D'Artagnon. "And you have enlisted the aid of the pup and the pack's embarrassment." His smile was devoid of any humor. "You think any of you are a match for *me*?" He angled his sword at Aimon. "*You* are but three years turned. *You*" — he pointed his sword at Ulrik — "have barely had you head out of a wine barrel for years. And *you*" — he swung his sword around to D'Artagnon — "I cut you down once. I will do it again. *This* time I will make certain you are — "

"How about me?" Gaharet pushed into the room. "And them?"

Edmond, Aubert and Farren stood behind him in the doorway.

A muscle ticked in Lance's jaw. "Well, I guess there is no point in proclaiming my innocence."

D'Artagnon blocked Gaharet with his body and advanced on Lance. The room was small, with little space to swing a sword, but that would not stop him from taking Lance's head.

Lance backed toward the window, but Ulrik outflanked him, blocking his escape. Lance snarled, but he did not appear cowed.

"Where is Godfrey, Lance?"

At his brother's words, D'Artagnon halted. Lance had nowhere to go, and they needed answers.

Lance shrugged. "Somewhere you will *never* find him."

D'Artagnon pressed forward. You could do a lot of damage to a werewolf before killing him. Of that, D'Artagnon was living proof. And if that is what it took to get information from Lance, D'Artagnon would not hesitate.

Lance scowled at D'Artagnon. "Why could you not have just curled up and died?" He jabbed his sword at Gaharet. "And *you*. Why were you not more like your father? Why did you remain so strong? It was meant to be *mine!* All of it. *You* took it from me. *She* was meant to be mine. And Jacques took *her*."

Spittle flecked Lance's lips, his veneer of civility slipping. He had fooled them all. They tightened the circle, hemming in their betrayer. There was no escape for him. Time for his debt to be paid.

Lance threw back his head and laughed. "You think yourself so *powerful*. So *untouchable*. I showed you. I showed you *all*. It was me. *All* of it. I may have used Renaud, but it was *I* who took away your pack and reduced you to a handful of men." He shook his head, focusing on Gaharet. "And still you believe in your own power." There was a smugness to his smile. "You were stupid coming here. With all of your men at your back. You have left your most prized possession unguarded." His face contorted, his eyes filled with an unholy rage. "I will have my due! The d'Louncrais *will* fall!"

The growls of his pack surrounded him.

Gaharet stepped forward, his brow furrowed. "There are seven of us, and but one of you. What makes you think you will leave this room alive?"

Unease slithered in D'Artagnon's gut. His brother was right to be cautious, to be curious. Faced with six werewolves and an experienced chevalier, why was Lance so confident? His reactions were not those of a cornered man. One facing his own death.

"You think you are the only one with access to a witch?" said Lance. "That is the benefit that comes with age, Gaharet. I know things you do not. *My* witch once cooked a man's blood, boiled him alive from the inside out. Can yours do that?"

Cordelia. How is that possible? Tumas had been but a boy. Lance might be older, and werewolves lived longer lives, but would a witch? She would have to be very old.

Lance raised his sword, but did not brandish it at D'Artagnon or Gaharet. Instead, he sliced the blade across his palm. Blood dripped to the floor. "Did your witch teach *you* blood magic?"

Lance began to chant. *No!* D'Artagnon roared and lunged for him, but clutched on empty air, colliding with the wall. Lance was gone. His nemesis had vanished. Only his scent and the hum of his bitterness lingered in the room.

Merde. D'Artagnon spun around to the shocked expressions of his pack mates.

"We left our most prized possession unguarded. That is what Lance said. He has gone to the keep." Gaharet's face paled. "Erin."

The blood in his veins turned to ice. With blood magic like that, no amount of guards or fortifications would keep him out. *Constance.*

D'Artagnon pushed past the twins and Farren and pounded down the stairs, Gaharet, Aimon and Ulrik close on his heels. They had all left their mates behind. He plunged from the rank air of the pleasure house and out into the street, and skidded to a halt. Lothair, surrounded by his keep guard, blocked their way.

Merde.

With a slow shake of his head, Comte Lothair crossed his arms. "Gaharet, Gaharet, Gaharet. You have you been keeping secrets from me again?"

Lothair eyed D'Artagnon up and down, settling on his scar, and D'Artagnon fought the instinct to hide it beneath his hair. Curiosity and a myriad of questions brimmed in the comte's eyes. Questions D'Artagnon had no intention of answering. Not now. His brother's mate and unborn pup were in grave peril. And Constance was with them. He took a step toward the comte, with a mind to shoulder his way through the keep guards. A ring of steel snapped into place, swords leveled at his chest.

Lothair sidled up to him. "Now, now D'Artagnon. What is the rush?"

D'Artagnon stood his ground. It would take more than Comte Lothair and a handful of his keep guards to stop D'Artagnon from going after Lance. Ending this once and for all.

Gaharet stepped between them. "Now is not the place for this discussion. Nor the time." He leaned closer to the comte, keeping his voice low. "Lance was Renaud's informant."

"Well, then." Lothair gestured at the pleasure house. "Let us apprehend him."

D'Artagnon snarled his frustration.

"He is no longer inside," muttered Gaharet.

Lothair's brows shot up toward his hairline. "No longer—" He waved his hand at them. "Lance got past all of you?"

"We need to get back to my keep. *Now.*"

Lothair scrutinized them all, then gave a nod to his men. "Lower your swords." He looked around. "Where are the rest of your horses?"

Gaharet pointed beyond the wall. "In the forest."

"Capitaine," Lothair called the man over. "Send two men to fetch their horses. And bring me a score of mounted men, and my horse saddled and ready to ride. Meet me at the gate. Go."

The capitaine issued orders and scurried off with the guards.

Lothair turned toward the gate. "Walk with me."

D'Artagnon gritted his teeth, but followed. At least they were heading in the right direction. And the keep guard was gone. Their drawn swords had made his skin itch, his wolf bursting to come out.

They hustled out of the alley, the few people in these narrow back streets scurrying out of their way.

"I guessed you were after Lance when you all converged on the pleasure house," said Lothair. "I have spies, too, Gaharet. There is nothing that goes on in my county that I do not know about." He gave D'Artagnon a hard look. "Mostly. But why are we heading for your keep? Would we not be better served going after Lance?"

Lothair was helping them?

"Lance has gone after our mates," said Gaharet, the fear for Erin and his pup in the pace of his strides and the terseness of his voice.

Lothair grunted. "It is a wonder your kind has survived this long. Threaten your women and it brings you to your knees. How *did* Lance evade you all? He did not leave through the door as you did. Out the window, perhaps?"

D'Artagnon could not stop the growl that rumbled in his chest at the thought of Cordelia. "He has a witch on his side."

Lothair stopped abruptly. "A witch?" He shook his head and caught up with them. "Werewolves, magical amulets, a chevalier who comes back from the dead. It should not surprise me witches also exist." Lothair sighed. "Best we keep this information from that witch hunter, Faucher. Or maybe we tell him and use Faucher to track her down."

D'Artagnon tightened his grip on his sword. Risk Faucher finding Constance? If he had to silence Lothair himself, he would not let that happen.

Gaharet halted. "This is pack business, Lothair. Do not involve yourself in it. It gives you plausible deniability if Faucher does become involved."

"On no." Lothair squared off with Gaharet. "Lance is as much my problem as he is yours. Do you not remember your vows that you so recently swore to me? You serve me, and in return, I grant *you* my protection. You are my most trusted vassal, Gaharet. Dare I say you are my friend? I protect what is *mine*. If you are going to face Lance, then so am I. With my keep guard at my back. Let them all see we are a united force."

D'Artagnon rounded on Lothair and his brother. "We are wasting time."

"Very well, Lothair. Your men may prove helpful," said Gaharet. "They will grant us clear passage to my keep. But I warn you, no one, not even you, will interfere with pack justice. And if the witch should make an appearance, leave her to us."

His brother trusted Lothair? Wariness leaked from his brother. No, Gaharet did not trust their comte. Not completely.

"Of course." He held his hand out in front of him. "Shall we?"

They hastened through the square, murmurs of Mon Seigneur Comte following them. D'Artagnon's skin crawled. So many people. Too many. He quickened his pace. He wanted to be free of the village and on his way back to the keep. If the spell Lance had used was anything like the one on the amulets, Lance was already there.

It was a half day's ride to the keep. If they pushed their horses hard, they could cut that time down, but the horses had already done the journey once. Riding them beyond exhaustion would not get them there any faster. His wolf could.

They reached the gate as the keep guard returned, mounted and in force, with their horses in tow. Gaharet handed him a set of reins.

Ulrik nudged him. "As much as riding with Lothair is unappealing, shifting now would not be wise."

The keep guard gathered around them, their horses agitated.

D'Artagnon grunted. Was he so easy to read? His wolf screamed at him to shed his armor and slip into his animal form, but Ulrik was right.

Gaharet took up his reins. "Remi, give your horse to the Comte and take his." He turned to Lothair. "Best you keep your men and their horses at a distance. They do not like our presence."

Lothair accepted the reins and mounted up. "I did wonder how you managed that."

D'Artagnon swung into the saddle and spurred his horse into a canter. Lothair could keep up or fall behind. He did not care. All that mattered was he get back to the keep and stop Lance. He prayed they were not already too late.

* * * *

Lance landed in the dirt with a thud, his body screaming with the pain of a thousand stab wounds. The witch's spell had sent him through space, but not with effortless ease. Not as it did when one used an amulet. It was as though the spell had forced his body through a rent in the fabric of the cosmos, its jagged edges ripping and tearing at his flesh and his soul. He would hate to think what it had been like for Godfrey — when he had spelled him through time *and* space.

He coughed and spluttered, spitting out dirt, saliva and blood. He must have bitten his tongue. Lance grunted and pushed himself to his feet. He was a werewolf, not some weak *human*.

He stilled. Moonlight glinted in the many eyes staring at him. Villagers, pitchforks and scythes in their hands, watched him, some rising to their feet and advancing. On the hill, looming like a sentient being, the d'Louncrais keep mocked him. Above it, the almost full moon was high in the sky.

Merde. How could this be?

It was barely dusk when he had left the pleasure house. Had the spell sucked away time as it had pulled him through? Had Gaharet returned already?

He eyed the villagers firming a circle around him. No. The villagers would not be on guard if he had. *As if they could pit themselves against me? A werewolf.*

Old man Tumas approached him, his pitchfork held in front of him. "Seigneur Vautour?"

"What eve is this?" he snarled at the old man.

Tumas narrowed his eyes, but did not answer him.

"Has Gaharet returned to the keep, old man?" Lance called his wolf close to the surface and put power behind his words. Some of the villagers shrunk back. Not Old Tumas, but no human could resist a command from a wolf, not one like him who was alpha enough to rule the pack. Who *should* be leading the pack.

"No. Seigneur Gaharet left the keep this morn and has yet to return."

Lance stared at the moon, tracking high in the night sky. *Stupid witch.* She had not said her spell was inaccurate, that it ate up time. And it had spat him out, not inside the keep, behind the lowered portcullis and beyond the reach of Gaharet's men lining the ramparts, but in the wretched village. He glanced at the road leaving the village, weaving its way to Langeais. If Gaharet pushed his horses hard...

"*Merde. Merde.*"

An evil grin twisted Tumas' craggy face. "By yer cursin', Seigneur Gaharet is soon to return. Perhaps we will wait right here until he does."

The circle of villagers thrust their tools at him, stepping forward and tightening their ring around him. He snarled, raised his sword and sliced his hand. Once again, he chanted the spell. The angry voices of the villagers faded as pain pierced him, as the cosmos push-pulled him once more, and it damn well better take him exactly where he wanted, or Cordelia would feel his wrath.

* * * *

Didier pressed himself against the wall of the blacksmith's hut, peering around the corner at the confused villagers. It was not every day a man disappeared in front of your eyes. It was no surprise to Didier. He had witnessed such things many times. His mother did it all the time. The spell Lance had used came from her.

He glanced up at the d'Louncrais keep. That was where Lance would have gone — the chevalier's hatred of the d'Louncrais matched only by Didier's mother's.

It did not take long for the villagers to come to the same conclusion. Armed with farming implements, they stormed up the road to the keep gate. Drawing the hood of his cape over his head, Didier followed them. He had a mind to get a closer look at the woman who he had spied going to the farmer's cottage. She had returned that morn, in the company of the white-haired chevalier. No sign of the black wolf. There was something about her. She reminded him of someone. Someone he used to know.

When the guards raised the portcullis to let the villagers in, Didier slipped through the gates along with them.

Chapter Thirty-Nine

Constance paced in front of the fire. She was too full of nerves to sit. The fluttering in her stomach at the thought of D'Artagnon returning to claim her as his mate had long since been replaced by concern for his safety. It seemed an age since the men had left for Langeais, but in reality, it was not that long. Too soon for cause for concern. So Anne said. It *was* a half day's ride to Langeais, and back again.

She twirled on her heel and did another lap in front of the fire. At the table, Erin sat hunched over the journal. Now and then she would read something out loud to them — memories of the past, anecdotes she found interesting. Constance could not remember a single one of them.

Kathryn, sword in hand, lunged, stabbed and feinted, practicing the moves Aimon had taught her. She was getting good at it. To Constance, it looked exhausting, but... Maybe, if D'Artagnon did not claim her, did not make her one of them, she could prevail on

Kathryn to teach her. Such a skill would be helpful if she ever had to face that priest.

Bek lay on the table — *on the table* — unconcerned at the impropriety of such a thing, staring up at the ceiling. She tossed a rectangular object, cracked on one side and shiny green on the other, into the air and catching it again. Repeating the process over and over. A phone, she had called it. What its purpose was, Constance had no idea. Erin had nodded sagely.

Bek caught the *phone* and rolled over onto her stomach. "Constance, I don't suppose you have anything in your grimoire that could help make tattoos stick?"

Bek's grasp of the language had improved much in the few days she had been at the farmer's cottage. Werewolf blood truly was a marvel.

Kathryn paused, lowering her sword arm. "What is a tat too?"

"You would call it stigmata," said Erin, looking up from the journal as Anne entered the room with a fresh jug of wine. "Bek had lots of them, all over her arms, her shoulders, some on her back. They disappeared during her turning. Werewolf blood heals almost everything, including the things we inflict on ourselves."

Bek scowled. "I *liked* my tattoos. I paid a lot of money for them. You know" — she slid off the table, resting her hip against its edge — "I once read a shifter romance where they laced the ink with small amounts of silver. I wonder if that would work?"

"Nope." Erin shook her head. "Silver is one of our weaknesses. It burns. Adding it to your ink and sticking it into your skin permanently would give a whole new meaning to the pain of getting a tattoo."

Bek's shoulders slumped. "I forgot about that."

Anne filled the goblets on the table. "You lasses should think about getting some rest. The men might not return until the morrow."

Kathryn screwed up her face in a frown. "What is a shifter roma—"

A loud thud had them turning around. Kathryn raised her sword, Erin got up from the table with a scrape of her chair and Bek straightened.

"Constance." Erin's voice had an edge to it. "Come here. Get behind us. Now."

Constance backed away from the man on the floor. The one who had appeared out of nowhere. He rose to his feet, and the three women, the three she-wolves, closed ranks in front of her.

Anne lumbered forward, hand on her hip and wagged her stubby finger up at him. "Begone, Lance Vautour, you traitorous wretch."

Lance? The traitor? Constance peered between the women. If he was here, then where were the men? Where was D'Artagnon? And how did he get here? Lance's hand dripped blood. Was it—? No. The slash on his palm—she had seen that before. Many times. On her own palm. *Oh, dear.* Lance Vautour had found a witch to aid him. That did not bode well for the wolves of Langeais. For D'Artagnon.

"You have taken enough from this pack, and I will not let you take anymore." Anne lunged forward, faster than Constance thought the old woman capable of, and slapped Lance hard across his cheek.

His face twisted in a furious snarl. "No." He struck out, knocking Anne to the floor.

Horrified gasps from Erin and Kathryn, a growl from Bek. Constance covered her mouth to silence her scream.

Lance stood over Anne. "When I claim this pack, this keep and all that belongs to the d'Louncrais, no longer will your lack of respect for your betters be tolerated, *peasant*." He kneeled over her and wrapped his hand around her throat. "You will learn your place, if I have to beat it into you."

"Stop!" A defiant Kathryn thrust her sword at him. "Let her go."

Lance released Anne, rising to his full height. "You think to threaten me with a sword, little she-wolf? Me?" He slapped his blade against Kathryn's.

Kathryn parried and jabbed the blade in his direction again, forcing him to take a step back from Anne.

"I *made* you, you ungrateful wench. You will kneel at my feet." He pinned them each with a stare. "All of you."

"Like hell we will," muttered Erin.

"Sod off," said Bek, lifting her chin. "Over my dead body."

"So be it." Lance lunged.

The ring of steel against steel echoed as Kathryn blocked Lance's strike. Angry growls, the ripping of fabric and the popping of bones filled the hall as Erin and Bek shifted.

Two wolves, one blonde and the other dark brown with green streaks, faced the chevalier, snapping and snarling at him. As women, they were extraordinary. As wolves, they were fierce. Kathryn with her sword was no less ferocious. She swung her blade again, but Lance fought her off, knocking her sword from her hand. It skittered across the floor beyond her reach. She abandoned it, and shifted into her wolf, gloriously red and angry.

Kathryn snarled and lunged. Lance leaped out of her path and she skidded across the floor, sending meadowsweet rushes in all directions. Bek and Erin were not far behind her, forcing Lance to dodge teeth and claws.

"*Wretched* women."

Kathryn, the most experienced of the three, latched onto Lance's sword arm. He lashed out with his boot, catching her on the flank. She yelped, and he shook her off, but not before Bek leaped at his back, almost knocking him to the floor. Lance threw his elbow back and connected with her jaw. Her teeth tore into his tunic, exposing his skin to her sharp canines. She drew blood. Lance roared, throwing her away from him. Erin worried at his side, dodging his sword.

The she-wolves were not letting up. Lance had underestimated them and the training they had received from their mates. But he had yet to call his wolf forth. And if he did?

Constance retreated from the struggle. She must do something, but she was no use to them in this fight. Unless... She had a few spells, ones her mother had taught her. She searched the table for something sharp. Platters, goblets, her grimoire—no knives.

In the meadowsweet rushes by the stairs to the kitchen, Kathryn's sword gleamed.

The chevalier's gaze snapped to Erin, and he sniffed the air. A malicious grin spread across his lips. "You are with pup."

Oh, no. Dread curdled in Constance's stomach and she raced for the sword, snatching it up. Lance lunged for Erin. Without taking her focus from the fight, Constance sliced the blade across her palm, a spell on the tip of her tongue.

Noise filled the hall. The villagers, Old Tumas in the forefront, his pitchfork brandished like a weapon, poured through the doorway. They had come to their aid, and with them Seigneur Gaharet's men. One look at Anne, prostrate on the floor, and rage flickered across Tumas' lined face. Fixated on Erin, Lance turned too late, and Tumas plunged his pitchfork into Lance's side, the tines sliding between the links of his hauberk.

But Lance did not go down. He roared, wrenched the pitchfork out and cast it aside. With a mighty swing of his sword, he sliced his attacker's head off. Tumas dropped, his head rolling across the floor.

Constance gasped, and stumbled. *Tumas.* A wail so heart-wrenching split the air. Anne.

Lance slumped to his knees as more men entered the hall, their weapons at the ready. Constance sagged against the wall, her palm stinging and sticky from her blood. Help was at hand. They would prevail. Lance slumped to his knees, wrapping his hand around his blade. The chevalier sliced his palm.

No. He cannot get away. He cannot live to haunt them still. "Stop him! He's going to—"

A hand banded about her waist and pulled her backward through the doorway and into the stairwell.

The sword, knocked from her grasp, clattered to the floor and a hand clamped over her mouth. "Oh, no. No spells for you, little witch."

Constance struggled and kicked, but he was too strong.

"But I have one for you."

He began to chant, and as blackness closed in, as he dragged her away from the hall, she glimpsed lank dark hair with streaks of gray, then nothing.

* * * *

Constance stirred and blinked open her eyes. She squinted, her head pounding. *Where…? Why am I in the forest? Why… Am I in someone's arms? D'Artagnon.* Had he returned? She shook her head and winced. No. That did not feel right. Her memory danced in and out of focus. Snatches of three wolves — one blonde, one red and one with green streaks. A chevalier, angry, blood dripping from his hand. Villagers storming into the keep with pitchforks.

Lance. She remembered.

But who…? Why…?

Whoever carried her was moving fast. Moving where? She had blacked out and… Constance froze. Someone had grabbed her. The man who held her?

Constance struggled, flailing her arms and kicking her legs. The man grunted, dropping her to the forest floor. She scrambled to her feet, but not before he grabbed her arm.

He tugged her forward, and she almost lost her balance. "Now you are awake, you can walk." He propelled her forward.

"No. Wait." She dug her heels in and locked her knees, but he continued to drag her along. "What do you want? Where are you taking me?" She was not supposed to be here. Out in the forest. She was… She glanced over her shoulder. The d'Louncrais keep, silhouetted by the moon, moved further away from her with each step. No. *She* was moving away from the keep.

"You will see soon enough."

"I'm a healer. They need me at the keep. Tumas…"

The haziness in her head cleared. Tumas was dead. He had no need of her skills now, but someone else might. Erin, Rebekah, Kathryn. Anne. "I have to go back. Anne needs me. Did you not hear me? I am a healer."

"I know what you are, woman. You are far more than a village healer. Those eyes of yours do not lie. And you are far more valuable than your *soft-hearted* mother."

Constance squinted through the dappled moonlight at the back of the man's head. "Who are you?"

"Who am I?" The man laughed. "The question you want to ask is, who are *you*? The very image of Helene and with the same eyes as my mother, you can only be one person."

She tried to wrench free of his grip, but he was too strong. "I do not understand."

"Your mother never told you about me? Never mentioned the name Didier?"

Constance gasped. "Didier?"

He halted in front of a horse, untying its reins from around a tree. "Yes. *You* must be my daughter. And you are coming with me to Langeais."

Chapter Forty

D'Artagnon rode up to the keep, the Langeais
wolves and Lothair at his side and a full contingent of
keep guards at his back. The ride had been long and the
horses were tired, but at the sight of the raised
portcullis, he pushed his horse to canter up the hill. He
had known something was wrong when they had
ridden through the village, the peasant women urging
them to hurry on to the keep.

D'Artagnon reined his horse in and leaped down,
racing through the open main door, Gaharet close on
his heels. He caught a scent, familiar and yet out of
place, but he brushed his concern aside, ran down the
corridor and burst into the hall.

The room was in chaos. Villagers and guards from the
ramparts milled around. Torn clothing, women's
clothing, lay scattered about the floor. Anne and Erin
clutched each other, Erin, a cloak wrapped around her
and Anne's face red and puffy from crying. Erin was
safe. Gaharet's relief filled his senses, matching his own.

"Where is Lance?" asked Gaharet.

Erin shook her head. "Gone. He zapped himself out of here the same way he zapped himself in."

D'Artagnon looked around for Constance. Both Bek and Kathryn hovered beside Erin, also wrapped in cloaks. The she-wolves had shifted. Then he spotted it. The body, covered in a blanket, a pool of blood seeping from beneath it. Two separate shapes beneath it. One large, one small. A torso and a head.

No. He stumbled forward and sank to his knees. With trembling fingers, he lifted the blanket. The rheumy eyes, glazed in death, of Old Tumas stared back at him.

"It is Tumas," he croaked.

"Yes. He saved us," said Erin, a heavy sadness in her voice.

"Where is Constance?"

"I..." Erin frowned, looking over her shoulder and around the room. "She was right here."

D'Artagnon searched the crowd. "Constance!"

The room fell silent.

"Constance," he roared, pushing through the crowd of people. Where *was* she? Was she hurt?

"She would not have left, do you think?"

D'Artagnon sought the tentative voice, his gaze landing on Aimon's redheaded mate, Kathryn. "Why would she have left?"

Erin and Kathryn shared a glance.

"Because she thought you didn't want her as a mate," said Bek, stepping forward. "Ridiculous, I know, but that's what she thought. That she wasn't enough for you."

Not enough? No. She was... She was *everything*.

The crowd parted, allowing Lothair, flanked by his guard, through. "We need to hunt Lance down. We cannot have him on the loose."

"He's injured," said Erin. "Tumas skewered him in the side with a pitchfork. Won't that slow him down?"

"It will," agreed Gaharet. "That should give us an advantage."

Lance. The traitor to the pack. His nemesis. He should want to go after him, be eager to exact his revenge, but he could not dredge up any enthusiasm for the task, or any of his old rage. Constance had gone. She was his everything. How had he not seen that?

Constance's riddle, her vision. He clasped his head in his hands. She had warned him. He had misunderstood. Chosen wrong. It was not her that was never meant to be his, but *revenge*. *L'enfer*. Constance was right. His brother was right. Revenge belonged to all of them. The greater reward, if he had the courage in his heart…

The realization sliced through him, cutting away his years of exile, his anger and his sense of failure, leaving but one thought. The only thing that truly mattered. Constance. His mate. *She* was the greater reward. And with his driving need to take his vengeance gone, there *was* room in his heart for her. For them. And a life they could forge together.

He spun away from the crowd. The noise, the people, the ache in his chest and the deep well of emotions that boiled up in him too much. He had lost her. Constance was gone. D'Artagnon eyed the doorway leading to the back stairs of the kitchen, and he stumbled toward them. He needed air. He needed the forest. The weight of his brother's gaze tracked him across the hall. D'Artagnon paused in the doorway and glanced over his shoulder, an apology on his lips.

He stilled. *Wait.* There was that scent again, familiar and yet wrong. It was strong, pulling him into his memories. Of a time before Lance had cut him down. When he was but a young lad. It teased at him, brought to mind a stable hand with lank hair and a greasy smile. Didier. Overlaying it all, the fragrance he would, *could,* never forget. Constance. It carried the taint of her fear. And the coppery scent of her blood. He spied a sword on the steps.

She did not leave. She was taken. By Didier. And she was injured.

D'Artagnon unbuckled his scabbard and dropped it to the floor. He wrenched at his vambraces.

Gaharet strode across the hall toward him, a curious Lothair right behind him. "D'Artagnon?"

"She did not leave, Gaharet. Didier took her."

Lothair quirked a brow. "Didier?"

"A miscreant stable hand my father threw off our estate when I was a boy," said Gaharet.

D'Artagnon firmed his resolve. "I am going after her."

"What would this Didier want with this Constance? Is she your witch?" asked Lothair.

D'Artagnon paused. *Her vision. Constance bound and pleading before a priest. Faucher.* From what he remembered of Didier, he could believe him capable of selling Constance out for money. How had he known she was a witch? How had he known she was here? What was Didier doing here, back in the keep?

"I think he has taken her to the witch hunter."

Gaharet blanched. "Go, D'Artagnon. Find Constance. Save your mate and bring her home."

D'Artagnon stripped away his greaves, and removed his hauberk and gambeson.

"Everybody out! Now!" Gaharet roared, his voice layered with alpha command.

The villagers, the keep guard, the servants all turned and fled. Lothair flinched, but remained where he was. D'Artagnon ignored him, stripping off his boots, tunic and breeches.

"Aubert, Edmond, take fresh horses and go with him." Gaharet scooped up D'Artagnon's armor and clothing and shoved them into Aubert's hands. "You don't know what you'll face, or where Faucher will be."

Lothair's curiosity blazed in his eyes. "Go to the chapel. There are storerooms beneath it, perfect for holding prisoners. That is where I would keep her if I were Faucher."

D'Artagnon nodded, surprised the comte had offered the information.

"Try not to kill him, if you can. The last thing I need is for another high-ranking churchman to go *missing* in my county."

D'Artagnon grunted. He would try, but nothing, not Didier, not Faucher, would stand in his way when it came to Constance. If they did, their life was forfeit.

Gaharet beckoned Remi over. "Take the boy with you. He could prove useful."

D'Artagnon nodded. "Gaharet"—he faced his brother, shaking out his limbs in preparation for his shift—"when you find Lance, kill him slowly."

Gaharet squeezed his good shoulder, a hard glint in his eyes. "You have my word."

Lothair might be certain Faucher would confine Kathryn beneath the Langeais chapel, but D'Artagnon would trust his nose over the comte any day. He called forth his wolf. Dark hair sprouted across his naked body, and with a crack and pop of bones sliding, readjusting and realigning, D'Artagnon dropped to all fours. The awe, the longing in Lothair's eyes, he ignored. His brother could deal with the comte. D'Artagnon had his mate to find.

On swift paws, he flew down the back stairs, through the kitchen and into the bailey. He skirted the keep guards, their shouts, their wary eyes following him, and raced down the hill and beneath the portcullis. All the while, he kept his nose to the ground, following the trail left by the banished stable hand and Constance.

He had barely made it into the forest when the trail went cold, but the pile of fresh manure told him what had happened. Didier had mounted a horse. It did not matter. D'Artagnon could track the horse as easily as he could Didier. He picked up its scent and set off after it. As he bounded through the forest, Aubert and Edmond, mounted on horseback, flanked him. The boy, Remi, bouncing along in his saddle behind them. As D'Artagnon crossed out of d'Louncrais territory, a familiar presence tracked alongside them. Vladimir.

He settled into a loping gait. *I am coming, Constance.* He would not return without her.

Chapter Forty-One

The early rays of morn were turning the walls of Langeais a soft golden color as Didier guided the poor lathered horse from the gloom of the forest. Constance's whole body ached — from sitting behind Didier on the horse, jolted by every stride, and from holding on tight, her arms clasped about his waist so she would not fall off.

Many a time on their journey through the night she had contemplated letting go, sliding off the back of the horse, but Constance had tended many a patient who had fallen from a horse. Broken bones, a cracked skull. A fall at that pace could have been fatal. Perhaps she would have a better chance of evading him in the streets of Langeais.

Didier — Constance could not bring herself to acknowledge the man as her father — dismounted at the gate, dragging her from the horse and into the village.

He handed the animal to a beggar boy with a few coins. "Take her to the stables." He fisted his hand in the boy's worn shirt, dragging him close. "Do not think of double crossing me, boy. I will hunt you down and you will regret the day you were born when I am through with you."

The boy nodded, his eyes wide. "*Oui*, Monsieur. I will take the horse to the stables, as you say."

Didier let the boy go, cuffing him across the ear. "See that you do." The boy hurried the horse away, and Didier hauled her along the street.

If she could get free, maybe she could lose him in the crowd. She struggled against his grip, but he was too strong. "Where are you taking me?"

Didier smirked. "I never imagined I had a daughter. But now I know I do, you are going to earn your keep."

What did he mean by that?

As Didier weaved his way through the streets, Constance searched the people they passed—merchants, nobles, villagers—looking for a kind face, someone who might help her. Madam Dufont, her little boy in tow, turned her head away as they walked past. A merchant, whose boils she had prepared a poultice for, refused to look at her. The drunken blacksmith who had burned himself in his own forge, the girl from the pleasure house with the unwanted pregnancy—all these people she had helped, and none of them would come to her aid.

Constance was on her own. She eyed the dagger strapped to Didier's leg. Unlike Kathryn, she had not the skill to brandish it like a sword, but Erin was right. She was a powerful witch. She was not without a weapon. All she needed was a drop of her own blood.

She would have to be careful. Cries of witchcraft in the Langeais village would attract the comte. And

Didier knew what she was and what she was capable of. She would need to distract him.

"You say you are my father. How can you be certain?" She edged closer as he tugged her along, keeping her hand low. "My mother never mentioned you."

Didier shoved his lank hair out of his eyes. "Just like Helene, always asking questions, demanding answers. You women never learn when to hold your tongue."

Constance swallowed but pushed on as they entered the busy square. "You said I have your mother's eyes. Is she still alive? Is she a healer, too?" A man jostled her shoulder and her fingers brushed the sheath. If she could grasp the hilt, she need not draw the full blade. A nick of her skin was all she required.

"Healer?" Didier snorted, dragging her close. "My mother is a witch to the core."

She grasped the hilt and tugged. The blade slid up, but before she could nick herself, he stepped back. She eyed the crowd, waiting for the moment she would have reason to bump into him, get close again. "I would like to meet her. I have never met another like me."

"You think you are stronger than Helene, girl? That you would be a match for your *grand-mére*?" Didier barked out a laugh. "Meeting my mother was enough to make Helene flee."

Villagers gathered around a market stall of fabrics. If she could...

"Once boiled a man alive because he crossed her, she did."

Constance gasped. Nausea swirled in her gut and Constance shivered. "Cordelia?" Could it be...? No. Tumas had been but a boy when the witch Cordelia had boiled the blood of farmer Brun.

"Heard about that, did you? About her? From grouchy old man Tumas?"

"It cannot be the same Cordelia. It is not possible."

Didier snorted. "Anything is possible if you have the knowledge. Time itself is no barrier."

Time is no barrier?

A group of women stepped back from the merchant's wares, bumping into them, pushing Constance into Didier. She grabbed for the dagger, heedless of doing serious injury, but a large hand slapped over hers.

"Uh, uh, ah." Didier squeezed her fingers tight, forcing her to release the hilt. "Do not try that again, daughter. Behave, or I will truss you up like a pig for roasting."

Constance wrenched her hand free and clutched it to her chest, her fingers smarting.

"Eveque Faucher will not care how he receives you, only that you are alive."

Eveque Faucher? The one Seigneur Gaharet spoke of? The betrayal burned a path down her throat and settled heavy in her chest. All her life, she had longed to know who her sire was. To have him in her life and live like a normal family, as everyone in every village she had lived did. But Didier was not who she had envisioned him to be. Small wonder her mother had kept Constance's existence a secret.

They left the square, following the main road up to the keep and the chapel. Constance struggled harder. Didier released his grip on her arm, but before she could run, he had dipped at the knees and flung her over his shoulder.

"No."

He carried her, kicking and screaming, through the village, past the gate guards and up to the chapel. Not one soul came to her aid.

In the quiet chapel, her shrieks echoed.

Running footsteps pounded toward them. "What is the meaning of this? What are you doing with that woman? Put her down."

Didier dumped her unceremoniously on the chapel floor, and pain shot through her hip. She tried to scramble away, but he grabbed a fistful of her hair.

"Unhand her."

Tears smarted in her eyes and Constance glanced up at her champion. The aumônier.

Another set of footsteps, brisk and purposeful, strode out of the sacristy and across the nave. "Aumônier Touissant, what is the cause of all this noise?"

Constance's blood froze. An angel-faced priest rushed toward them.

"They say you are a witch hunter," said Didier. "I have brought you a witch."

A witch hunter? The Fates protect her.

"What proof do you have this woman is a witch?" asked Aumônier Touissant. He turned to the witch hunter. "This may be but a man who wishes to rid himself of a wife. Or she has refused his advances."

"She is my daughter, and I say she is a witch." Didier wrenched Constance's head back, forcing her to look up at the men. "Look at her eyes."

Aumônier Touissant frowned. "You would condemn a woman because she has eyes of different colors?"

The witch hunter pulled her from Didier's grasp. "To the storerooms with you, witch."

Didier grabbed hold of her arm. "Not so fast. A witch of this caliber is valuable." He held out a hand. "Payment is required before I release her into your...care."

The aumônier recoiled. "You would hand over your daughter as a witch for *coin?*"

Didier shrugged. "Duty to the community, to the church, is all very fine, Aumônier"—he rubbed his fingers together—"but coin is far more useful."

"Pay him," commanded the witch hunter. "Two *livre.*"

"Four," countered Didier.

"Three *livre*. No more."

Didier released her and the witch hunter dragged her to her feet and propelled her further into the chapel. Constance sought the aumônier, pleading with her eyes.

"Eveque Faucher." The aumônier chased after them. "I do not think—"

"You know naught of these matters, Touissant. Two different colored eyes is a sign she has the second sight. She is a witch, there is no doubt. Now pay the man."

The witch hunter pushed her through the door of the sacristy. The aumônier, wringing his hands, did not follow.

Constance's heartbeat wildly in her chest. "Please, please. I am not a witch. That man lies."

The witch hunter ignored her, dragging her down a set of stairs.

"He says he is my father. I only met him last eve. When he snatched me from the keep and took me into the forest."

He opened a door and dragged her into a dark and dank room. "Be that as it may, I know a witch when I see one."

From a hook on the wall, barely visible in the flickering light from the oil lamps in the corridor, he took a loop of rope and bound her wrists together.

He shoved her to her knees. "Say your prayers, witch. Perhaps God may see fit to forgive your black heart."

"Please. I am begging you. Please believe me. I am not a witch. Ask Seigneur Gaharet d'Louncrais. He will vouch for me."

"D'Louncrais?" The witch hunter smiled. "Little witch, you have just sealed your fate." He turned on his heel and left the room, slamming the door behind him. A scrape of wood and a thunk echoed in the darkness as he barred the door. Constance slumped to the floor. Of the two visions of herself yet to prove true, it was this one that would come to pass.

Chapter Forty-Two

D'Artagnon buckled the last of his armor on and stared at the walls of the Langeais village. It was no consolation his assumption Didier would bring Constance here had been right. He prayed to the fates he was wrong. That Didier was not taking her to Faucher.

Sniffing her out with the miasma of odors from the village would take time, even if all three of them walked the streets. But time was not on their side, so they had sent the boy, Remi, in to scout ahead. First to the chapel. If the witch hunter had her...

A gray wolf slunk out of the forest and brushed against his leg. He dropped his hand to Vladimir's ruff, taking comfort in the old wolf's presence.

"Friend of yours?" asked Edmond.

D'Artagnon jerked his head.

Edmond shrugged. "Good enough for me."

"Here comes the boy," said Aubert.

Remi ambled along with the other villagers down the road until he got further from the gate, then he slipped away, heading toward their concealment.

"Something is sure going on in the chapel," said Remi, as he joined them in the forest. "Aumônier Touissant is in a right state."

A fist tightened around D'Artagnon's heart. "Do they have Constance?"

Remi held out his hands. "If I had to guess, I would say yes. Aumônier Touissant was on his knees praying as though the devil himself had paid him a visit when I entered the nave. When he saw me, he grabbed me. Told me to go find you." He pointed at the twins. "Said it was a matter of great urgency."

D'Artagnon grunted. "We go to the chapel."

"Do we need a plan?" asked Remi.

D'Artagnon unsheathed his sword. "I have a plan."

"Very direct. Is he always like this?" Remi asked the twins.

Edmond and Aubert drew their swords.

"It saves time," said Edmond. "We do have this, too." Edmond held up a piece of parchment with a wax seal on it. The comte's seal. "Lothair gave it to us as we were leaving. He said to show it to the guards at the gate and tell them by his order we are to keep our weapons. It should get us through without fuss."

Another boon from Lothair, but D'Artagnon did not have the time nor the care to wonder at it.

He strode out of the forest toward the gate, Edmond and Aubert flanking him and Remi trailing behind. Vladimir remained behind in the forest, guarding their horses. They marched through the square, villagers darting out of their way. The gate guard tried to stop them, demanding their weapons, but Edmond thrust out Lothair's seal and the guards stepped aside.

At the chapel, D'Artagnon threw open the door and stormed toward the nave.

A startled aumônier appeared from the sacristy. "Praise be you are here, Mon Seigneurs. I did not know what to do."

"Where is she?" D'Artagnon growled.

"Which one?"

D'Artagnon halted. *Which one?*

"The first young woman is so sickly I cannot imagine her a witch, but Eveque Faucher insisted she had appeared in front of him from thin air." The aumônier wrung his hands, his expression troubled. "Then, this very morn, a disgraceful man brought his daughter to us. *Sold* her as a witch to Eveque Faucher, for the crime of having eyes of two different colors. She begged him."

So Didier *was* Constance's father. Not much of one.

The aumônier's face flushed an unhealthy shade of red. "I spied on the eveque when he took her below. I am not proud of it, but I heard her say Seigneur d'Louncrais would vouch for her. Then Remi came to the chapel, and he has done work for you before, and I thought..." He glanced at the twins, his eyes pleading. "You are Seigneur d'Louncrais' vassals."

"You did the right thing," said Edmond, squeezing the aumônier's shoulder. "She is indeed under our protection. Tell me, are the women in the storerooms?"

Aumônier Touissant nodded and pointed to the sacristy doors. "Through there, to the end of the corridor and down the stairs."

D'Artagnon was off running.

"Please hurry," the aumônier called after him. "Eveque Faucher will soon return from the keep."

Aubert tossed his purse at Remi. "Find us a horse and cart."

The twins were at his heels as he descended the stairs. Two doors greeted them, both barred. He lifted the timber from the first one and dropped it to the floor. He swung it open. The room was dark and dank and empty, save for one thing. Lying in the corner was a sickly looking young woman, dark curls matted to her forehead and shivers wracking her body.

"Take her," he growled at Edmond, and went to the second door, lifting the timber plank and tossing it aside. He flung open the door.

Her scent hit him, earthy and of the forest, layered with his own, but now tainted with fear and misery. She scrambled back into the corner, her hands bound, her face grimy and streaked with tears. His heart bled. He could have lost her. In his thirst for vengeance, he had put her life at risk.

Never again. She was his. His wolf had known it from the moment he had first laid eyes on her. He should have claimed her then. Or at his family's keep. Or at the cottage. He had almost missed his chance.

Faucher and Didier would suffer for every bruise, every scrape they had given her. He gazed down at her disheveled blonde hair, her tear-stained cheeks smudged with dirt, his wolf hovering perilously close to the surface.

Mine.

Constance pressed back against the cold stone wall as the large shape kneeled before her. The priest? A keep guard sent to fetch her for her execution? Or perhaps someone to torture her. The priest had seemed in no hurry to send for firewood or a long coil of rope. No. He had been too curious about the Langeais wolves, about Lance Vautour, and about her abilities. Constance had never been so grateful her grimoire remained at the keep. Their lore, her spells, were safe from him.

A hand reached out and gently brushed away a tear. She flinched.

"Constance, it is I, D'Artagnon."

D'Artagnon? But...?

He took her bound hands and raised them to his face. With trembling fingers, she traced the familiar puckered flesh where his eye had once been. "D'Artagnon?" she breathed.

"Yes, Constance."

She flung her bound hands over his head, and he pulled her to him, cradling her against his chest as she sobbed.

"Ssh, ssh. I have got you, little healer. Come, let me untie you, and we will leave this place."

He eased himself from her embrace and made quick work of the knots, rubbing her wrists and working the blood back into her fingers.

"How did you find me? How did you know I was here? You were yet to return, and Lance came to the keep, then—"

"We arrived at the keep not long after Lance. When I could not find you, when I thought you had left..."

"It was Didier. He took me from the keep."

"I know. I tracked you through the forest." He touched his forehead to hers. "I am so sorry, Constance, that I was not there to protect you. I gave you my vow, and I—"

Constance pressed a finger to his lips. "Confronting Lance was important to you."

D'Artagnon took hold of her hand. "Nothing, Constance, is more important than you. Nothing will ever be more important than you."

Her heart soared. "But Lance...?"

"Gaharet, and a few of the others, are hunting him. He has Lothair and a score of keep guards, too."

A dark shape loomed behind them, and she cowered.

He pulled her into his embrace, cradling her against his chest. "It is but Aubert, my little healer. The twins and Remi came to help me save you."

Remi? They had brought the boy here? This was no place for a boy. As if to confirm her thoughts, a low moan, faint and full of pain, reminded Constance she was not the only woman the priest had confined down here.

She tugged at D'Artagnon's tunic. "You cannot leave her here. Please."

"Hush now, Constance." He dropped a kiss on top of her head. "Edmond has her." D'Artagnon picked Constance up, cradling her in his arms.

"I can walk. I am bruised, but not truly injured."

D'Artagnon's answer was to hold her tighter. She dropped her head against his chest and let him carry her, settling into the comfort and protection of his arms.

D'Artagnon swept out of the door, the faint light in the corridor little relief from the darkness. "We must hurry. Faucher will not be happy when he realizes he no longer has you, or the other woman, captive."

He climbed the stairs and raced her through the sacristy and into the nave, Aubert behind them and Edmond bringing up the rear, a woman in his arms.

The aumônier, another beggar boy beside him, rushed over to them. "Quick, quick. Remi is waiting at the gate with a horse and cart. You must go." He ushered them toward the door.

"I am sorry about this, Aumônier," said Aubert as he crashed his fist into the aumônier's face.

The man crumpled to his knees, clutching his nose, blood seeping through his fingers.

"Tell Faucher you could not stop us. You tried, but we were too strong, too many," called Edmond over his shoulder. "If you could not mention us by name, that would be helpful. But do not fear if you must."

They pushed through the chapel doors and hurried down the hill, crossing the bailey and passing quickly through the gate. Remi waited with a horse and cart, and their horses he had fetched from the forest.

"We will split up. It will make us harder to track should Faucher try to follow us." D'Artagnon turned to Edmond. "You and Aubert have the cart."

Aubert jumped up to take the reins from Remi, and Edmond settled himself in the back, resting the woman against his chest.

Constance pushed to be let down, and D'Artagnon set on her feet. She hobbled toward the cart, but D'Artagnon pulled her back.

"I must go to her, D'Artagnon." The woman needed a healer. She was in far worse condition than Constance. How long had she been in the clutches of the witch hunter?

"There is naught you can do for her here now, and we do not have the luxury of time." He led her over to their horses. "Edmond will take care of her."

D'Artagnon took two sets of reins off Remi and helped her to mount up. She glanced at the cart.

Edmond brushed the woman's hair from her brow. His lips moved. Words of comfort, perhaps. They were too soft for Constance to hear them. She did not like leaving the woman, but D'Artagnon was right. She had no herbs with her to create a poultice or a tonic. Nor the time to prepare them.

Aubert flicked the reins, starting the cart off toward the square, Remi trailing along behind them.

D'Artagnon mounted up and gathered his reins. "We must go, Constance. We have a long ride ahead."

Constance urged her horse into a trot, eager to be beyond the reach of the witch hunter. They left the village of Langeais behind, hope fluttering in her chest. Faced with the priest, his burning devotion to stamp out witches more frightening for his saintly beauty, Constance had feared the worst. Yet, she had survived. D'Artagnon had saved her. Had forsaken his vengeance to rescue her. If one of her visions had come to pass, could the other?

Chapter Forty-Three

D'Artagnon rode in silence but kept a close watch on Constance. Without complaint, she rode beside him. *L'enfer*, her first thought upon escaping had been for the other woman. In truth, the woman would most likely not survive. Something was very wrong with her. The pallor of her skin, the sheen of sweat on her brow and the underlying sickness tainting her scent were a sign of something beyond her visible injuries. Something he doubted Constance could heal. Had he let her, she would have tried all the same despite her own ordeal first at the hands of her father, then Faucher.

Constance might not be as determined as Erin, as fiery as Kathryn, or as bold as Rebekah, but she had a quiet strength about her that would outlast them all. She was a survivor. Like him. D'Artagnon could not have asked fate for a better mate.

They pressed on, keeping a steady pace so as not to tire the horses. From the moment they had entered the forest, Vladimir had joined them, keeping stride beside them. He was glad the old wolf had stayed. Another wolf against Lance. An experienced wolf with an age of wisdom. If they must fight against the witch Cordelia, too, every extra wolf would be a boon.

The sun was at its zenith, Constance's shoulders sagging with fatigue as they rode beneath the portcullis of his family's keep. A few of Lothair's keep guard milled around the bailey and they stared at him, at the old gray wolf at his side. He ignored them, helping Constance from her horse, handing the reins off to a stable hand.

"Come meet my brother, my alpha," he said to the gray wolf.

Vladimir jerked his head and followed them inside.

D'Artagnon found his brother and fellow wolves in the hall, and Lothair sprawled at the head of the table. The women crowded around a forlorn figure bundled in a blanket by the fire. Anne.

Gaharet was already walking toward him. "D'Artagnon, Constance. It is a relief to see you both."

"Constance." Erin rushed over and flung her arms around his mate. "I'm so glad you're back and you're safe."

The other women crowded around her, drawing her into their circle as though she were one of them. She *was* one of them.

"Anne?" Constance queried.

The corner of Erin's mouth turned down. "She is taking Tumas' death hard."

Constance went to the old cook, wrapping her arms around her, offering her solace. Her heart was so big for those in need, he marveled at it.

"She will make you a good mate," said Gaharet.

"Did you find Lance?"

Fatigue and concern reflected in Gaharet's eyes. "No. We have searched the entire estate. Nothing. Lothair has sent men to the Vautour demesne and back to the pleasure house. He has them scoring the forest between here and Langeais. Lance is injured. He will need to go to ground for a while and heal. Avoiding Lothair's men should keep him quiet for a while. Give us a chance to rest, to regroup." His brother clapped a hand on his shoulder. "We will find him, D'Artagnon. He will pay for his crimes."

Yes, he would, but this time, it would be different. No more hunting alone. He would fight beside his brother.

The old gray wolf, Vladimir, pushed past him and padded over to Anne, resting his big head on her knee.

"Who is your friend?" Gaharet tilted his nose into the air and breathed in. "He has the scent of... Is he a Rus wolf?"

"Yes." D'Artagnon cleared his throat. "They took me in, sheltered me when I needed it most."

"Then they have my thanks."

Ulrik sidled over to join them. "So that's where you were hiding?"

"Yes." He frowned. "Why did you not visit?" D'Artagnon had both dreaded and longed for the day when Ulrik would turn up in Rus, but it had never happened. Not once in all those years.

Ulrik shrugged. "Why would I? What cause would I have to visit the Rus wolves?"

Did he not know? "Because your parents are there. And your sisters."

"What? My...?" Ulrik spun to face Lothair.

The comte had straightened in his chair.

"You did not...?"

Lothair grimaced. "Seems like no one's secrets stay buried forever. Not even mine."

"My family is alive?" Ulrik spluttered, lunging toward Lothair.

D'Artagnon caught him and held him back. Attacking Lothair would not be wise.

The comte threw up his hands. "So now you know. I made a deal with Jacques d'Louncrais to spare your family. And now *I* know there is another pack of werewolves in Rus. I wonder, is there, perhaps, a third pack in Bretaigne?"

Ulrik struggled against him. "You let me think..."

Lothair got to his feet and sauntered over to stand before Ulrik, unfazed by Ulrik's snarling. "I let you believe what I wanted you to believe. What I wanted *everyone* to believe."

Ulrik fought against D'Artagnon's hold and he tightened his grip.

"I made a mistake." Lothair pulled a sour face, as though admitting he was not infallible left a foul taste in his mouth. "Introducing that tax was stupid. I was young, inexperienced and too trusting of my father's advisers. But once it was done, I could not change it. Repealing it would have made me look indecisive. Would have left me open to challenges from other comtes. Letting you go unpunished for your hand in the uprising would have made me seem weak. Ruling a county is no simple matter, Ulrik. It is much easier when everyone thinks you are a monster."

Ulrik's face turned a mottled red. Rebekah glared at Lothair with a fury that could topple mountains.

"Enough," said Gaharet. "We are all weary. Let us leave this for another time when we will not make hasty decisions we will come to regret." He gave Ulrik a stern look. "We will rest and convene again in the morn. After we have buried Tumas."

Ulrik looked as though he would argue, but Gaharet growled at him, and Ulrik clamped his mouth shut. He shook him off, and D'Artagnon let him go.

"Gascon," Gaharet called over his steward. "See that Lothair's men are settled and prepare a chamber for Lothair."

"Give him mine," said D'Artagnon. "I am not staying." His neck prickled with the heat of Constance's regard. He smiled at his mate. "Constance and I are returning to the farmer's cottage."

The concern in her eyes faded, and she smiled back.

Gaharet nodded. "Very well. Gascon, show Lothair to D'Artagnon's chamber."

Lothair waved him off. "I must return to Langeais. This county will not rule itself." He beckoned his man over. "Let us rally the men, *Capitaine*. We ride for Langeais."

D'Artagnon tracked Lothair's retreat from the hall.

"There is more to that man than I once thought," said Gaharet. "The days ahead may prove interesting indeed." He turned to D'Artagnon. "Will you return on the morn?"

Constance's blue-green gaze fixed on him. It would all depend on what Constance was willing to settle for.

"She loves you, D'Artagnon. Everyone can see that."

"I cannot give her the life she wants."

"Are you certain of that?" His brother rested a hand on his shoulder. "Forget about Lance for now, and our talks on the morrow. Go. Make things right with your mate."

D'Artagnon nodded. If she rejected what he had to offer… He could only hope she would not. For he could no longer imagine a way forward if she were not in his life.

* * * *

Faucher clenched his fists and with considerable effort, throttled his rage. It was all he could do not to add to Touissant's battered face. He had had her. The d'Louncrais' witch. Right there in the storerooms below the chapel, and the aumônier had let them go. Let *both* witches go.

Worse. From his talk with the gate guards, he had more than the d'Louncrais to contend with. He had Lothair, Comte Anjou.

"Argh!" He released his rage on the altar, scattering the heavy cross, the candlesticks and the chalices across the nave.

"Have I come at a bad time, Your Grace?"

There in the doorway, resplendent in a gown of deep red and gold, stood Comtesse Marguerite. He straightened, his chest heaving, and got his temper under control.

"My spies in the keep guard tell me my husband has interfered with your work." She pouted her pretty lips. "Perhaps I could be of some assistance."

Chapter Forty-Four

Constance and D'Artagnon rode in silence through the forest, his words to his brother ringing in her ears. *I cannot give her what she wants.* Had she misread his meaning when he had said there was nothing more important than her? Had he meant important to the pack? As a healer? No. Erin, Kathryn and Bek all said D'Artagnon was her mate. And Anne, too. And he had said, back at the cottage, he had wanted her then. But... She had wondered when she had first set eyes on him, that first day in the keep, if he was too far gone, too wounded. Mayhap he would never fully heal.

He *was* taking her to the farmer's cottage with him, not leaving as she had first suspected.

Oh, Constance. How can you think of yourself at a time like this?

Tumas was dead. Anne, Georgette, the entire village was grieving and the man who caused it all, the man who had robbed D'Artagnon of his parents *and* his eye, still roamed free. He had told her she was his everything. That should be enough. Could be enough. Far more than she had had living alone in the forest. Their days spent in the farmer's cottage had been wonderful. If that was to be her life, she had no cause for complaint.

The little cottage sat waiting, expectant, as they rode into the clearing. D'Artagnon dismounted, helped her from her horse and strode inside without a word. Constance sighed and followed him. She must be patient. He would speak when he was ready.

Nothing had changed since they had left it. It seemed an age ago Aimon had come to fetch them. So much had happened she could forgive herself for thinking everything would be different.

He lit the fire, and with a brief nod at her, headed for the door. "I must tend to the horses."

She rinsed the mugs from the table, and set them on the shelf, then straightened the linens on the cot, left tangled from their night of passion.

The door closed behind her and D'Artagnon's presence filled the room. Gentle hands grasped her shoulders and turned her to face him. She stared at his chest, at his surcoat with the d'Louncrais crest, wanting to know what this was, fearing it might not be what she was hoping for.

He gave her shoulders a gentle squeeze. "Look at me, Constance."

The rumble of his voice sent shivers up her spine. She did as he asked.

"You are the most extraordinary woman I have ever met. Kind and generous and selfless."

He thought her extraordinary? Her heart was fit to burst.

"You give *everything* of yourself to others with no thought of your own needs. You deserve to take your rightful place as my mate at the keep amongst the other women — Erin, Kathryn and Bek — but..." He bowed his head. "I am not the man I used to be, Constance. Too long have I been in the wild living as a wolf, surviving on instinct alone. I no longer belong in a fancy keep, dining off pewter plates and drinking wine from bejeweled goblets. Nor do I belong in any village, surrounded by civilized people."

A solid lump lodged in her chest, all but choking the breath from her lungs. Would he stay here with her? Or... She could not bear to finish her thought.

He raised his head, his eye full of anguish. "I know you wished for a life in the village, to live as others live, surrounded by people, by friends, but I cannot give you what you want, Constance. What you deserve."

Constance swallowed, waiting.

"I cannot exist as I once had, but... I also cannot not exist without you." He cupped her face in his large hands, his blue eye blazing with emotion. "You are my mate, Constance. My heart is yours, but I cannot offer you more than a life lived here, in the forest, in this cottage. Is that enough for you?"

Constance's face crumpled. Tears pricked her eyes and ran down her cheeks. His heart was hers? He wanted her as his mate?

D'Artagnon's sigh was heavy, and his hands slipped from her face. "I understand. It is too much to ask of you to set aside your dreams of a diff—"

Constance grabbed his face, pulled it down to hers, and kissed him. "Yes."

D'Artagnon opened his mouth, but no sound came out.

"Yes, I will stay. Yes, I will be your mate and live here in the forest with you. I can visit the village, or the keep, any time. What I want most is *you*."

"You will? You do?" A slow smile spread across his face, then he swept her up in his arms and held her tight. "Constance, my love. You have me. All of me. And I will do everything in my power to make you the happiest woman in this county."

Constance closed her eyes, a vision of a cottage — this cottage — dancing across the back of her eyelids. A one-eyed black wolf lounged in the grass as two little girls placed garlands of wildflowers in his fur. And there she was, a little boy balanced on her hip, her stomach already swelling with another pup. Constance hugged D'Artagnon closer and smiled. "I know."

He set her back on her feet. "Make your potion, Constance. The one to ease the turning. Hurry! I want you." His canines peeked out beneath his upper lip. "I need to make you mine. Now."

* * * *

Lothair squeezed the grip of his sword so hard he might leave an imprint of his hand on the metal. On the table before him, his meal fresh from his kitchen. Dead at his feet, the keep guard who had tasted his food. A man he knew to be in the employ of his wife. If he did not loathe Marguerite and her simpering stares, or fear her reach and her connections, he might have found their little dance a challenge. But too many times she had come too close to succeeding.

No matter the risk of a turning, he must become a werewolf. If he did not, his days were surely numbered.

Epilogue

A sennight later

D'Artagnon lounged in the grass with his brother, Ulrik, Aimon and Farren, watching the women splash their bare feet in the cool waters of the pond. The leaves in the trees had started to turn. Soon autumn would be full upon them, winter following on its heels. Constance, still recovering from her turning, laughed at something Erin said, and he smiled. He had never known such contentment, living in the quiet of the forest, his beautiful mate tucked beside him — or under him — each night.

Not far from them sat Anne, grief etched in the lines on her face and the puffiness of her eyes, but she was not alone. His mentor and friend, Vladimir, sat by her side, letting her stroke his fur. Why his friend chose to remain wolf, he was not sure, but he suspected it had something to do with Anne.

D'Artagnon did not voice his suspicions about the two of them, not even to Constance, but the gentle smile on her face when the old wolf refused to leave Anne's side told him she already knew. Anne's life had not been easy. She deserved happiness, too, and Vladimir was a good male. The Langeais wolves' connection with the Rus pack was about to get stronger. Especially with Ulrik planning a trip to see his family in the spring.

Of Lance, there had been no sign. Old Tumas had landed a grievous wound on him with his pitchfork. It would take time for him to recover, and Lance was not foolish enough to risk a confrontation with them at less than his full strength.

Faucher had made no mention of the missing women. At least, not to Lothair, but he had continued to ask too many questions about the Langeais wolves. Lothair had spies in the chapel monitoring him.

Still, worrying thoughts niggled at him. Things that made little sense. Did they bother his brother, too?

D'Artagnon plucked at a blade of grass, twisting it in his fingers. "How did Lance arrive at the keep so long after he vanished from the pleasure house?"

His brother frowned. "It is a conundrum that I cannot figure out. If the spell he used was similar to the one on the amulets, he should have arrived there mere moments after he vanished. Yet, we rode in from Langeais, a half day's ride, and he had appeared not long before we had if the villagers spoke true. I have no reason to doubt them."

Constance, followed by Erin, Bek and Kathryn, joined them, her expression clouded. It was uncanny how, more oft than not, she knew exactly when her counsel was needed.

"Didier," she sighed, "my father…"

D'Artagnon clenched his fists. He would like to get his hands on Didier for what he had done to Constance, but he had also vanished. His father had made a mistake not killing him. D'Artagnon planned to rectify that as soon as Didier surfaced.

Constance slipped her hand into his, and his anger seeped away.

"My father," she addressed Gaharet, "mentioned my *grand-mére*, the witch Cordelia. The one your *grand-pére* banished. I believe it is her spell Seigneur Lance used."

D'Artagnon growled. "Do not grant him the respect of a seigneur. He is but Lance. Or Traitor. Nothing more."

Constance squeezed his hand again. He pulled her down beside him and nuzzled her neck. How he loved his little mate.

Gaharet shook his head. "That is not possible. It cannot be the same Cordelia. Humans, witch or no, do not live that long."

"My father hinted Cordelia had mastered the ability to travel across time."

Gaharet frowned. "That still does not explain why Lance arrived at the keep so long after he vanished from Langeais. Why would he delay his arrival? And why would he not, as Erin would say, zap himself right into the keep?"

"Bending the laws of nature is no small thing," explained Constance. "A spell like that, cast by one person, has its limitations. The one worked into your amulets required the power of my entire coven. Thirteen powerful witches. The weight of a spell like that, performed by one person, could lead to significant distortions. You could not depend upon its accuracy. One could end up anywhere, at any time. It is possible Lance had *planned* to arrive at the keep much, much earlier. He was but one man, and he did not take time to prepare for such a complex spell. Nor does his blood have the power of a witch."

"What a minute." Erin plopped herself down on the grass beside Constance. "Are you saying this Cordelia, your grandmother, can zap herself into anywhere on the time continuum?"

Constance shrugged. "It is not beyond the bounds of possibility."

"Then" — Erin chewed on her bottom lip — "could it be that *all* the women mentioned, *all* the Cordelias we have come across, are the same woman?"

D'Artagnon stilled. Could it be? He glanced at his brother. Gaharet was no longer relaxed, his body taut with tension. D'Artagnon had yet to tell him of their origins, of the woman named *Cordoylla*. The scorned woman to whom they owed their entire existence.

"It could also mean," said his brother, grimacing, "if what Lance hinted at is true, Godfrey could be anywhere in the past or in the future. We may never find him."

"We need to put this in your father's journal, Gaharet," said Erin. "All of it. This information is too important to be lost again. In the centuries to come, they might need it. We don't want them to be in the dark like we were."

Gaharet pulled his wife into his lap. "A good idea, my love. I will attend to it upon our return to the keep."

"What of Lothair?" D'Artagnon asked his brother. "It surprised me how much he helped us."

Gaharet grunted. "Lothair wants to be a werewolf. Claims he has his reasons."

"Lothair could have killed my family. He let everyone think he had, but he had made a deal with Jacques and let them live," said Ulrik. "And he let you go in the forest, Gaharet."

"He could have taken Kathryn from me," said Aimon. "He did not."

"And he let me go," added Ulrik, "though I had offered him my life in exchange for Rebekah's. Even after I bit *and* killed Renaud."

"Do you think, maybe, he never intended to sentence Rebekah to death?" asked Aimon.

Ulrik clasped his mate's hand in his. "It is possible. I know I am beginning to wonder if Lothair is not the monster we all thought him to be."

Gaharet nodded. "I agree. There is much deceit in his court and all around him. And there is something amiss with the Comtesse Marguerite. It is not a happy union. But I would wager it is more than that."

He shared a glance with his brother. He suspected there was much more to Lothair than anyone had ever imagined.

They all turned as hoof-beats approached. D'Artagnon leaped to his feet, tucking Constance behind him. As the rider drew closer, he tilted his nose to the air. "Remi."

The boy rode into the clearing as though he had been riding all his life, reined the horse in and jumped to the ground.

He grinned at them all facing him, protecting their mates. "My apologies, Seigneurs. I figured you would all smell it was me from a fair way off. Perhaps I should take more care if you lot are going to be this nervous. I do not want you to mistake me for someone else."

"I trust you, Edmond and Aubert made it back safely?" Neither D'Artagnon, nor Gaharet, had seen the twins since Langeais. "And the woman? Did she survive?"

Gaharet's eyebrows rose. "The woman?"

"Constance was not the only captive Faucher was keeping in chapel storerooms. She was in a far worse state than my mate. Who knows how long she had been down there."

Remi rubbed the back of his neck. "That is why I am here. The woman." He held up his hands. "I am only the messenger. Please do not be mad at me, but..."

"Speak, Remi." A touch of alpha command echoed in Gaharet's voice.

Remi quailed, but he did not run. The boy had courage.

"Well, you know how Edmond likes to rescue those less fortunate?"

They all nodded. D'Artagnon had a suspicion where this was going. From the stormy expression on Gaharet's face, his brother did, too.

"The woman was dying and Edmond... Well, to be fair, Aubert was in agreeance. You see, Edmond bit her. To save her life. And they have sent me to get one of those turning potions from Constance."

"Neither of them could come to me and tell me of this." Gaharet's voice was pure steel. "To *ask* for this?"

Remi held up his hands and shrugged. "Neither of them would leave her, and they growl at anyone who comes close. They are extremely protective of her. Both of them."

D'Artagnon shared a startled look with his brother. "Both of them?"

Sign up for our newsletter and find out about all our romance book releases, eBook sales and promotions, sneak peeks and FREE romance books!

Want to see more from this author?
Here's a taster for you to enjoy!

The Wolves of Langeais:
Wolves' Witch
K.E. Turner

Excerpt

Isobella Rodriguez centered herself in the clearing and, with shaky hands, pulled supplies out of her backpack. A dozen burly Langeais wolves formed a protective ring around her as she hitched her skirts and kneeled on the ground. It would take a bit of getting used to wearing layers—a chemise, a heavy dress—but she couldn't go back in time dressed in jeans and T-shirt.

"Hey." Stef, her friend and Langeais she-wolf, crouched in front of her. "Remember, don't take on Eveque Faucher on your own. Find the Langeais wolves. Work with them."

Go back in time, find the Langeais wolves, don't get dead. Stef made it sound so simple.

"It would be easier if I knew *exactly* what I was supposed to do." Isobella placed a bowl in the dirt, along with candles, matches and a Ziploc bag of ingredients—herbs, berries and snail shells. Two sets. Gabriel, head of pack security and her step-sister's mate, had said she would survive *and* thrive in the tenth century, hinting she may not be returning. Isobella was willing to put her faith in him, but only so far. If things all went to hell in the tenth century—not an unlikely proposition—Isobella wanted a way home. A way back to modern hospitals and chemotherapy, if it turned out they all had it wrong.

Stef squeezed her hand. "I've given you as much information as I can. It should be more than enough to get you where you need to go. I promise. Now, you remember everything I told you about the Langeais wolves?"

She took a shaky breath and nodded. "Thanks, Stef."

"And stay away from Comte Lothair. He's bad news."

Isobella wasn't sure how one twenty-first century witch was supposed to prevail against a tenth century bishop with a reputation as a successful witch hunter, but that was her task. Bishop Faucher, *Eveque* Faucher — she must think in Old French from now on — had to be dealt with. Somehow.

The fear that had plagued her from the moment her doctor had called with her test results tightened in her chest. Was she doing the right thing? Going back in time? She was putting a lot of faith in the Langeais wolves. In Gabriel Montagne and Stefanie d'Louncrais.

"All right everyone." Gabriel clapped his hands. "We need to get this started. We have a limited window before the Kings or the Faucherians get wind of this. Given they've taken to working together, if they find out, they may descend on us with bigger numbers than we can counter." Gabriel turned away to organize his men, shaking his head. "Faucherians. Stupid name."

Yep. Even in the twenty-first century, Eveque Faucher had followers. *Go figure.* And the Kings... Cordelia King... You'd think a woman in her eighties, who knitted Christmas sweaters for her many descendants, would be content to bake cookies and spoil her grand-spawn. Not Cordelia. The woman ruled the King family with an iron fist and had more arcane power at her gnarled fingertips than any one person had a right to. Isobella had only met her a few times, but she'd made an impression. Cordelia was one scary old lady. With any luck, she wouldn't encounter anyone like her in the tenth century.

"You're going to be fine. You've got this."

"Yeah." Maybe. It'd be nice to have Stef's confidence. The she-wolf didn't back down from anything. Or anyone. She more than held her own against any of the male shifters. Or half of Annabelle's boldness. Never was there a more kick-ass witch than her step-sister.

She was glad they were both here with her for moral support. She might have bailed if they weren't. But it wasn't Annabelle or Stef going back to the tenth century. According to the Gabriel, only Isobella could change the fate of the Langeais wolves and rewrite the history of witches. All she had to do was…take out the eveque?

Annabelle wrapped Isobella in hug. "You know I wouldn't be letting you go if I didn't believe it was for the best." A grand admission from Annabelle, since she'd been the one most against Isobella taking on this mission. She released her step-sister.

"If something goes wrong, if for some reason I don't come back, take care of my papa, yeah?"

"Of course."

That Annabelle didn't argue was another hint they weren't expecting her to return.

"Tell him…" What should she say to her father? He was going to be beside himself. Worried. Heartbroken.

"I'll explain it all to him, Bella. Your illness, why you're going on this mission, everything. I promise."

Gabriel's phone dinged. "We have incoming. Stay alert."

Annabelle let her go, and Stef hugged her before stepping back to give her room. "Trust us, Isobella. Trust me. You're going to like the outcome."

The sparkle in her friend's eyes, and her knowing smile, sent her stomach fluttering. Isobella wasn't stupid. With the Langeais wolves' bite capable of turning humans into werewolves, it didn't take a genius to read between the lines. She was going to survive because the tenth century Langeais wolves were going to turn her. Nothing else was capable of curing stage four ovarian cancer. Especially not in the dark ages.

But the Langeais wolves didn't go around turning people into werewolves on a whim. Only the alpha could sanction a turning, and Gabriel had made it clear that while they *could* turn her here, now, they wouldn't. The one exception — when a Langeais wolf met their mate, and the mate was human.

Was Isobella ready to be in another relationship? Ready to put her trust in another man after what Douglas had done?

Isobella pushed her concerns aside. She was doing this. She drew a pentacle in the dirt, then lit her candles and placed one at each point. Her bowl, she set at its center. This was her best chance to survive, and she'd be helping her coven, the Langeais wolves and thousands of witches who'd come before her.

She kneeled on the ground, mixed a pinch of each of her ingredients together, and stirred them through. With her athame against her palm, she held her hand over the bowl and closed her eyes, shutting out all sound, and focused on her breathing, settling herself into a meditative state.

It wasn't a simple spell, and from what Annabelle and Gabriel had told her about their experiences, it would hurt. Anything that broke the laws of nature, that was conceived to do harm and not good, would always have a price. That the spell came from a grimoire with darker spells than this one, that they suspected it belonged to Cordelia King herself — though how the old crone's grimoire had ended in an antiquarian bookshop was still a mystery — did not bode well for Isobella's journey. All she could do was prepare her mind.

Awareness of her surroundings slipped away, her steady breaths and the lazy beat of her heart the only sounds penetrating her calm. In her mind's eye, she brought up the images she'd created of the Langeais wolves — Gaharet, Erin, D'Artagnon, Constance — and held them there, focusing her intent on joining them at the d'Louncrais Keep.

She sliced her palm, the familiar sting of the blade grounding her. Squeezing her hand into a fist, she let her blood drip into the bowl.

"Blood and bone and hair and skin,
Rend a hole in time so thin."

As she spoke, acrid smoke teased her nostrils. The spell was working.

"Thy body held not in place — "

A growl broke her calm. Then another.

"Keep going, Isobella," Gabriel ordered. "Stef and Annabelle, stay close to her. Nothing must stop Isobella from completing her spell."

Isobella steadied herself, refocusing. They would protect her.

"Instead to thine imagined space."

More snarls and sounds of fighting echoing around her. A gun went off, breaking her concentration.

"Don't stop." Stef, her voice guttural and deep, as though her vocal chords were changing, hovered close.

"Bleed mind and soul to point, to plunder,
To change, to bend, to tear asunder."

"Douglas, *no!*" Annabelle this time.

Douglas? No. He'd taken enough already. He wasn't taking this chance away from her.

"So mote it be."

A hand gripped her arm with bruising force. "I can't let you go after Faucher."

Douglas.

The vision in her mind's eye blurred and changed. Gone was the face of the tenth century alpha of the Langeais wolves. Replaced by a man in the flowing robes of a priest. *No!*

Her eyes snapped open. "Douglas, what have you done?"

She tried to regain her calm, to get back the image of the Langeais wolves, but it was too late. Darkness descended and a silence so thick blocked out the forest, Annabelle, Stef, the werewolves fighting, everything but the grip on her arm.

Pain ripped through her. Douglas shrieked. Isobella gritted her teeth, biting back her scream. When it was almost more than she could bear, a force so strong propelled her forward, pushing and tugging at her, and Isobella feared it might tear her apart. Douglas let go. Then Isobella slammed to a stop, winded, hurting and gasping for breath.

The darkness eased. With a groan, Isobella raised her head. A set of boots, leather and fur-lined, filled her vision. Had it worked? Was she in the tenth century? Was this one of the Langeais wolves? The man kneeled before her, his black robes billowing about him. Priest robes. Isobella swallowed and raised her gaze. Staring down at her was a young priest. Malevolent glee flickering in his eyes, he scooped up her Ziploc bag of ingredients. From Stef's descriptions, this could only be one person. Eveque Faucher.

About the Author

K.E Turner can't remember a time when she wasn't writing stories or reading books—as a teenager in class instead of doing math, in her lunch break at work, or at home when there's housework to be done. With a love of history, mystery, suspense, paranormal, and romance, she likes combining more than one element in her stories.

An award-winning author, she writes spicy paranormal romances and romantic suspense, with strong but good hearted heroes, smart, sassy heroines and an often unexpected villain or two, to shake things up.

A Western Australian based author, she lives with her husband, two dogs, two cats and a menagerie of farm animals on their property in the southern region of the state. A hopeless romantic, she enjoys beach sunsets, sitting by the wood fire with a good book, a nice shiraz and good food.

K.E. Turner loves to hear from readers. You can find her contact information, website details and author profile page at https://www.firstforromance.com

ENTWINED PUBLISHING

www.ingramcontent.com/pod-product-compliance
Lightning Source LLC
Chambersburg PA
CBHW030400030726
47497CB00002B/411